Books by Mary Catherine Campbell

Prince of Cwillan

Prince of Cwillan - Revised 2014*

Forest Lake- Revised 2014*

Tomorrow Is A Long Time

The Golden Coin

*Originally sold as one book under the title
Prince of Cwillan, Yellow Cover with the Cliffs
of Moher photograph

Prince of Cwillan

Forest Lake

Mary Catherine Campbell

ISBN: 0988360977

ISBN 13: 9780988360976

Library of Congress Control Number: 2014917352

Thistle and Shamrock Publishing, Shelby Township, MI

Book Two

In The Prince of Cwillan Series

Forest Lake

"Fair." Mánus finished for him and
shook his head. "Lad,
who told you life was fair? You have to
hold onto the good
times. Not one of us knows when it will
be our last."

Mánus Scanlon

PROLOGUE

As soon as Donal passed through the portal, back into the world where he lived with Cynthia Long, he pulled on his parka. He had to move away from the portal before he was able to make the call on his cell phone. She must have been waiting by the phone, she picked up immediately.

"Oh Donal, I am so glad to hear you're back."

"I'll hitch a ride into Chicago. Can you arrange a evening flight."

"Of course. How did things go?"

He couldn't hold back his happiness. "I have a son, Cyn. His name is Feargus Cullan Cormac."

"Donal, that's great news." Her voice coming over the miles sounded happy for him. He sensed rather than heard a question in it, as well as a little worry. "Did you bring him with you?"

"No. We'll talk about it when you pick me up at the airport. There is nothing to worry about Cyn. After the wedding we will come out here together."

"I know, darling."

CHAPTER ONE

Donal helped Cynthia down from the horse.
She looked around the overgrown meadow.
"This is where you lived?"

"For over a year when I first came here."

Scrub trees and bushes almost obscured the small two-room cabin where he had lived with Fred Tolan, slept on the floor in front of the fireplace, learned American English and the ways of this New World. They lived here with no plumbing, no electricity, not that he was used to such conveniences. They carried water from a spring that fed the lake three miles away as the crow flies, for cooking and drinking. For washing they used a rain barrel.

"Fred told me the Native Americans who lived in the area stayed clear of this land. They called the island out on the lake 'The Place of Strange Dreams.' Early settlers to the area stayed clear of it too, because strange things were seen around the island."

"Did you see or have strange dreams there?" Cynthia asked.

Donal smiled at Cynthia and shook his head. "Fred left me his parcel of land. I want to buy the rest so we own the whole tract of land as far as the county road. Then once we are established, the land on the other side of the gravel road."

Cynthia looked around. "You don't want much." There was indecision in her eyes. "Sure, why not. We can clear this meadow and build our house right where the cabin stands."

She walked to the edge of the hill. "Down in the valley we can build my studio. And a stable too, for your horses."

"I'd love that, Cyn."

"We'll call it...we'll call it Forest Lake," she said.

"I'll have to work for your father another year, maybe two."

"You'll go crazy."

Donal heard the worry in her voice. "We need the money."

"I know, Donal. You know I have..."

Donal cut across her words, "I could take Mánus up on his offer."

"I'm...I'm not sure which would be worse."

It took them over an hour to ride out to the lake.

Dark rocks with silver veins running through them protruded out of the shallow lake, like strange, ugly creatures stranded in water not deep enough to swim in.

"I don't understand," Donal said, as he looked around the lake, the water level in some places now only several feet deep.

They rode along the shore to the source of the water. Not even a trickle of water fed the lake.

On foot, Donal followed the dry stream to the place where a spring burst out of the ground. A few feet from the spring a dam made of wooden planks sent all the water off at a new angle, to feed a new stream. Why? Were there other homes in the area?

Donal stepped over to the dam, he intended to pull the boards up. As he bent at his work, the memory of his first encounter with Fred Tolan came to him. He stood and let the memory flow though him. It took him back to the time when he still went by the name Cullan.

His memories were as real as life. Right down to the smell of wildflowers, the warmth of the sun, and the gentle breeze that blew from the west. He knelt again at the outcrop filling his water bag.

"You can drink that without boiling it. It's safe."

Startled, Cullan stood; he fumbled the stopper back onto his water bag, in time to save most of the water.

Before him stood an old man with scraggly gray hair and beard, and dark piercing eyes that looked out of a weathered face. He held a long branch that was thicker than a spear at one end and as thin at the other, but shorter.

"This is private land, no hunting. If that's your buck back yonder, hung up to bleed, you're in big trouble, boy."

Cullan grasped the tone of the stranger's words, but not the meaning. The way he kept the stick across his chest told him it had to be a weapon.

"I have no weapon."

The stranger would not understand him. He let the water bag slip to the ground, held his hands out palm forward to show that they were empty.

"God, what language is that? You best not be faking it, there aren't many strangers around these parts. And don't give me any bull about your family starving, that you need that buck."

If Cullan could get close to the man, he might be able to make contact. Perhaps even be able to learn the man's language. The old man spoke again; when he didn't get a response he placed his free hand on top of his head, emphasized this with an upward movement of the branch.

With slow movements Cullan raised his hands and placed them on his head.

"Good, for a second I thought you might be dumb or something."

Nervous, sweat broke out on Cullan's palms. What did the branch do? Not just wood, a combination of wood and metal. Could he get to the dagger hidden inside his right boot before the stranger could react? The old man wore a short black cloak with close-fitting sleeves over a tunic tucked into dark-blue, baggy leggings. He had never seen dress like this, not in Wyneth where he grew up, nor to the north.

"Now we're going to head back to where you left the buck. We'll take it with us. You look healthy enough to carry it back to my cabin. No use wasting it. I can carve it up for steaks. Maybe even trade it for some groceries, or a few beers up at Stan's place."

The stranger made a motion with the branch, pointed it back toward the trees where Cullan had left the stag. The old man stepped back to let him pass. For now, Cullan decided he would go along with him. He moved with caution, stayed well clear of the weapon, and started for the trees across the meadow.

Over the treetops soared a huge bird. The twitter of small birds in the tall grass, the wind in the trees, every sound was drowned out by the strange sound made by the bird. Cullan's eyes went wide with surprise. He had never seen a bird this large.

It flew straight at him.

What kind of bird made this strange droning noise instead of the usual hunting cry? He dove to the ground, expecting at any minute to feel the talons sink into his skin. When nothing happened he looked up, then over his shoulder. He watched the bird soar over the treetops to the west.

"Gave you a fright, did it?" the stranger laughed, then stopped to stare at him.

Cullan lay spread-eagle in the tall grass, what a fool he must look. The older man had stood his ground, showing no fear of the huge bird. Cullan rolled over and sat up, his long legs stretched out before him. As he made a show of adjusting his boot, he loosened the strap that held his dagger in place.

"God in heaven, is it possible?" the stranger asked.

Cullan watched the man. There was a new look on his face; a look of wonder.

"Speak up boy. You one of those people the old-timers talk about?"

"This is getting us nowhere." Donal had to make contact with this stranger before he decided to use that weapon.

What would Niall do?

Wait?

Is that what his friend would do?

No.

"Are you one of those island people? My great-great grandfather claimed he saw one when he was a boy. But I've been all over that island, inch by inch, and there isn't a place anyone could hide out there."

What was the problem?

"You sure have on some funny clothes. Old Charlie Three Feathers said that those rocks leading up to the knoll on the island are steps, made long before his people settled here."

The stranger gave him a curious look, stepped closer, and held his hand out to help him rise. Cullan hesitated for only a second before he took the hand offered. That had been the beginning of their friendship.

Donal pulled himself back to the present. He decided to leave the boards in place, for now at least, even though the land was legally his.

This property was important to him; the lake around the island acted as a natural moat to keep someone from stumbling onto the island at the wrong time.

As he cleared the low bushes and scrub trees, Donal waved to Cynthia. She sat by the edge of the lake on an old, fallen tree trunk.

"What's the problem?"

"Someone has dammed up the spring. Now that Fred has passed on, I guess someone thought it was okay to do that. I'll worry about that later."

All through their wedding, he tried to figure out how to explain his past to Cyn. Where to start, how much to tell her? Now it was time for him to tell her the truth.

He had been amazed when Mánus and Liam showed up at the church on the day of their wedding. It drove home the realization that he would have to tell Cynthia soon. The two men had joined him in the side room where Donal waited with his best man, John Stills, for the ceremony to start.

John excused himself, saying he needed to check on something.

Liam handed Donal a card.

Donal slid his nail under the edge and pulled the flap up. Inside he found a wedding card and a print-out of a legal notice from the Chicago Tribune. As he read the notice, he couldn't believe his good fortune. Could this be true, were they really looking for him?

"I don't understand?"

"Fred Tolan didn't have an heir, he named you," Liam said. "You need to contact the attorney at the bottom. The land is rightfully yours, there's a man, Terrence Strickland, who hopes to buy the land when it goes up for auction for back taxes."

Donal looked from Liam to Mánus. "Why do you want to help me?"

"This goes beyond us being distant cousins," Mánus said.

"You see, lad," Liam said, "We, Mánus and I, think you're running away from something. You'll have to face whatever devil drives you. Sooner or later you will have to make a stand. You wanted to find your people. But that is only an excuse to avoid something else."

They were wrong. He chose to come here. His need to find his people wasn't just an excuse, the reason not to stay in Cwillan. He had found his people, found where they came from. Somewhere in Ireland was where he would find the other portal. He wasn't sure where to look for the third one, but when he had time he intended to find it too.

Niall's words came back to him, *You are the special one. The one to unite our people.*

Mánus and Liam wanted the same thing that Niall had wanted of him. What if this is what he was supposed to do all along? To unite his people here in the world they came from.

"We both would still like you to come into the business with us," Mánus said.

"It's not going to happen."

"Why, lad? Because of our business?"

"Sooner or later you or your computer expert will make a mistake and get caught."

"Not likely to happen," Liam said. "We've never even been close to getting caught. Have you told your lady yet?"

Donal shook his head.

"You're afraid she won't understand. In the end, you will have to do what you have to do."

Mánus was right.

Liam told him to give it some thought. They would contact him later, after his honeymoon.

When Donal contacted the attorney, he was surprised to find out that the parcel of land left to him was larger than he had expected. Fred Tolan owned all the land along the gravel road, as well as the strip of land from the cabin back to and including the lake.

Now it was time; he had to address the problem of how to tell Cyn about his past. He decided to start with Cullan's return to Cwillan. His plan was to do it out on the island, where Cullan's new life began.

Cynthia's voice pulled him back to the present.

"Should we eat here or over on the island?"

"We'll eat out on the island. The water is low enough for us to cross on horseback."

They ate lunch on a flat oblong boulder near the center of the island.

"This looks as if it were dressed stone," she said as she ran her hand over the surface.

"Perhaps it is. It looks like it might have been placed upright at one time. It might be the mate to the boulder almost completely buried over there."

They walked over to take a look at the other boulder. On the side sticking up out of the ground, there were no markings of any kind. Perhaps one day they would dig it up. He hoped to find ogham markings on the buried side.

Donal helped Cynthia pack up what remained of their lunch. With their backs against the sun-warmed stone, Donal told her the tale of Cullan, the boy-prince. Cynthia listened to him without interrupting.

The tale was short. The memories of his early days were only a few brief glimpses into his life and the day his mother died.

When he finished, Cynthia waited.

"I know there's more."

He went on and told her about the farm where Cullan, lived until he was called back to Cwillan. He told her about the long days and hard work. Up before dawn with a late meal, to bed only after the sun went down.

Now, it seemed like a hard life; at the time it was the only life he knew. He smiled at her, reached over, and took her hand. He told her not to be afraid that no matter what she saw, it was the past. Nothing could hurt her. They were only memories, no matter how real they seemed.

He didn't think she would fight him.

She didn't.

They were one, standing in the icy water of a tributary that joined the Glas River farther south.

"It's only a memory," he reminded her. "Nothing can hurt you. Think of it as watching a video-show."

"It seems so real."

"I know, Cyn. But it can't hurt you."

She relaxed, and he went on with the story. He let his memories flow through him into her.

CHAPTER TWO

Cold water chilled Cullan to the bone. Beneath his bare feet the flat, slippery stones threatened to undo him. If he slipped now, everyone back at camp would know. Sylva would shake her head and Rad, her son, would laugh at him.

Rad had turned cautious of late. Cullan had never threatened the boy, but his size, now a full head taller, gave him a marked advantage; one he liked. Even the hired farmhands treated him with respect now that he had grown as tall or taller than they were.

Two men on horseback galloped out of the woods making for the river. Cullan's dun mare and their packhorse trailed behind the first rider. The second rider led two more horses. Instinctively he put his fingers in his mouth and whistled. The mare's head came up. When she hesitated, the second rider brought his whip down hard along her flank. The mare whinnied in pain, jumped sideways, and almost broke loose from her captors.

Cullan scrambled up onto the grassy bank, letting the water bag and the rabbits he had trapped earlier slip off his shoulder. With long powerful strides, he ran to intercept the lead rider before he reached the river. He hoped his height and strong body, hardened by years of hard labor, would give him an advantage.

His fingers curled around the headstall of the lead horse, he leaned his shoulder into the beast's neck. By sheer strength, he tried to halt the horse in its tracks. He dug his feet in for leverage.

It almost worked.

The rider yelled at him in a strange language. His whip came down so fast Cullan barely had time to turn his head and save his eyes. The metal-tipped leather sliced across his forehead. Searing pain made him lose his concentration. Pulled into the icy water, his feet slipped from beneath him. He had to let go and roll to the side to avoid being trampled.

Dark green water closed over his head. When he managed to find his feet again, he scrubbed water and blood out of his eyes. His hand went to his chest, feeling for the slight bulge beneath his tunic. He whispered thanks to the gods that he still had the pouch that held his talisman. He shivered as he climbed up onto the riverbank and watched, powerless to stop the thieves as they made for the forest on the far side of the river.

Angry, he shook his fist at them and uttered a curse in the language of Wyneth. He almost slipped off the riverbank when two more horses raced past him. This time both riders and horses were familiar to him. His companions were only minutes behind the thieves. Perhaps they would be in time to catch them.

Niall slowed his horse, the powerful black gelding answered his every command and turned in a tight circle. He rode back to where Cullan stood. "Are you all right?"

At first, Cullan only blinked, surprised at Niall's concern. His wound began to throb; the reality of why he was standing here soaking wet, with blood running down his face jolted him out of his silence. "They have our horses."

"A man on horseback. Has a greater advantage over a man on foot."

Cullan's heart sank. Niall had seen his failed attempt to stop the thieves.

"Only a brave man would attempt it. Go back to our camp." Niall turned his horse. The gelding pranced, anxious to be off. "Have that wound looked after," he called over his shoulder.

Niall let his horse pick its way across the river, once on dry land he urged the horse to greater speed. At the edge of the forest Rónán waited for him; they disappeared, swallowed up by gloom created by the tall trees.

Brave. Niall thought him brave.

With his sleeve, Cullan scrubbed water and blood out of his eyes. He hurried back to where he had dropped the water bag and rabbits. If Niall and Rónán did not catch the thieves, this would be their only food tonight. It was not much for four men and a woman. He retrieved his boots from their hiding place under a bush.

As he ran back to their camp, he prayed to the gods that Sylva and Rad were unharmed.

"I see the thieves got by you as well." Sylva didn't sound surprised. "It looks like we will have to walk all the way to the fortress of Cwillan."

"Niall and Rónán will catch the thieves." He kept his voice normal, so it did not betray himself, that he was relieved that she was unharmed.

"They are no more than boys, playing at being men. We might as well have sent you to get our horses back. It will be a long, hungry walk," Rad said.

Cullan gave Rad a hard look. The older boy moved away from him.

"Let me look at that wound."

Evening shadows had darkened the forest around them by the time Niall and Rónán returned. The stolen horses trailed behind them, along with a dun with a strange design painted on its flank. What had become of the thieves was never mentioned.

After their evening meal, all but Niall and Rónán lay down to take their rest. The two youths sat under a huge oak tree well away from the sleepers. In low voices, they talked while they cleaned their weapons. Both boys rode with long broadswords in scabbards across their backs, as well as shorter swords on their hips.

Pretending to sleep, Cullan lay on his back with his eyes closed. He listened to their quiet voices, understanding nothing. They spoke in a guttural language, the same language the thieves had used. It sounded familiar yet foreign to him. It stirred strange feelings in him, strange memories. Each time, as he almost caught some meaning to the words, the memory slipped away from him like the tiny silver fish that slipped through his fingers as a child.

Cullan drifted into a troubled sleep.

He ran through an endless forest pursued by a man in black. No matter how fast he ran the man gained on him. Talon-like fingers reached out to catch him. The world around him changed, he stood at the edge of a high wooden bridge, beneath his feet a deep gorge. Hands jostled him from behind, his grip on the railing slipped and he fell forward.

Jagged rocks rushed up to meet him.

Startled, as if he had fallen in his sleep, he woke and cried out. He looked around in the darkness half expecting the man in black to step out of the forest to take him.

What did the dream mean? He closed his eyes tight to shut out his fear.

"Cullan, are you all right?" Niall asked.

"Leave him be," Sylva said, from her place on the other side of the fire.

"Silence, woman."

It was the first time he'd heard Niall raise his voice.

"Cullan, sit up."

Rad was right about one thing, these two were no more than boys, their facial hair was new, more like reddish down than hair. He felt guilty at his unfair judgment; after all, they had caught the thieves.

Niall spoke to him again. Something in his voice told Cullan to do as commanded. He eased himself into a sitting position. Niall reached over and threw another log on the fire, sparks crackled and flew up into the night air, flames licked at the dry wood. Strange shadows danced around the trees. He turned back to Cullan.

Rónán stood near by with his drawn sword at the ready.

"Does it hurt, Cullan?" Niall's soft voice reassured him as his fingers moved across Cullan's forehead. His touch was light, and only a slight tingling marked the movement of his fingers. Not only did the pain ease, the fear from his dream drained away.

"No. Not now."

"Has it been hard?"

"Hard?"

"Living with that one." Niall indicated Sylva on the other side of the fire.

"It is not as bad as you think. They took me in, did they not?"

"Aye, but that one shows no respect."

"Perhaps she should for you, lord, not for me, a foster son." Cullan paused, then went on, "It has been so long. I began to think she lied about my uncle, who had left me with her. Who now all of a sudden calls me back to a land I no longer remember, to this fortress I have never heard of."

"Old Sundra was to tell you about your uncle, make sure you did not forget your people, or that he would send for you one day," Niall said.

"The old one died before my eighth summer. Sylva, his sister, took over the farm." Without thinking, Cullan felt for the pouch that hung around his neck. He removed his hand; perhaps Niall had not noticed. "She sent me to the barn to sleep with the beasts." Guilt nagged at Cullan for being ungrateful. "As I said, they took me in."

"Your time with Sylva is over, though I donot think your uncle will find fault with you. You have turned into a powerful youth. Though angry he might be when he learns that you have forgotten your native tongue, your God." Niall paused. "Are you all right now?"

The tone of his voice this time had a soothing quality to it. He would sleep now, without dreaming. He nodded and offered a small smile.

Before Niall stood, Cullan put out a hand to stop him.

"Did you know my parents?"

Niall paused, for far too long.

He does not want to speak about them.

"I met your mother once long ago. When she died, your uncle had you fostered to his friend in Wyneth."

"Why did they send you? Why did not my uncle come for me?" Cullan was aware that Niall said nothing about his father.

"Your uncle asked us to come." The older boy smiled at him. "We are related, far back. Sons of the sons of the great man who brought us to this land."

Cullan searched Niall's thin face, looked for some likeness to himself besides the color of his hair, the lightness of his eyes.

"Rest now. In the morning we cross the Glas River, from there it is not far to the fortress. You will meet your uncle soon."

Niall stood.

"Will I live with my uncle? Does he have a wife, children?"

"Get some sleep, tomorrow is soon enough to answer your questions."

Cullan lay back and closed his eyes. Aye, tomorrow would be soon enough. This time he found it easy to sleep.

CHAPTER THREE

Niall pulled his cloak tighter. This morning felt more like winter than spring. Last night's rain still dripped from the trees. Cold water managed to work its way down his neck, chilling him to the bone.

He shivered, a bad omen for what the future held for him. He turned to check on the others in their small band. Sylva rode third in line, Cullan came next, Rad brought up the rear. Satisfied that they were keeping up, Niall turned forward again.

"Do you believe he is the chosen one?" Rónán asked, as he slowed his horse, dropping back so he could ride next to his friend.

Niall wondered where he had heard of the chosen one. Only the holy men were able to read the old books. Their history had become legend to many, no more than myths. His own father, Lord Uaid, who should know better, had lost faith when his oldest son, Cathaír, died.

"What do you know of the prophecies?"

"My family knows the old stories too."

"Before my brother died, he told me how I would know the one," Niall said.

Did Cathaír know he would die soon? Is that why he told me?

Rónán turned in his saddle. Niall turned his head enough to watch his friend while he studied Cullan. Rónán turned to face forward again.

"They say his mother was near relative to his father. Perhaps he is not right." Rónán tapped his forehead.

"Aye, very near, they wanted to make sure that one of the Ard Ri's sons had the Power. Nothing to worry about, nothing is wrong with the boy."

"It doesn't matter if he is or is not."

Niall reined his horse to a stop. Rónán did the same.

"Why do you say that?"

"The council will never accept a young boy. They will go for one older, with more experience like Artúr."

When the small band of riders gathered around them, Niall realized they had stopped. He was glad that they were speaking in their native language. He told them that all was well, turned forward and made a clicking sound with his tongue. His gelding broke into a gallop.

Cathaír's words came back to him. "Artúr is of northern blood. More one of our enemy, than one of us. Many will not want to follow him." After half a league Niall relaxed his grip on the reins and let his horse slow to a canter then a walk, so they could talk.

"'Tis true," Rónán continued. "He is of few summers, and if the Old One dies they will go for a young man rather than a mere youth." He paused, then went on. "My father feels that a marriage between Artúr and Briana would unify our people."

"And you, do you think she would accept Artúr?"

"No man has been able to please my sister. She finds fault with every suitor." They rode in silence for a while, before Rónán went on. "Has Cormac named his tanist? If not, perhaps my father would back your clan's claim to the throne."

Niall studied his friend. "My father will side with the council. Your father will side with them too. I need to know where you stand."

"Me? Need you ask? 'Tis a low mood you are in this morning." Rónán cocked an eyebrow at his friend, a slow smile spread across his broad face. "The Old One is not dead nor ill, so tell me what is on your mind."

"There may come a time when we are forced to stand against our fathers for the good of our people. If Artúr sits on the throne, it will be in name only. His uncle, Darlisca, Lord of Nortcora, will be the real ruler."

In their language the northern lands were simply ó thuaidh, the land to the north.

"We must get as many on our side as soon as possible. Artúr and his uncle have been content to bide their time. Word will spread like wildfire that an heir still lives. If we are not ready, we will not be able to help Cullan."

"I will speak to my kin. Have you spoken to Ciarán yet?" Rónán said.

"Yes, before we left."

His thoughts were low indeed, low and very dangerous. If their fathers learned of their scheme, there would be the dark one to pay. Rónán was his anam chara, soul friend, more of a mentor in many ways. If Darlisca learned that Rónán and he were doing more than just playing at the old ways...His blood turned cold at the thought. He didn't want to end up like Cathaír or his brother's Guardian.

"Do you remember Catháir?"

"Yes. And my older brother, Kleeta. Did you know that Briana found them?"

Niall shook his head. "All I know is that Catháir had a spear through his chest which pinned him to a tree. They cut off both his hands. That is what the enemy does to those with the Power. Your brother had several spears though his chest. They laid him at Catháir's feet."

"My sister never talks about it. It was a warning, is that why you never told your father the truth? That you are like your older brother?"

Niall could not tell his friend that he feared to end up like Catháir. If their enemy found out the truth, what would they do to any that stood in their way?

He had two on his side. Who else could he recruit? Athdar, Cullan's uncle? Perhaps; more likely he would stand with the council. Ciarán had many friends in Cwillan and the village below. He could speak to them. He put his fingers to his lips, and a sharp whistle split the air. His horse eased into a canter.

Tomorrow when they reached Cwillan it would begin.

The sun had reached its zenith when they turned left off the roadway onto a path that took them through old growth woodland. In a small glade they came upon several standing stones; at the tallest they turned right. The slender stones looked like the bones of some huge, long-dead creature. The trees thinned; now they rode through scattered young trees, and then into an open meadow.

At the crest of a low hill, Niall reined in his horse and waited for the others to catch up.

෨෨

Cullan stopped his horse beside the youths. He followed their gaze.

Near the foot of a high rocky outcrop spread a large village. His eyes moved upward to the summit. So this is where the High King lives. The fortress of Cwillan sat like a crown of stone upon the crest of an outcrop that had thrust straight out of the earth to form a high plateau.

At the highest point, a curtain wall ran around the edge; tall inner walls surrounded a central tower with windows set high in its sides. The road left the village and entered a dense forest. It later reappeared to wind its way around the curve in the plateau.

Cullan stared with wonder at the fortress. From the top of the central tower a standard of blue and saffron with a white horse flapped in the afternoon breeze. Had Cwillan changed? Had he stood here before, gazing up at the fortress? If he had, he no longer had a memory of this place, these people, nor this uncle who had sent for him.

He turned to Niall. The young man watched him, his eyes alert.

"It is very impressive. Who rules here?"

"Cormac, son of Artúr II," Niall said. "Come, your uncle awaits your arrival."

They crossed the meadow and after a league they came back to the main road. As they neared the village, they passed carts and travelers on foot as well as men on horseback going to and from the village. Only a few were going straight through to the fortress. Cullan noticed most of the people on the road were tall and fair with near red to dark-brown hair.

He looked around, fascinated by what he saw. On each side of the road men and women moved along paths formed by split logs placed side by side to form a wooden lane for the villagers to walk on. Most of the shops were single story, with thatch for roofs, much in the way of Wyneth.

Youths standing in the open doorways called to the men and women, calling out their Master's wares. One brave youth moved closer to the roadway to get Niall's attention. He nodded at him and rode on.

Cullan had never been anywhere larger than the small village at the crossroads in Wyneth, with no more than a dozen shops and cottages. It was tiny in comparison to the village of Cwillan.

The village had a long main road that ran up to meet the path that went up to the fortress. Off the main road ran two lánai, lanes, following the direction of the sun, with a few smaller shops that gave way to thatched cottages.

How many people lived in this village? Far more people than Cullan had met in his entire life.

As soon as they left the village the road begin to climb. Coming around a turn they passed a high stone wall; the ancient black stone blocks were splotched with lichen. Stout wooden gates barred entry. To the right of the small door set into the gates hung a single pull-rope.

As they rode on the forest closed in around them.

It was cooler here, peaceful. Soon the path came out onto an open hillside. He moved his horse closer to the edge so he could look down into the valley below. Green farmland stretched as far as he could see. The road wound up and around to the far side of the outcrop. Near the top, they entered a natural tunnel. It ran with a slight incline half a league. Rush torches set into brackets along the wall gave off an acrid smokey light. Cullan's eyes watered from the smoke. He was glad when they emerged into the sunlight and fresh air again.

They came out onto a lower shelf of the plateau, a stone parapet marked the outer edge. The fortress loomed above them. At the far end gates gave access to a wooden bridge. The gates were guarded by tall muscular men, who questioned each man and woman, each wagoner, seeking entrance to the fortress.

Niall and Rónán urged their horses forward, moving ahead of those who waited their turn. Men grumbled in the language of the land. Cullan did not have to understand the words to know they were angry with those unwilling to wait their turn.

When a tall man with auburn hair stepped forward to grab at the headstall of Niall's horse, Rónán moved so fast his sword seemed to jump into his hand. The closest guard stepped forward. His hand on the hilt of his sword, he leaned close to the man to say something to him in private, moving him out of the way. Fear replaced the look of anger on the man's plain face; he bowed to Niall and moved back into the crowd that had gathered to see what would happen.

When the guard moved over to Niall, he leaned over to speak with him. They spoke together for a time, before the guard called to his comrades and hurried to his horse. He rode through the gates, heading up toward the summit. Another guard hurried out of the guardhouse to take his place.

"Cullan's uncle will meet us in the garden within the time it takes us to cross the second bridge."

They rode out onto the wooden bridge, their horses' hoofs making hollow thuds on stout wooden planks, the sound echoed around them. The bridge swayed on ropes that held it in place.

Cullan leaned over, only to sit up and jerk his mare to a stop. Fear took him; his heart raced. Last night's dream returned. In his mind he saw again the man in black, the bridge where someone pushed him.

He closed his eyes and mumbled a prayer.

"There is no time to daydream, Cullan!" Sylva yelled at him.

Cullan face grew warm. He opened his eyes. With caution, he moved his horse forward to catch up with the others. He glanced back; it was only a coincidence. This could not be the bridge from his dream.

Grooves were cut into the stonework on each side of the road to form a series of terraced steps to make it easier for the horses to manage the grade. Carts stayed in the middle, those on foot, had to move from side to side to avoid both horses and carts.

After crossing a second bridge they turned left off the road to an open area with a stone parapet around the outer edge. In reality the garden was no more than a narrow grassy area, too small to build upon.

Niall and his companions dismounted.

Cullan walked to the edge and looked out over the land. In the distance, he could just discern the glint of a river snaking through the bright green fields of spring. He sat down on the parapet with his back to the countryside.

Niall sat down beside him.

"Is that the Wyneth River?"

"Yes, it marks the end of Cwillan. Eastern Wyneth is on the far side. Once this was called the Valley of Fire, perhaps some act of the Father caused this outcrop of rock to thrust up to the sky. It is the only one in this area. Our holy men live at Alibie to the east."

Presently, two men joined them. One old, though he still walked with a firm step, the other younger, red-haired and tall.

This must be Niall's father, Cullan thought, *or a near relative.*

Niall and Rónán stood.

"So you are here at last," said the older man. "Let me have a look at you." When Cullan did not stand the man repeated his words in the language of Wyneth.

Cullan rose to his feet, uncomfortable, as if he were a horse the older man intended to buy. He seemed to weigh Cullan in his mind. Whatever he thought, nothing showed on his face.

After examining Cullan, he turned to Niall. "You took your time."

"There were thieves on this side of the river. We found it best to take the long way around."

"You mean you decided, and your companion agreed," the red-haired man said. Youth and mature man stared at each other. Niall's face colored, he lowered his gaze and sat down.

"Sundra is not here, who speaks for the boy?" the older man asked.

"I do," Sylva said.

"Come, we will talk in private."

ॐ

Sylva followed the two men out of the garden and up toward the fortress. After a dozen paces they entered a half-round recess in the wall with strange narrow windows.

"I am Airell," the older man said speaking in the language of Wyneth. "Sundra, why did he not come?"

"My brother went to our ancestors many summers back. He told me on his death bed of the agreement with you for the care of the boy."

"The youth was to be educated? He looks and acts like a peasant."

"He is a willful boy. Hard to train, much less educate. My brother called him Cullan, a strange name. Perhaps it has some meaning in your tongue."

Sylva hoped the lie would pass. That it would stave off any inquiries about the gold coins to have the boy tutored, coins that would guarantee her son, Rad, a good marriage. She had no love for Cullan, looked forward to seeing the last of the overgrown boy. Every young woman within a league looked at him first before her son, the real heir to the farm.

"My brother spared the whip out of some mistaken kindness toward his foster son."

"Is the horse his?"

She turned to the red-haired man, who until now had used the narrow window to watch the youths below. She wanted to keep the mare; the animal was too valuable for the likes of this foreign boy, but something told her to be careful. She weighed the gold that rightfully belonged to Cullan against the value of the mare. She decided to let him keep the horse.

"Yes, my lord. It was arranged by my brother that he would get a horse in his thirteenth summer."

The red-haired man watched her, his eyes were a strange light color. Something about him made her nervous. She was relieved when he turned back to the window. The men and women on this side of the river had strange ways. They worshipped only one god. She had heard that there were men here who were witches.

"Watch him, my lord. It will take a hand firmer than mine to make him mind."

The red-haired man turned at her comment to stare at her.

Sylva tried not to fidget.

He doesn't believe me. It would be best to have this over with and return home.

"If there is nothing more, lord, my son and I will start back for Wyneth. We need to get back as soon as possible; a neighbor and two hired men are watching the farm. It's best not to be away too long."

"Very well. I will send men with you as far as the river crossing." Airell nodded toward the other side of the road.

For the first time, she noticed the men waiting with their horses on the far side of the road. One tall, heavy set man with auburn hair hanging below his shoulders, the other two shorter but just as imposing. The big one never took his eyes off her.

Airell signaled for her to start back down. He followed a few paces behind. The three men crossed over to their side and followed them. She could hear the men speak to one another. She slowed, to catch a word or two. They spoke in the language of Cwillan, only a word or two did she understand.

At the entrance to the garden, Sylva signaled to her son. Rad rose and joined her.

"We go."

She walked over to where Cullan sat talking with Niall and Rónán. "I've tried my best to show you the way, Cullan. May the gods be with you."

Sylva turned away and hurried back to her horse. She noted that the two men who would see them back across the river were ready to lead them back down. Before Sylva had a chance to follow them, Airell stepped forward and offered her a small pouch.

"For your trouble with the boy. You will be able to stay at an inn on the other side of the river and still be back at the farm in good time."

"Many thanks, my lord."

She took the pouch, hesitating only a second, weighing the contents in her hand. The pouch disappeared into the pocket sown into the lining of her cloak. She bowed her head, showing a respect she did not feel for this tall, foreign man. She signaled her son to follow. It would be good to be home again, among civilized people.

Chapter Four

Niall's father, Uaid, watched the youths make their way down to the upper village. Once they were lost to sight, he crossed over to the parapet where Bran, the tall, heavyset man, watched for Sylva and her son to appear with the men that would take them as far as the Western Bridge. It would be awhile before they cleared the lower village.

Athdar joined Uaid and Bran.

"Airell?" said Uaid. "Athdar, what is the meaning of this?"

"Airell is the name Sundra and I agreed on. This way no one would connect the boy to my sister.

"Why now? Why bring him here now?" Uaid asked. "He should have stayed in Wyneth with those farmers."

Athdar turned on his friend of many years, his face dark with anger. "Do you forget that he is the tánaiste, heir to our Lord? In four summers he would have returned to the fortress. It is over time Cullan met his father and learned his duties."

"Are you sure the council will accept him?"

"I know what you and the other chieftains hope for. That Cormac would name one of you as his tanist."

"The brehon should have forced Cormac to name a new heir."

"Never, Cormac knew that his son lived and would return. If his father accepts him, the people will too. And the council will have to accept him as heir to the throne. Would you rather have Artúr on the throne?"

Cormac was old.

The people needed to know who would replace him, who would keep the ways of Déaglán. Could this youth be the answer? Perhaps Artúr would be better suited for taking the throne of Cwillan. Heir or not, these were hard times; a firm hand was needed.

What they needed was an alliance with the north, to put a stop to the raiding across their northern border. In private he would speak to Bran about Briana.

Athdar waited for his answer.

"Prove he is the one, then I will tell you what I think on the matter."

"May Niall and Rónán continue in my service?" Athdar looked to Uaid, then to Bran.

Both men agreed.

"Good. They can keep an eye on Cullan for me. Until we decide when the boy is ready to present to his father."

"There they are," cried Bran.

Below the riders came into sight making for the river crossing west of Cwillan.

"Do you think she knows who he is? She seemed ill at ease at times," Bran said.

"Old Sundra never told; if he had, his sister would have expected more money. There has not even been a whisper of a rumor of his existence. Cormac has looked forward to the day his son would return to take his rightful place at his side. Only the Ard Ri and the three of us know of his existence."

"And Niall and Rónán," Uaid added.

"No worry there, they are sworn to secrecy."

Uaid had doubts about Niall, his youngest son. If only Catháir had lived. His oldest son would have known, if Cullan was the boy the women claimed him to be. He sighed and turned to follow his friends up to the fortress.

∽

Cullan followed the two youths back down the roadway. Before they reached the lower bridge, they turned off to the right into an open area. There were a dozen small thatched cottages. At the far end the farrier had set up a stall in a barren area against the rock wall that stretched up to meet the roadway above. Across from the farrier, with its back to the outer edge, stood the stable, a large timber hut with a thatch roof.

At the stable, Niall signaled for the boy who appeared at the entrance to take their horses. "Where is Ciarán?"

"The new horses are being brought in from the east. He wants to get the best for the Ard Ri."

Niall turned to Cullan and spoke in the language of Wyneth. "For the time being you can stay with the farrier, live with his family until other arrangements can be made."

Before Cullan could ask if he had a choice, a man spoke.

"Why do you bring this foreign boy here?" The youths turned, startled by the gruff voice. "Who says I am to take in another to feed and care for. Do I not have enough of my own to see to?"

Cullan studied the newcomer. He had long dark hair he tied back at the neck with a piece of rope. Over his tunic and leggings he wore a leather apron, his muscular arms were burned, scarred by sparks flying from the forge.

"Lord Athdar needs a place for the boy."

"And you thought of me," the man said. "Do me no favors, boy."

Cullan understood only one word out of five. Even without knowledge of the language, the older man had insulted his companion. Niall stood half a head taller then the older man. Rónán's hand went to the hilt of his sword. The air around them became charged with tension between the youths and the dark-haired man.

"Please, Baltice, we want no trouble with kin or near kin," said a woman back in the shadows. She stepped out into the light.

Once she must have been beautiful, now after many summers of hard work she looked worn beyond her time. She stood tall as a man with a regal countenance on her thin face. Her light brown hair was pulled back and tied, rather then braided.

Baltice grumbled, "I could use his help in the forge."

"He can help Ciarán with the horses. Your youngest can work the bellows for you," Niall said.

Baltice scowled at him, then at Cullan. He pointed at the open stable door, "You can sleep in one of the empty stalls."

Sensing the older man's intention, Cullan said, "I would rather sleep up in the loft." This would be no different from the farm, up early and work hard all day. In the loft he would have some privacy.

Niall repeated Cullan's comment to Baltice.

"Arrogant and demanding like all your people. What makes you think you are so special?" Baltice asked. "No fire up there. Understand! Down here we do not care who your friends are above."

After giving Niall and Rónán a meaningful look. Baltice pushed by them to cross over to the forge. He made no effort to introduce the woman. Only when he disappeared into the back of the forge did the woman step forward.

"Welcome, young lord. I am Émer. Baltice says you cannot have a fire in the loft."

She spoke again in the language of Wyneth when Cullan did not answer her. Discomforted at the title, he mumbled that he was not a lord and to call him Cullan. In the shadows, a young girl watched his two companions. She took no notice of him.

He wondered which of the youths she favored.

The woman followed his gaze.

"This is my daughter, Mór." Again, she spoke in the language of Wyneth.

At the mention of her name, the girl moved out into the fading light of day. She looked at him for the first time. Mór was tall and slim, green-eyed like her mother, with hair more like her father's. This is what Émer must have looked like many summers back, beautiful, with the bloom of youth and good health on her. Before life had a chance to wear her down.

Cullan's first night in the loft was no different than his life back on the farm. He found a place for his meager belongings in a niche in the back corner and made a place to lay down with his blanket, used his cloak to cover himself. He fell into a troubled sleep. When he woke toward dawn, he found a small cat huddled close to him for warmth.

In the dim light, he could just make out the striped animal. He slid his thumb under the cat's chin and rubbed and was rewarded with a soft purr. From a cloth wrapped packet he took the remnants of yesterday's fat-soaked bread. He broke it into small pieces. He placed the pieces on his palm and held it out toward the cat. The small cat sniffed at the bread, tried a piece, before finishing off all the scraps.

The small furry animal nosed around for more.

"If I get any food this morn, I will save a bit for you."

Cullan scrambled down from the loft. Outside it was cold; he shivered in his thin tunic and bare feet. The cat joined him at the well.

"So my friend, how did you get down?"

He brought up a half bucket of water. The cat ran ahead of him as he carried the water back to the stable.

"Morning."

Cullan looked up to find Mór standing in the stable door.

He nodded at her.

"I see you have made a friend."

Cullan glanced at the cat, understanding only that Mór had referred to the animal.

"She is an orphan, her mother and the rest of the litter were killed by a hound that went crazy. My father had to put it down," she said in his tongue.

She followed him into the stable, "Do you know Niall and Rónán well?"

"Not really," he said. He wanted to pull off his tunic and wash himself. "They accompanied me here, that is all."

She looked disappointed.

"I have come to fetch you for the morning meal. We eat early each morning. I feared you would still be asleep."

Cullan glanced out the stable door. Already men and women moved among the cottages. On the farm, they were usually up before first light.

"I'll be right in," he said, hoping to dismiss her.

"Our cottage is the one with the blue door," she said, pointing to the cottage only a dozen paces from the stable.

As soon as Cullan was alone he took the bucket of water to an empty stall. He poured the water into an earthen basin he found in the back, and washed as best he could. When he was done he put on a clean, but well-worn tunic and leggings.

He had to stoop to enter the low cottage door.

Five people sat around a small rectangular table.

Besides Baltice, his wife, and his daughter, there were two dark boys, one looked older than Mór, the other younger. Neither of the boys appeared old enough to be in charge of the stables. He guessed there must be an older boy, perhaps older than Mór.

Their meal consisted of a slice of bread with a thin layer of butter and a hot liquid brewed with rose hips.

The meal was almost identical to those Cullan had on the farm.

Baltice watched Cullan. He kept silent, only speaking when asked a direct question. Baltice left first. He scowled at Cullan as he passed him.

As Cullan rose to leave, Émer spoke.

"Lord Cullan, a word with you."

One look from Émer the boys stood and left the cottage to attend to their duties. Mór followed her brothers out.

"There is no need to call me lord, I am only a farm boy. It angers Baltice."

Cullan didn't say "your husband." It was strange to think of these two different people as being married. From the woman's bearing, she was highborn. How had she fallen to this low state?

"Please, stay out of Baltice's way for a few days. I want no trouble with your uncle or his friends. Nor with those two youths who brought you here. They are boys who think they are men, Cullan."

She had dropped the lord. Still, she said his name as if it were still there.

Women were strange creatures.

He found himself addressing her as a lady, using the same manner as she used.

"Later, I will help you with our language."

"Thank you."

⟲

Two days later, the oldest son, Ciarán, returned. He tossed his horse's reins to Cullan.

"So you are here at last."

With Émer's help, Cullan's knowledge of the language of Cwillan had improved. He was glad they no longer had to switch between the two tongues.

The medium-height youth had sandy-brown hair, paler skin than his brothers and sister, with green eyes like his mother. Meeting Ciarán explained many things. His father was not Baltice, even if the man had taken him as his own.

As Ciarán looked Cullan over, his young face creased into a frown.

"Is something wrong, Master?"

"When I heard about you, I expected someone older," Ciarán said. "Could my kin be mistaken about you?"

What was the youth talking about? Perhaps he had misunderstood him.

"What do they call you?"

"Cullan."

The youth smiled, "Do you know what your name means?"

"No, Master. What does it mean?"

Ciarán smiled again, shook his head and said, "It is not important." He turned and walked up and down the open stalls, moved to the back to the box stalls to see if all was in order.

He stopped at the stall with the thief's horse inside, stepped inside to examine the animal. "Where did this horse come from?"

"Niall or Rónán relieved a thief of this horse."

"I will speak with them. They should have taken it up to the fortress stables." Ciarán continued along the stalls giving the mare a quick glance, then moved on. "Well done. You have done a man's work here," he smiled. "Call me Ciarán, I am no more a master here than my father yonder is. Keegan, the Master of Horses, resides above in the fortress, he leaves this stable to my care."

Cullan nodded. He wondered what his name meant.

The days passed, one much as the one before. He brushed horses, saddled them, unsaddled them, and mucked out stalls. He hauled water from the well to fill the trough in front of the stable and carried water to the forge.

Ciarán showed him how to repair leatherwork. The youth was surprised how fast Cullan learned, his long thin fingers worked the leather with ease and at a speed that surpassed even Ciarán's younger brother, who had been at it for years.

All the bridles and saddles were repaired after seven mornings.

Each morning, Niall and Rónán came down to the stable on the pretense of speaking with Ciarán.

Cullan had the feeling that they were checking on him.

The days grew hot as spring turned to summer.

Early one morning Ciarán received a message. He was to report to Keegan, the Master of Horses, as soon as possible. He left Cullan to handle the stable.

Late in the morning, a young girl entered the stable.

Cullan had watched her approach. She was fair to look at, with hair that hung down her back in a cascade of red-gold curls.

"I need to speak with Émer."

"You need to go to the cottage, the one just across the way with the blue door."

He watched as she went to the cottage. No one came to answer her knock. He stepped over to the cottage to speak with her.

"She may have gone up to the fortress with her son."

She watched him with her cool light eyes. He had never seen such beauty before. When she looked at him his heart skipped a beat.

"You are new here?"

He nodded, conscious for the first time of how dirty he must look to her.

She favored him with smile, before she turned to go.

"Please, your name? So I can let Émer know you were here."

She tossed her head; the sunlight glistened on her hair turning it to burnished gold. "Medb," she said over her shoulder.

He watched her until he lost sight of her among the people moving about the village. He was surprised at his interest in Medb. In Wyneth, he had met many of the daughters from the surrounding farms; none had caught his attention. Medb was different; he would find her hard to forget.

When Ciarán returned, Cullan told him about Medb.

The young man thought about it then shook his head. "I do not know anyone with a daughter called Medb. Are you sure about the name?"

"Yes. She is tall, and fair to look upon. With long red-gold hair."

"Was she shy, Cullan?"

"No." He didn't think she was. But then, what did he know of women?

"There are few girls who could be described like that. However the one who comes to mind is very shy and her name is not Medb."

"What is she called?"

"Females are trouble. It is best to stay away from all of them." Ciarán paused, "I will let my mother know about her. Perhaps it is someone she knows."

Cullan found himself thinking about Medb at odd times.

Why had she come to the stables looking for Émer?

Three mornings later, just as he was about to step over to the cottage for his meal, Medb appeared at the stable door.

"If it is Émer you seek, she is with her family."

"I need your help." There was worry in her voice. "It will go hard on me if I have ruined one of my father's horses."

Men held their horses and hounds as dear as their wife and children.

"Where is the horse?"

Cullan followed her over to a place halfway down the village. There she had tied a large roan gelding to a ring set into the boulders that rose up to form the foundation of the wall that ran along the road above. He had her walk the gelding for him. He did not see a problem with the horse's gait.

"The horse looks sound."

"It doesn't happen all the time, but now and then he favors his right foreleg."

With care, he lifted the large hoof to examine the shoe to check for a stone or other debris, which might cause a problem. He found nothing, nor was the shoe loose; an expert had shod the horse.

"Give the horse rest for a few days. That should remedy the problem."

The warmth of her smile washed over him, warmer than the sun above. Her nearness made his heart beat faster.

"Thank you," Medb said.

Medb walked her horse toward the gate. Cullan watched until he lost track of her at the far end of the village.

When he returned to the stable, he found Ciarán inpatient about his absence.

"I was needed to look after a horse."

Cullan didn't mention Medb. He was not sure why.

Ciarán gave him a thoughtful look. "In the future let me know if you will be away from the stable."

"Yes. Of course."

"You better hurry, or one of my younger brothers will eat your meal."

CHAPTER FIVE

Fear prickled Cullan's spine as he ran down a leaf-strewn path, pursued by the man in black. Around him, the forest caught fire. Flames jumped from branch to branch turning the old trees into giant torches. He gasped for breath as the forest became an inferno of heat and smoke. Burning pine needles rained down from above singeing his hands and face.

Cullan struggled across a wide stream. He staggered on only to find the man in black waiting for him. Firelight reflected off the broadsword the man held before him, ready to strike. Cullan stood rooted to the ground, unable to move. Fiery metal sliced toward him.

With a start, Cullan woke up, his heart pounding in his chest. He pushed back his cloak and pulled at his sweaty tunic. His usually cool sleeping place was as hot as an open hearth and seemed to grow hotter as he lay staring up at the roof timbers.

His dream had been so vivid, he could still smell the smoke.

His furry, striped companion, whom he simply called Cat, jumped onto his chest and began to yowl. Sharp claws cut through the thin linen to pierce his skin.

He sat up, pushing the cat off.

Was he still dreaming?

He shook his head to try to clear it. Below, the roar of flames, the smell of smoke filled the night. Now it was not the smell of burning pine, the stench of pitch. Added to the usual odor of manure and warm horse-flesh, he smelled burning wood and hay. The horses below began to whinny in fear and stump around in their stalls.

The stable was on fire!

In the flickering light he pulled his pouch from its hiding place and pulled it over his head and dropped it beneath his tunic. He hurried on his leggings. With Cat held against his chest he climbed down the ladder. On the ground he ran to the bell by the well. He gave the rope several hard yanks. The huge bell clanged, its loud warning in the silent night.

He ran to Baltice's cottage and pounded on the door.

Cullan was surprised when Émer opened the door.

"Fire," he yelled and pushed Cat at her. He ran back toward the well.

Men, women, and children, pulled from their sleep, emerged from the cottages, and begin to run toward the stable.

Baltice organized two lines of men and older boys to bring water from the well. Émer with the help of her daughter gave orders to the older women and smaller children, handed them grain stacks soaked in water to beat at sparks carried by wind. Many of the younger women helped pass the buckets of water.

Amid the chaos of screaming horses and shouts from the water lines, Cullan helped Ciarán and his brothers bring the horses out of the stable.

Men shouted for more buckets, the fire had to be contained. If sparks jumped to the thatch on Baltice's cottage, their small village would be in peril.

Cullan ran his hand along his mare's neck, trying to soothe her before he led her through the burning stable and out to a pen set up at the far end of the village. After checking that all the horses were safe, he relieved a man at the front of the second line of men, waited for the bucket to reach him. They were trying desperately to save the stable. Reinforcement came from the fortress to help contain the fire.

The village must be saved at all cost.

As Cullan waited for another bucket of water, two men, strangers, came from around Baltice's cottage. One carried a miller's sack. It must have been a trick of the light that made the bag seem to move. He was too busy to do more than then yell for the men to join one of the bucket lines.

They stared at him, but made no move to help. The man with the sack moved off, but his companion stood watching the frantic labor of the villagers.

Cullan grasped the pail thrust at him and threw the water on the smoldering thatch. He was not sure when the man with the sack returned. He was there again, standing by his companion.

"Is the cat yours?"

"What?" Cullan said, turning his attention from his duties to the two men. "The striped cat, yes." He grabbed another bucket of water and aimed it at the cottage roof.

"Too bad, I just saw it run back into the stable."

"Are you sure?"

"Yes," said the second man. "Just now, I saw it run in that direction."

The open stable doors framed the inferno within. Cullan swore under his breath. The cat had become his responsibility. How did it get out? If he did not look now, soon it would be too late. It might be too late even now. He gave up his place to another man and hurried back to the well, doused himself with water and ran toward stable.

Inside the stable the intense heat threatened to overwhelm him. Bent over, Cullan had to force himself to concentrate.

Where would Cat go?

The furry animal often slept in the box stall he kept his mare in. He hurried in that direction. There was not time to wonder why the cat would have come back into the burning stable. He had heard an old tale that a horse would return to a burning barn.

The side window stood open.

Cullan was sure Ciarán had closed it earlier.

Just discernible above the roar of the fire he heard an eerie sound that came from somewhere in the back. As he made his way along the closed stall doors, he remembered he had left each one open to show that they were empty. Ciarán or one of his brothers must have closed them.

In the second from the last box stall, Cat crouched in the left-hand corner. Cullan stepped inside to catch her. There was a sound behind him; something hard hit him across the back of the head. He stumbled forward into the hay; a heavy weight came down on his back, pinning him down. His head was jerked up by the hair, then slammed down hard. Sparks flew before his eyes as he slipped into darkness.

Somewhere, in another place, Cat screamed.

Niall pushed his way through the crowd that surrounded the burning stable. Panic grew within him as he searched for Cullan and failed to find him. He was not among the men and boys passing buckets of water. He sent Rónán to look for Ciarán.

Rónán returned with Ciarán.

"Have you seen Cullan?"

"He helped get the horses out. He should be around here somewhere."

"I think he's looking for the cat," said the man at the front of the second line as he grabbed the water bucket to throw on a tree that had caught fire.

"Are you sure?"

The man handed back the empty bucket and took a full one, turned for a brief moment. "I took his place. I saw him head in the direction of the well. Ask there, they should know where he went."

At the well, Niall learned that Cullan had headed toward the stable.

Ciarán and Rónán caught up with Niall.

Rónán grabbed Niall by the arm, pulling him away from the stable. "Would you throw away your life for this boy? If he is in there, it is hopeless."

"This is no common boy," Niall said. "Nothing is ever hopeless, nothing." He gave no thought to his sudden boldness. Nor any thought to the fact that for the first time in his life he was not worried about his own safety. "Stay here, my friends."

Niall grabbed one of the full buckets and doused himself with it. He moved closer to the entrance, took a deep breath and hurried into the stable. The fire was a living thing that wanted to knock him to the ground.

Flames cut off the first and second row of stalls. Only the back row was open for Niall to check.

Rónán and Ciarán joined him.

They moved down the back row where Cullan stabled his mare. The open side window fed the flames as they consumed the dry timbers. Flames raced up the supporting beams, licked at the loft, caught wisps of hay hanging between timbers, raced along the edge as if it were a living creature. In minutes the entire loft was burning.

Calling for Cullan was useless, even if it were possible. The roar of the fire filled their world, blocking out all but the loudest sounds.

The smoke was so thick it stung their eyes and burned their throats with each breath. Soon they were coughing and forced to gasp for each breath. Niall pulled the top of his tunic over his mouth to give himself some protection. His friends did the same.

He was about to signal for them to leave when Ciarán stopped and turned to stare back toward the corner as if he had heard something. He hurried back the way they had come.

It was useless to try to speak, Niall pulled at Rónán's arm to get him to follow him.

Ciarán moved along the row of box stalls. He flung the top door open, listened, then moved to the next. At the second from the end, he pulled both doors open.

Coughing, Niall hurried to join him.

They would have to leave now or this inferno would be the death of them. Inside, he found Ciarán trying to lift a heavy beam that had fallen into the stall. Above, the loft gave an ominous groan. Niall glanced up, before he hurried to help Ciarán. The high-pitched bean sí scream seemed almost part of the noise from the burning stable. Now Niall heard it as a separate sound.

First Cullan's head appeared, then an arm, as Ciarán cleared away loose hay from around the beam. Bits of burning hay began to rain down on them.

They would have to work fast. They lifted the beam off Cullan. Niall helped Ciarán place the unconscious youth across Rónán's shoulders. Then he grabbed a sack, reached down, and caught the frightened cat, dropping the struggling animal inside.

Flames cut off their escape through the front entrance. They hurried to the side window. Ciarán jumped out first and helped pull Cullan to safety. Niall and Rónán joined him. Together, they managed to move the unconscious youth a few paces from the stable as the loft collapsed into the lower level.

The sound of the dying stable thundered around them. Burning hay singed their faces and clothing. Niall smiled at his friends. They were all thankful to have found Cullan and to have escaped with their lives.

As Cullan turned over, rushes crackled beneath him giving off a scent of water and old linen. He had had another dream, like the dream about the fire. The insistent cry of Cat cut through his foggy thoughts to bring him to full wakefulness. He tried to sit up; his head throbbed, he felt dizzy.

He lay back waiting for the dizziness to pass.

With a start, the heat and chaos of the fire came back to him. He eased himself into a sitting position, was startled to find that he did not know where he was.

In the dim light from the dying embers on the hearth, the room was a place of indistinct shapes.

His right hand flew to his chest. His talisman was gone. Desperate to find the pouch he ran his hands over the rush mattress. He lowered his feet to the cold stone floor. He had to find his talisman. The room turned at a crazy angle, he clutched at the bed frame to steady himself. When the room returned to normal, he forced himself to stand.

Behind him wood creaked, someone was there in the darkness. He managed to turn; a woman sat in the corner near the hearth.

"It is too soon for you to be out of bed, lord."

Sick again, he swayed. Strong hands steadied him.

"Easy, Cara is here." She helped him to lie down again. Cat began her insistent yowl.

"Where is Cat?" Cullan asked, his voice no more than a croak.

Only a shadow in the dim light, she moved over to the hearth. From the mantle-shelf she took a braided length of straw and thrust it into the embers. With a tiny flame she lit a candle and placed it on the table by his bed. She moved to the corner of the room.

From a wicker cage she pulled the striped bundle of fur. Cat leaped from her hands, bound across the floor and up onto the bed. Cullan reached out toward Cat as she moved to his side. After working the mattress with her front paws, the cat settled down beside him and began to purr.

"Water, please."

He was helped to sit up; a cup of water was pressed to his lips. He tried to hold the cup and drink deep, to soothe his parched throat.

"Easy, not too much," the women said.

When his stomach started to protest, he pushed the cup away and was helped to lie back again.

"Rest now, lord."

Cullan stared up at the ceiling. The only sound in the room was Cat's soft purr. What had happened to his talisman? The stable had caught fire; he remembered going back into the stable to find Cat. Then pain as something struck him on the back of his head. There was nothing beyond that point.

How did he get here?

Where was here?

༄

Athdar paced the floor.

Niall watched him go back and forth. After a long time the older man stopped in front of him.

"You never told your father?"

Under Brehon Law, Niall was supposed to tell his father, who would then get in touch with the holy men. Young men with his gift needed training. Everyone who came forward had died. His brother had told him to keep it a secret and had instructed him in some of the things that he would need to know.

"It was safer that I told no one."

"Because of your brother?" Athdar said. "Now you tell me this is not about Cullan."

"Lord, not entirely. It was a trap set to catch one of us," Rónán said. "Or perhaps to catch us all. I would guess there is a spy in the village."

"Who?"

"Baltice."

"Careful who you name spy, Niall," the older man said. "Lord Cormac brought him and his family here. I heard that they were starving in a village to the north. At least now he can take care of his family."

"It was done for Émer and her children. Not for him and he knows it."

"Do not hold it against him because he comes from the borderlands. Tell me again what you suspect."

Niall started from the beginning with the orphaned cat that Cullan had befriended. The cat represented a bridge to help him to reconcile himself to his new life.

"When he realized the stable was on fire, he sounded the alarm, gave the cat to Émer. She said that she placed the cat in the cottage. Ciarán found Cullan in a box stall, a beam across his shoulders. The cat was with him."

"Not a trap I would say, then," Athdar said.

"The timbers above were still intact, it was made to look like an accident."

"I see," Athdar said. "And Cullan knows nothing?"

"I think for the time being it is best to keep this our secret."

"Where is he now?"

"In a room off my quarters," Niall said. He noted that Athdar did not say my nephew. "Watched by a servant that has been in service to his family for years."

"Do they know who he is?"

"Perhaps. He is his father's son, after all. Soon we will have to tell Cullan the truth."

"Do you know that your father is upset about my bringing him here?"

Niall nodded. From his pocket he pulled a pouch on a leather strap. "I think you have the mate to this."

Athdar loosened the laces, pulled from it a carved horse head. He closed his hand around the game piece. "Yes, I have the piece given to Pól on that horrible day. I kept it all these years. You are right. For the time being this will remain between the three of us. Hopefully we can keep the truth from Cullan for a while longer."

"The four of us, lord," Rónán said.

"Four? Of course, Ciarán."

They looked up, startled by the quiet knock on the door. Rónán moved to the door, his hand on the hilt of his sword. He called for the person to enter.

"I know you," Athdar said to the woman who entered. "You attended my sister."

She bowed to him, and turned to Niall. "He is awake, lord."

"Good. May I have his pouch back."

Athdar placed the carved game piece into the pouch and handed it back to Niall.

"If you will excuse me. I will see how Cullan is feeling."

CHAPTER SIX

Cullan slipped out of his room. He turned left, heading for the back stairs, hoping to avoid Niall and Rónán. When he heard familiar voices coming his way, he ducked down a side hallway on the first level. At the end he found a wooden door. He entered to find himself in the gallery above the great hall. Below, tables and benches were arranged on either side of a main aisle.

Those of the highest rank would be seated closest to the dais where the Ard Ri's table and high-backed chair were placed. It had never been required of Cullan to take his meals here or come for the evening entertainment.

The room was cold; the huge hearth near the dais stood empty. Above, the high windows caught the morning light. As the day waned servants would light the rush torches placed in brackets along the length of both walls. Near the far end of the room a huge, round, iron candleholder hung on iron chains from a thick beam.

Before returning to his investigation of the castle, he checked to make sure the hall was deserted. Farther down he found a stairway to the ground level. After a search he found the back entrance to the great hall.

His footfalls echoed around him as he moved down the empty room. Birds calling to each other caught his attention. Behind a tapestry placed before an alcove to keep out drafts, he discovered a cage filled with birds. He let the tapestry fall back into place behind him. Taller than a grown man the iron framework was large enough for a boy to enter to clean it. Small birds flitted from branch to branch on tree limbs anchored to the sides.

In Wyneth, single birds or pairs were kept in small wicker cages. He had never seen a large cage of birds before. The drabber grays and blacks flocked together. The single yellow bird kept to itself.

"Good morning."

He turned to find a young woman watching him; she was tall with long dark hair. Her open stare made him uncomfortable. She pulled back the tapestry and tied it off.

"You must be the youth who is friend to Niall. How is your head?"

"I am better, hardly any headache at all."

"If you need something, do not hesitate to seek me out. I can make willow bark tea to ease the pain."

"I am fine," he said. Then changed the subject. "Are the birds yours?"

"Indeed," she said, as a manservant entered the hall on his way to lay new logs on the hearth. As he passed she said, "Only the yellow one sings. The rest I keep for amusement.

When the servant had passed beyond hearing, she said, "A word of caution, young lord."

Surprised, he turned his full attention on her.

"You should not go about alone. Only a blind man would not know who you are. There are men, even here in Cwillan, who do not like this new turn of events."

What did she mean?

Puzzled, Cullan did not know what to say to her. Another manservant entered the hall. She turned to the birds.

"Do not let the birds out on penalty of my wrath." She watched out of the corner of her eye as the servant joined the first one at the hearth. In a kinder tone she said, "Tell Niall that Aoife says he is playing a very dangerous game." She patted him on the arm. "Take care, young lord."

Could it be his imagination, or had her hand lingered on his arm a little longer than necessary?

Later, when he ran into Niall and Rónán, he told them about his encounter with Aoife.

"Cormac never married after his wife died. Aoife is a near relative. She sees to the running of things inside the fortress. Sees that the servants keep to their tasks."

"She is a beauty. Making conquests already?" Rónán winked at Cullan.

Cullan's face grew warm. To cover his embarrassment he told them of her warning. About her hesitation, of not wanting to let the servants over hear her words.

Niall and Rónán exchanged looks.

Smiling at Cullan, Niall said, "She makes a mystery of everything. Life here can be very boring for a woman."

His friends were not telling him the entire truth. What were they keeping from him? Rather than press them he would let it go, for now.

Within days, Cullan learned the layout of the fortress. It was almost as if he had lived here before.

Ciarán brought his mare up to the stable in the fortress. Keegan, the Master of Horses, assigned him to care for his mare and the horses of his two companions. Otherwise he let Cullan do as he pleased.

When his duties at the stable were finished he sometimes sought out the company of Niall and Rónán.

Most of the time he kept to himself.

After a full moon at Cwillan, Cullan decided to disregard Aoife's warning and to strike out on his own. He made friends with the head cook, a jovial heavyset woman. She gave him bread made fresh each morning and a bowl of a hot liquid with a little honey added to sweeten it. After breaking his fast he slipped out of the fortress and hurried down the roadway to the village below.

For a while he was content to stand with the men and boys and watch while workers built the new stable. His friends had saved his life. He owed them more than he could ever repay. Still, he relished his time alone.

When Ciarán joined the group. Cullan ducked his head, moved behind a large man before he moved off toward the gate. He crossed the promenade to gaze out at the fertile valley that stretched for leagues to the east. In the distance, he made out another outcrop of stone. From here it was hard to tell if there was a fortress on it as well.

"Impressive, isn't it?"

Cullan turned to confront a young girl wearing a tunic over leggings. Women in Wyneth seldom dressed in the manner of men. So far here, he had noticed few girls dressed in this manner. He smiled to himself; she had her hair braided and wound around her head, still he recognized her.

It was Medb.

"Yes it is."

She smiled at him. "You're the boy from the stable?"

"I was moved up to the fortress. Even though they have more than enough help up here."

"I am pleased to have run into you," she said and smiled at him again.

For a moment he savored the thought that she had come looking for him. "How can I help you?"

"My horse, my father's horse, is lame. I wonder if you could look at him again?"

He tried to keep the disappointment from showing on his face. Amadan, he whispered and pulled himself back to reality. "Where is the horse?"

Cullan followed her to the far end of the promenade, to a place just before the ground sloped down to enter the tunnel. A young boy waited with the horse. Medb pressed a coin into the boy's hand in thanks.

"The problem is the left foreleg."

Medb led the gelding as he asked, then back. He bent to check the horse's leg. The gelding did not seem lame. He adjusted the foot irons and mounted the horse. Slowly he walked the horse down toward the tunnel, stopped, and had the animal execute a turn. The horse responded to his slightest command.

At a canter he returned to Medb.

He dismounted and handed her the reins, and checked the horse's foreleg again. He still did not find a problem. As he bent to check the leg it came to him. The gelding was sound. Medb had said last time it was the right foreleg.

What game is she playing at?

"Do not ride the horse so hard," he said in a stern voice. Medb frowned at his words. "Did you give him rest?"

She nodded, her mouth pulled into a thin line of disapproval.

"Give him rest for a day or two more."

"Many thanks," she said.

"Your father must be one of the lords from above. Would I know him? Your horse is well trained, very valuable."

"My father is a minor chieftain, we are a sept of Lord Cormac's clan. The horse is valuable, it would go hard for me if I lamed the beast," she smiled at Cullan. "And you? I am often at Cwillan, but I do not remember seeing you before the day I needed to speak with Émer."

Medb's voice was low and sweet, a pleasing soft purr to his ears. Her voice evoked in him feelings he had never had before, unfamiliar and strange. It made his blood run hot.

"My parents are farmers from the west."

Her eyes showed relief. He wondered why she was pleased that he was of even lower status than she was. He did not think on it too long. This daughter of a minor chieftain was fair to the eyes.

"Perhaps we could ride out together, there are ruins nearby. We could..." she stopped.

Her face went pale as she glanced past him. Cullan turned to see what troubled her. Niall and Rónán were coming. The youths searched the crowd as they rode by. They were looking for him. When he turned back to Medb, there was fear in her eyes.

What connection did she have to them?

"As you rode up," she said, moving over to mount her horse. Cullan adjusted the foot irons for her. "Do you remember the stone wall?"

He nodded.

"Go along the wall into the woods, there is a trail there. At the end it splits, left to the village, right takes you to some ruins. Meet me there, as the sun reaches its zenith, in two mornings..."

"Cullan, my name is Cullan."

"Cullan," she repeated. "At the ruins."

His name spoken by Medb made him feel as if he were truly a lord. He helped her to mount, then watched until she entered the tunnel and disappeared into the gloom.

He moved to the parapet and sat down to wait for Niall and Rónán.

CHAPTER SEVEN

Cullan waited on the stone stairs in what had once been a small courtyard. The old walls were gone, only the foundation, the hearth and the stairs he sat on remained.

The day had turned hot.

His heart skipped a beat as Medb rode out of the woods. Her hair pulled back to hang in a cascade of red-gold down her back, to contrast with the simple brown tunic she wore over leggings of the same color.

He helped her dismount. She had a different horse this time.

"You came."

"Did you think I would not?" Cullan said, surprised that she doubted him.

"I brought bia and leann."

"When the others went for their meal, I slipped out to water my horse, then rode down here. I must admit I am glad you brought food."

Cullan helped Medb with the saddlebags. At the edge of the forest they found a shady spot to sit and enjoy their meal. Above them an ancient oak spread its huge branches. They reminded him of arms reaching to heaven, making a plea to the gods.

Niall had been telling him about the true religion. He corrected himself, a plea to the Father and Son.

Medb seemed shy; she concentrated on her food, and talked only to answer his questions. He had never tasted ale as strong as this before. It made him feel warm inside, lightheaded as if he no longer had control of himself.

He leaned back against the tree bole, felt the rough bark through his tunic, content to watch Medb as she gathered her things. Soon they would have to return to the fortress. For now it pleased him to relax and watched her every move.

Overhead in the branches birds flitted around, filling the air with song.

Was it Medb or the ale that made his blood sing? As he helped her with her saddlebags their hands touched. This simple act made his skin grow warm. They walked side by side through the woods, together, yet apart.

Had something changed between them?

Would a day come when he looked back on this afternoon and wish for this simple life again. This new thought puzzled him.

Even with the change between them, he hated to see the day end. They walked back to the place where they had left the saddlebags. Cullan picked them up and followed her back to where the horses were tethered.

After he helped Medb mount her horse, she leaned over and kissed him on the cheek.

"Three mornings from now, when the sun is overhead.

Long after Medb had disappeared into the woods. Cullan watched the spot where he had last seen her. In his heart he hoped that the next three mornings would go by with speed. He touched his skin where she had kissed him, felt again the strange stirring inside himself.

༄

Cullan waited on the stone steps. Overhead the sun climbed in the sky. Still he waited for Medb. Birds called in the woods around him. Two small fat animals ambled out into the sunlight to graze on the grass near the ruins.

When dusk came he left his place on the steps. He would never hear the end of it for being gone so long.

For the next two mornings he rode out to the ruins to wait for Medb. On his return, he would ride across the promenade looking for her in the crowd.

The days passed slowly for him.

What had happened to Medb?

Was it a game after all? Women were strange creatures at best. Cullan tried to forget her, found it was not so easy to do.

It became harder for him to get away from Niall and Rónán. Soon he would have to give up riding out to the ruins. On the fifth morning, he borrowed a horse from his friend in the kitchen. He reached the ruins just as the sun was overhead.

His heart sank when he found the ruins deserted.

Cullan sat down on the stone stairs to wait.

He did not have to wait long. He watched the rider stop at the edge of the woods, before he urged his horse forward.

Niall dismounted and led his horse over to where he sat.

"You have led us a merry chase. What brings you to this place?"

"It is the only time I am alone."

Niall sat down next to him. "I feared I would have to tell your uncle of a dalliance, perhaps with a kitchen maid or serving girl. Your friend who lent you the horse is a little old for you, do you not think?"

Niall watched him.

Does he know the truth?

"Please, do not tell my uncle. I would not want to get my friend in trouble."

"Cullan, I will not, but you must promise me not to wander off by yourself. We live in dangerous times. There are men who would cut you for your boots."

Niall was right. With reluctance, he agreed.

"Come, I have a surprise for you."

❧

Cara set the bowl and pitcher of water on the table and smiled at Cullan. He still felt uncomfortable having a servant wait on him.

"Your hair needs to be cut a little or some will wonder if you are a girl. Then you can tie it back or braid it." She pulled a comb and scissors out of the pocket of the long apron she wore over her shift. She placed them on the table. "And you must decide if you will let that fuzz under your nose develop into a mustache, like your friends here."

His friends had long braids on each side of their face, the rest of their hair flowed down well below their shoulders. To keep their hair out of their eyes the braids were pulled back and secured at the back with small silver ring-combs. Both young men had let their mustaches grow long and full.

Cullan slipped lower in the water as Cara approached. He looked to Niall for help. His friend lounged on the only chair in the room. Rónán leaned against the wall. He would get no help from either of them.

Cara unfolded an oblong piece of cloth, held it up for him. When he did not stand, she turned her head. He rose from the water, wrapping the cloth around his body, and stepped from the tub.

Dripping water on the braided mat, Cullan began to dry himself. From a trunk against the wall Cara pulled out clothes for him to wear.

"I will come back to see what we can do with your hair."

Sitting on the edge of the tub, Cullan had just finished pulling on his boots when the knock on the door announced her return.

"The chair, please," Cara said to Niall.

Niall moved over to the small window. Cat lay on the window ledge in the afternoon sun. Rónán moved over to stand next to him.

When Cara caught a snarl with the comb and tugged too hard, Cullan protested. She worked the rest of the snarls out with her fingers. She went to work combing out his long hair, and then cut it. After considerable clipping, she stepped back to admire her handiwork.

"Good, you no longer look like one of Niall's hounds. I see nothing of your mother in you; you have the look and coloring of your father, the Ard Ri...oh..."

Cullan blinked and stood. When Cara made to stop him, he pulled away from her. Niall and Rónán stopped to stare at her.

"Forgive me, lord, I..."

In a daze, Cullan moved over to the window to stroke Cat.

Niall dismissed Cara.

"What nonsense is this?" Cullan asked when they were alone.

"Would it surprise you to learn that you are the Ard Ri's son?"

"If I were, would I not have some memory of it, of this place?" Cullan ran his fingers through his damp hair. This was crazy.

"Come, I have something to show you."

Out in the hall Cara waited.

"Ask Athdar to meet us below, where his sister lies," Niall said.

Cara hurried off.

Cullan followed his friends down a servant's stairway. At the bottom, he paused. To the left a passage ran back to a cross passage that led to a narrow stairway that went up to the Ladies Bower. Something stirred inside him, something about that passage made him nervous.

Niall placed his hand on his arm, pulling him out of his thoughts. With a backward glance at the passage, Cullan followed his companions out to the main courtyard.

They crossed to the stable.

Seeing the youths approach the stable, the grooms hurried to get their horses ready. Cullan saddled his mare, refusing help.

There was only one cart coming up the road as they entered the tunnel. The rumble of the wheels on stone echoed off the walls. At the ancient stone wall they rode to the end and dismounted, leaving their horses tied in the shade beneath the trees.

At the gate, Rónán gave the hanging rope a hard pull. In the distance a bell rang. They waited for what seemed like a long time. Just as Rónán was about to give the rope another pull, they heard a shuffling sound on the other side, mumbled words. There was a scraping sound; the small door in the gate opened a slit.

"Who wishes entry here?"

"Lord Niall, his Guardian, and a friend," Rónán announced.

The frail old man poked his head through the door, squinted at the three youths, and mumbled an oath. The rusty hinges protested as the old man pulled the door open. Rónán stepped through first, then Niall signaled Cullan to enter. Niall entered last.

Cullan was surprised to find they were in an ancient burial place.

"Do you know the way?" asked the old man.

Niall nodded.

The old man turned to bar the door again.

"Another will be coming, please wait for him,"

When the old man started to grumble, Niall tossed him a coin. With surprising agility, the old man caught the coin in his gnarled hands. After examining the coin, he smiled, and slipped the coin into his pocket.

"This way," Niall said.

The three youths followed the weed-choked path straight back from the gate. Near the center, on a marble pedestal, stood a woman with wings who looked down at them as they approached. Cullan stared at the figure; he had never seen a statue before; nor a winged woman. Her face, weathered by the elements, smiled down at him.

From there they took a side path to the southern wall. Under a small ornamental tree, Cullan made out four graves, newer, more recently placed here than the ones they had passed.

Names were carved into the wall above each grave. First came Aislinn, carved in large letters, then below it: Finnbharr. There were three more names, children he guessed. All four graves were sectioned off by a low wall.

"Aislinn was your mother, Finnbharr your younger brother. He was only of one summer; they buried him in your mother's arms. Your grave is next, and your two sisters, Banba and Medb. The boy buried as you was your friend Pól."

Cullan shook his head, stepped back, at his side his hands fisted. "I know none of these people. My own mother I would remember."

"You found your mother where she lay..."

Startled by the voice, Cullan turned to confront Athdar.

"Your mother was my only sister. We were twins. I loved her with all my heart. I would do anything for her. Anything. I came with her to Cwillan when she married Cormac." He sat down on the bench across from the graves. "So when she told me to take you to safety, I did as she asked. Never realizing until it was too late that she would die and I...I would be witness to it, powerless to help her."

Athdar buried his face in his hands.

"You are wrong. I am not that boy. There has been a mistake."

Athdar looked up at Cullan. "I used to call you Cullan Og. You would not answer to your name, or any of your pet names, after your family was murdered. I stayed in Wyneth with you for a full moon. It was a full twelve moons before my friend sent a message to me that you accepted your name."

Cullan shook his head. "You are wrong I am not that boy!" he sat down on the end of the bench. Athdar reached over and caught his hand. Strange sensations leaped from the older man to him.

Once, a few summers back, Cullan had felt this same sensation during a confrontation with a farm worker. Cullan's head grew heavy, his eyes sleepy, would he be sick? He tried to stand, found it easier to let his body slump back onto the bench. Athdar held on tighter.

This only made Cullan feel worse.

Athdar's thoughts washed over him, filling his thoughts.

He tried to push them away, tried to ignore them. Nothing helped. Vivid images invaded his consciousness; a woman with long dark hair danced around a room. She danced with the abandonment of someone in love with life itself.

Somewhere in the room someone unseen clapped encouragement. In a heartbeat the scene switched to a summer day. Above, scattered white clouds like sheep on a field of blue, with a warm breeze blowing across a flower-strewn meadow. His friend, Pól, ran ahead of him.

They were chasing a fawn through tall grass. He heard his name called. The urgency in the man's voice scared him. He called to his friend; and turned to see what the problem was.

It was Athdar, the man who claimed to be his uncle, but a much younger man than the one he knew. Athdar picked him up and hurried back toward the ruins. Pól followed, he had to run to keep up with them. Two women came out of the fortress, yelled for Athdar to hurry.

Cullan smiled remembering the tall woman's joyful dance.

Her name was Aislinn. Northeast of the fortress was where her clan lived. She took him into her arms, holding on to him as if her life depended on it. Then she held him out to Athdar. Told him to take him to safety.

Reluctantly, Athdar took him from her. He begged Aislinn not to force him to leave her. Her companion pushed Pól forward.

"Yes," Aislinn said, "This will help just in case they find us. Our boys are similar. No one would guess the truth."

Cullan's clothes were stripped off him and he put on the clothes of his friend. Pól put on his.

"Do you have the horse game pieces with you?" Aislinn asked.

Cullan nodded, dug the game pieces out of a pouch he wore around his neck. He hesitated only a moment, before he held them out to his mother. She took only one and gave it to Pól.

Banba, poor sweet child, too young to understand what was going on, stood to the side and watched. Fear plain on her young face. He wanted to reassure her, but did not understand himself what was going on.

Suddenly Cullan found himself in a courtyard; Aislinn lay on the ground. Her sightless eyes looked up at him.

Mother, no...

With a start Cullan opened his eyes to find he was lying on the ground. He blinked. The sun hurt his eyes. He closed them, then opened them and watched the clouds drift by. Seeing them from this perspective made him feel small and insignificant.

Niall knelt by his side.

No one spoke.

Athdar broke the silence. "What happened? I was thinking of the night before Aislinn married Cormac. She danced around the room as if she were a giofóg, from the south." Athdar touched his forehead then his chest with his fingers. "The Father help me. What did he do to me?"

"Not what he did to you, but what you did to him. Unless he tells us what happened we will never know. Perhaps through you he went back to the day his mother died," Niall said.

"How could I doubt him?" He stared down at Cullan, as if he were seeing him for the first time.

"All you had to do was watch the way he would soothe his cat or his horse, never conscious of what he was doing. I wondered if he had ever tried to touch someone's thoughts. Yet you still doubted him."

What was Niall talking about?

"We were back at the fortress on the horrible day," Athdar said.

Niall helped Cullan to sit up.

"It's not true. That was not me."

"Somehow you managed to bury the memory of that day where you would never have to remember it.

Your uncle brought the memory back, even though I am sure you tried to fight it."

"It is time he met your father," Athdar said.

I am not the boy they claim I am, Cullan told himself. Still, they insisted. He had to get away, but how? It came to him. His plan was simple. "This is too much to take in. I need time to understand what is going on here. Please let me rest here in the quiet of this burial place. Later I will meet you back at the fortress."

Athdar agreed.

"We will wait for you by the gate. Take your time," Niall said.

Cullan had not fooled Niall. His friend would not leave him on his own. Another plan took form. He waited to make sure his friends had returned to the gate. Without knowing why, he cut wildflowers and placed them on the grave of Aislinn. He touched his forehead then his chest, much in the way Athdar had.

It seemed to come naturally to him.

The small tree near the graves would not support his weight. He walked along the wall until he found a place where a large rock lay close to the wall. If he stood on the rock, he could boost himself up onto the wall and move along the top.

When he came to a tree large enough to support his weight. He reached out to catch a branch, swung himself away from the wall, let go, and landed lightly on the ground. From there, it was a short walk to where they had left their horses.

Cullan was not pleased with himself; Athdar and his friends would be at the gate a long time. His need to get away outweighed his lie to them. He ran his hands over the mare's head to soothe her, so she would not whinny. Quickly he untied her, led her back along the wall to the place where the path headed down toward the village.

He circled around the village taking the road west. At the first crossroads, he reined his horse in, not sure where to go now. If what the youths said was true, that Athdar was really his uncle, then Wyneth was not his home.

Cullan turned the mare north. He did not stop to wonder why. He rode for the rest of the day. At nightfall, he found a place well off the road to tether his horse and make a place to sleep.

He dared not light a fire.

CHAPTER EIGHT

Cullan woke in the half-light of early morning. The birds in the trees around him called to each other in that time just after true dawn. Hunger gnawed at him, he had nothing to break his fast. He saddled his mare and continued north.

At the sun's highest point he slowed his horse, looking for something, not sure what. Overhead a tree branch had been bent to point downward, to mark the entrance to an old forest road. It had become so overgrown that a casual traveler would not even know it existed.

At the first stream he was forced to stop.

He tied his mare to a tree and walked out onto to a huge split boulder where water poured through to boil at the bottom, then tumble through a series of rapids. He could jump across, but he would not chance his mare breaking a leg. He rode upstream until he found shallow water. He dismounted and led his mare across. He had to backtrack over a league to return to the road.

Near sunset, he came to the ruins of an old fortress. At the edge of the earthwork he stopped his mare and looked across the dry moat to the curtain wall that had collapsed outward for a dozen paces along the south side.

He dismounted and led his horse through the ancient gates. Overgrown with weeds, the courtyard and crumbling walls gave their silent testament. No one had lived here in many summers. Halfway across the courtyard he stopped and stared down at the stonework.

For an instant, a woman lay at his feet. Fear forced him to step back and shake his head to clear it.

From the courtyard, he passed through an arch and down shallow steps to an overgrown garden. He took a rope from his saddlebag, fastened it to the mare's bridle, and tied the other end to a statue. She could graze on the grassy area at the center of the garden. As he walked back to the courtyard, several rabbits darted away from him.

In the main courtyard Cullan crossed to the well; the bucket and rope were new. Someone came here regularly to get water.

How close was he to the northern border?

This is where it happened. He was not even sure where he was; yet, he had found the place. Was he that little boy? How else could he have known to watch for the marker for the way through the woods?

Thoughts of sweet little Banba came to him.

He told himself that they were wrong. He was not that boy. His name was Cullan like the other boy. The man that claimed to be his uncle lied. Had the boy died? Were they trying to force him into a life that was not his?

Cara said that he looked like Cormac. He had seen the High King once as he rode in with his retinue, riding tall in the saddle, a gold circlet on his brow, a stern countenance on his thin face.

Was it safe to leave his horse in the garden? Better to find a place where no one would expect to find a horse. In a room in an intact section of the fortress, near stairs to the first level, he placed his mare. He would sleep in here as well. Tomorrow he would go east, see what the land looked like in that direction.

Remembering the new bucket and rope, he hurried out to the forest; on the backside of a low-growing tree he broke a branch off. He went three dozen paces into the forest, holding the branch like a broom he swept away his tracks, working his way all the way to the south gate and into the courtyard.

He paused halfway across the courtyard, waited for the vision to come again. He did not know if he was disappointed or happy when nothing happened.

Late in the night, Cullan woke to hear horses whinnying close by. He rose, held his mare, running his hand down her head to her nose. He did not want her to answer the horses. When he was sure he had soothed the animal, he made his way up to the first level. Concealed at one of the windows he watched riders to the east.

From the torch carried by the lead rider, he made it out to be a party of six. Four more came from the north to join with them. After a short meeting the riders headed north.

"Northerners. This place is closer to the border than I realized. Time to move on."

In the morning, there were more riders, northward and in the direction of the forest. He decided to stay in the fortress for a while.

As the sun passed its zenith, Cullan trapped two rabbits and skinned them. He found a cauldron to hang over a small fire he built in the underground kitchen. He added water, when it came to a boil he added the rabbit meat and a few wild herbs he found in the garden.

As soon as the meat looked cooked, he put out the fire.

After not eating for two days, the simple fare tasted like a feast. He wished he had meal to make bread. After eating he found a niche in the wall to place the cauldron, he scattered the ashes. At a glance, no one would know that he had been cooking down here. In time, the earthy closed-in smell would over-power the scent of burning wood and cooked meat.

On the fourth morning, Cullan watched from his first level lookout as a hooded rider rode out of the forest. The rider stopped at the edge of the trees. He dismounted, knelt, and scanned the ground before him. Then he stood and stared at the ruins. He mounted his horse and rode back into the forest, only to reappear again as the sun began to dip toward the horizon.

Again the rider dismounted and searched the ground. On top of the earthwork, he stopped his horse and placed his fingers to his mouth. Cullan hurried down the stairs to get to his mare in time. Too late, a sharp whistle split the air. Below, his mare answered with a loud whinny that would echo out to the rider.

Cullan waited in his room for the rider to find him. The sound of iron-shod hoofs on stone echoed through the silent ruins. The sun had almost disappeared in the western sky as he heard the footsteps approach.

Rónán appeared in the doorway holding a torch high as he inspected the room. "You made good your escape."

He stepped into the room placing the torch into a wall bracket.

"I am surprised you are alone. I have observed northerners coming and going."

"And how would you know about northerners?"

"The same way I knew how to get here."

"I followed your trail through the forest. Few people remember this old road. I backtracked to make sure that you did not leave the trail at some point. I sent Ciarán back to get the others."

"I should have left as soon as I saw you."

"To go where? To Sylva?"

Rónán was right. Where would he go? He had not even realized at the time that he was coming here.

"Two days ago from a hill west of here, well off the main roadway, we watched northerners. This is the farthest into our lands they have come in a long time."

"Who are they?"

"A war band of Artúr's uncle. No one lives up here because it is too close to the northern border."

Cullan watched the youth. This talk of war bands meant nothing to him.

"Who is Artúr?"

"The son of your fathers only sister. She married a northerner to help unite our people. To bring peace between us."

"Did it?"

"No. Artúr's uncle now has his eyes on all our lands, not just the marriage portion he was given. It would not surprise me that he gave the order to slaughter your family."

Cullan thought on the matter for a while. He tried to form a defense to prove that he was not the boy they claimed he was.

"Without an heir, Artúr takes the throne of Cwillan. That is, if something were to happen to Lord Cormac."

"That is why your uncle brought you back to Cwillan. To take your rightful place."

"My rightful place," Cullan said. "I still do not believe I am the son of the Ard Ri."

"As you said, how else would you have found this place?"

"The man who claims to be my uncle did something to me that day at the burial place. Those were not my memories. Somehow through him I learned to watch for the marker for the road up here."

"He claims you did something to him," Rónán said. "You can discuss it with your uncle and Niall when they get here. It may be a day or two. They will wait until they are sure they can avoid an encounter with warriors from the north." He glanced around the room. "Have you eaten?"

"I am tired of rabbit."

"I take that as no. I have some seasoned meat and bread. The packhorse is with Niall. We have enough for a few days. And some grain for your horse."

"Someone comes here. There is a new rope and bucket to get water from the well."

"Not a northerner."

"Why not?"

"By Crom, Lord Cormac put a curse on this place. If a northerner enters here, a horrible death will follow. As to the rope and bucket, it is most likely a shepherd, or perhaps your uncle comes here. His clan is not far from here."

Cullan doubted the youth believed the story of a curse. On the other hand maybe he did.

"Why did Niall send you?"

"I am Niall's Guardian." When Cullan made no comment, Rónán went on. "Niall is like you." As if that explained everything. "He can read thoughts, as you did that day at the burial grounds. They say you can remember things that when recalled are as real as life itself."

Fear prickled at the edge of Cullan's thoughts. The memory of what happened at the burial place still fresh in his mind still haunted him. He had heard of Guardians, what did it have to do with him?

"No one can read another man's thoughts."

"Think what you want. They say a properly trained man can even change another man's thoughts, bend his will. Make him do something he would not otherwise have done."

"What does that have to do with you being a Guardian?"

"In the old days, the Guardians saw to the protection of the entryways. Now the entryways have been lost. We now act as protectors to those who have the Power. Men like Niall and yourself. There have been Guardians in my family since Clontarf," Rónán said with pride. "Alas, many no longer believe the old ways."

"Why?"

"Few can read the old language. Many claim that Clontarf is only a myth made up by the holy men."

Cullan did not really understand this talk of having the Power and reading thoughts. Nor had he ever heard of Clontarf.

Since the south curtain wall no longer protected the old fortress from intrusion, they moved up to the first level to await the others. Rónán stayed awake late into the night to keep watch. Some nights, from their lookout they watched riders pass. Always the riders kept well away from the dark ruins of the fortress.

Three mornings later the clatter of hoofs on stone announced the arrival of Athdar and his friends. They led two horses in with them, a tall gray stallion covered with a blanket along with a sturdy packhorse.

Athdar dismounted first and came forward. "Forgive me, for doubting who you are."

He knelt, his left knee and hand touched the ground, his right hand he placed on his right knee. He bowed his head. Puzzled, Cullan looked to Niall for help. The youth signaled him to touch his uncle's head. Cullan did so, but only briefly, afraid that strange visions would come to him again.

Athdar rose and bowed his head again and stepped back.

When Niall moved forward to bow. Cullan put a stop to it. "No man bows to me, I am not your lord."

"But you are, Cullan. You are the son of the Ard Ri. You have my sword and my fealty."

Rónán and Ciarán kept silent, but their eyes said that they were in agreement with Niall. How could he stop this? Even if he was Cullan, the prince of Cwillan, he still hoped to put an end to any plans his friends were making.

"I am not the youth you seek."

"I know you are," Niall said. "My brother told me that you would have a talisman, a white carved horse head that will match the game pieces on your father's board."

Cullan fought to keep his hand from the pouch that hung beneath his tunic. When had he received the game piece? In his dim past, he recalled a game board in a large room. He had taken both white horse heads. Now he only had one. What had he done with the other?

Pól had the other game piece.

"Not saying that it is true," he said. "I will have no man bow to me."

"Come," Athdar said. "We will eat. In the morning we will return to Cwillan, you will meet your father. He sent a gift, Warlord, one of the finest horses in all the land."

The tall gray stallion pricked its ears forward at the mention of his name.

Warlord was a magnificent animal. Indeed a gift fit for a prince. If he accepted the gift, he would also accept all the duties that went with being the son of the High King.

Cullan made no move toward the stallion. He had his mare; for now it was enough for him.

At some point on the ride back to Cwillan, Cullan was sure, with only a few doubts, that he was the prince. Had he known all along? Had he refused in his heart to believe what his head was telling him?

It went beyond the game piece he carried all these years. It was his knowledge of Cwillan, their language, and the ease he felt after a few days of moving up to the fortress. He had tried to ignore the feeling that he had come home. Now he was to meet his father for the first time in many summers.

Cormac stared down at him from his high-backed chair. Does he see me for who I am, or does he see what the others have told him?

"Come forward, son. It has been too long." Cullan hesitated. "Do you remember? How you would scratch with a sharp stone squares on the steps to the bower. You would take the pieces from my board and play your own game."

In his mind, Cullan saw the narrow stairs that led up to a low doorway. A grown man or woman had to bend to get through. For a child it was easy to pass through to the bower, or down to the lower levels. He blinked. Cormac had not touched him, yet the memory came to him. In truth, he was that boy, yet he held back. He did not want to take on this new life. That meant people would bow to him; he did not understand why this bothered him.

With less difficulty than to recall what he ate the morning before, he remembered his earliest memory of Sundra and the farm. Sundra took him to the village at the crossroads. The old man carried him on his shoulder into a sweet shop and bought him several pieces of honey candy.

Cullan licked his lips as if tasting the candy again. He frowned, beyond that point there was nothing. Then a new thought came to him, one that he did not understand at all.

Did his father still have his stones?

Without thinking, Cullan stepped forward. Cormac, High King of the clan of Déaglán stood, stepped down from the dais to take him in his arms.

"My son, it has been too long."

That evening, Cullan met the chieftains that made up the clan at a great feast prepared in his honor. Most of the chieftains seemed to accept him as the heir to the throne of Cwillan. Only Uaid gave him a cool welcome. Did Uaid know the truth about him? Perhaps not; he suspected that Niall had not told his father.

Hardly had he settled into his new life, when the talk turned to finding a young woman for him to marry. Cullan was sure he was too young to think of taking a wife, but his father and uncle pushed the matter. His thoughts turned to Medb. He decided to make some discreet inquires about her.

Cullan tried in vain to get news of Medb. She seemed to have vanished from the land. He even went to Émer, hoping for information. She told him she had never heard of the girl.

As the year neared its end, the forest around Cwillan and the surrounding countryside turned to gold, and vivid reds and oranges. Winter would be upon them and it would be many moons before the new growing season came again.

On Samhain, summer's end, the countryside glowed with the fires marking the turning of the year. As the weeks passed the weather turned cold, daylight shortened as winter took its hold on the land. Even the short days stretched long for Cullan. His father included him in every meeting. The affairs of state took up most of his time. In a way, he longed for his days back on the farm.

Cullan went out with the hunting parties. Niall and Rónán accompanied him, as well as warriors assigned to him as his personal guard anytime he left the fortress. With Niall's hounds they hunted for game to the south of Cwillan.

Soon the snow grew too deep.

Life slowed.

They stayed in the fortress, content to sit by the fire and talk about what they would do in the spring.

Each of Cullan's friends talked of what they hoped for in the future. Only Ciarán kept silent. He seemed content to listen to his friends.

When the weather lightened, the chieftains returned to Cwillan. They talked and argued before Cormac about what to do about Darlisca. Raiding had began across their north border. Cormac sent warriors northward to drive the northerners from their land. After several brief but bloody battles the war bands pulled back into their own land.

As time passed Cullan found it easy to slip into the life of a privileged son. He wondered if given the chance would he choose to go back to the farm in Wyneth. At one time he would have said yes. Now that he knew that Wyneth was not his home, he no longer thought about returning there.

By early summer Cullan had lived at Cwillan for twelve moons. The land seemed calm, still he was sure some danger lurked around the next corner.

He let Warlord slow to a walk, matching the stride of Niall's gelding. Both riders fell behind their companions who had ridden into the dimly lit tunnel.

"You will need to choose someone to be your Guardian, Cullan."

"Who would I choose?"

"There is one who would consider it an honor to be of service to you."

"I do not know who you speak of."

"Ciarán."

Ciarán! Of course, that is why he never voiced his wishes. Cullan reined in his horse at the entrance to the tunnel. Thoughts of Ciarán vanished as he looked into the darkness at the other end of the tunnel. The night around them seemed too quiet.

Some inner sense made him hesitate.

"The others passed without incident, we should have no problem," Niall said.

With a nudge of his heels, the gray moved forward to follow Niall's gelding. Once they were deep into the tunnel the torches at their end of the tunnel went out.

Darkness swallowed the world around them.

"We are not alone here," Cullan said.

"I am afraid you are right. Hold your ground."

The sound of baying hounds made the hair at the back of Cullan's neck rise, sent chills down his back. The sound echoed off the walls and roof making it hard to tell how close they were. Beneath him the stallion shifted. He sensed rather than heard his friend soothe his horse. He did likewise with the gray.

When Niall told him to dismount. He did so. Not sure if they would be any safer on foot.

"We will send the horses on up, the hounds will follow them. Our enemy will be forced to come to us. For now they are as blind as we are."

With a slap on the rump Niall sent his horse on up toward the fortress. Cullan slapped Warlord. Listened as the clatter of hoofs moved away from them. Something large and hairy bumped against him, turned and snapped at him, then was gone as the pack moved off in pursuit of the horses. The horses left the tunnel, dark forms against the darker night, with smaller forms in pursuit.

Now all was quiet.

"Arm yourself, back to back, now," Niall whispered. "If they light the torches do not look into flame. It will ruin your vision for a time."

CHAPTER NINE

At the gate, Rónán stopped his horse to wait for Cullan and Niall. Athdar and Ciarán just behind him stopped also.

"Did they enter the tunnel?" Rónán asked.

"Do not worry, they will be along. They talk more than a couple of old women," Athdar said.

"What troubles you, Rónán?" Asked Ciarán. "We are safe in the fortress now"

"By Crom, we are not in the fortress yet. What is that sound?"

The words were barely out of Rónán's mouth when two horses emerged from the tunnel followed by a pack of baying hounds.

Rónán dismounted and drew his sword, told his bay to stand.

The two riderless horses ran on across the promenade to be lost from sight as soon as they moved out of the circle of yellow light created by the gate torches. The snarling pack made to follow them. Rónán stepped into the path of a huge beast that wore a spiked leather collar.

The hound lunged at him. With an agile side step to avoid the powerful jaws that could snap a man's arm in two, he drew his sword across the beast's throat. The smell of blood drove the pack into a wild frenzy. They turned on their fallen leader and tore at its lifeless body.

When the pack lost interest in the dead hound, they milled around, growling, ready to take on a new victim. Rónán moved back against his horse.

Ciarán joined him. "Athdar has gone to retrieve the horses."

In the distance a horn sounded on the night air.

The pack turned jostling each other as they made for the tunnel and disappeared into the darkness.

Rónán mounted his horse and rode after them. At the tunnel he was dismayed to see only darkness. He called to the guards to bring torches. He wheeled his horses in a tight circle as he waited for the guards.

When they arrived, they looked into the darkness, then at each other, eyes wide with fear. Rónán leaned over and grabbed the torch from the hand of the nearest guard.

He urged his horse down into the darkness. Behind him, Ciarán yelled for him to wait.

⁓

Cullan, sword drawn, stood back to back with Niall. He waited, alert to every sound.

From somewhere behind them a horn sounded, echoing off the walls and swirling around them. The hounds rushed by, black shapes in the darkness, heard but not clearly seen.

Nearby a sound made Cullan strike out with his sword. The scream of an unseen man told him that his sword had found its mark. Muttered curses came from all around them. The very air seemed to have a voice.

Every minute their unseen enemy delayed brought their rescue closer.

When the torches were lit, Cullan turned his head.

The tunnel entrance was blocked by men on horseback. With the light, the enemy came at them full force.

Cullan waited. Let the enemy come to him. His sword work was basic; fortunately for him these men were not seasoned warriors.

Down the tunnel rode a warrior in full charge, his war cry terrifying in its ferocity, the sound echoing around them.

"What new devilment is this?" Niall called over his shoulder.

Sword in one hand and a torch in the other, the rider bore down on them. Cullan relaxed a little when he recognized Rónán. Their friend threw the torch at the nearest enemy, and rode his horse into their midst, forcing them to scatter. Then a second rider joined him. The odds were with them now; their attackers turned and ran.

The riders blocking the tunnel turned their mounts and made their escape.

Thank the Father, Cullan thought, breathing a sigh of relief. Someone grabbed him by the arm, pulled him away from Niall. Weariness slowed his movements. In the second before he slid into darkness, Niall yell a warning. As he turned his head, something hard hit him, the world around him dissolved into nothingness.

∽

Cullan woke to find Niall leaning over him, he sat back with a sigh.

"You gave us quite a fright." Niall leaned over again to place his fingers on his forehead.

Cullan pushed his hand away. "What are you doing?"

"It is a simple thing that will calm you without any ill effects," Niall said as he returned his fingers to Cullan's forehead.

"You did that to me once before?"

"Yes. Only a little pain from the blow, that is good. It is a hard lesson to learn to not lower your guard too soon."

"Is everyone else all right? My uncle?"

"All are well. Rónán and Ciarán ran down several of the enemy. They would not surrender. The leaders on horseback made good their escape."

"Who were they?"

"Artúr or his uncle sent them. Rest now."

Cullan did not ask Niall for the details. He was not sure he wanted to know what had happened after he was hit.

Again, Niall placed his fingers on his forehead. Cullan made to protest. His friend shook his head.

"Rest now."

Cullan's eyes grew heavy as he slipped into sleep.

His last thoughts were that he needed to learn how to do this.

༄

Niall left Ciarán to watch over Cullan.

Cara hovered near, ready to help if needed.

In the outer chamber, Cormac waited with Athdar for word on the young prince.

"Will he be all right?" Cormac asked. "I have sent for a healer?"

"He is fine, pain from the blow, nothing more," Niall said, hoping to reassure the High King. "In the future we need to take care. Someone wants to see Cullan dead."

"Rónán," Cormac said as he turned to the young man standing guard at the door. "I need to speak with your father."

He nodded. "I will ride to my father's holding at first light."

CHAPTER TEN

"Why?" Cullan asked.

"Every time I tell you something, you ask why. You sound like a petulant child. If you must know, a marriage between the clans makes us stronger."

"I do not know this girl. There is one that I would chose."

"What girl?"

"Her name is Medb. She is the daughter of a minor chieftain."

Cullan stopped to adjust the gold circlet on his forehead. It was a little too big for him.

"So there was a dalliance," Niall said. He shook his head in disbelief. "The daughter of a minor sept is not for you. Briana is nothing like her brother if that is what worries you. She is considered to be a quite a beauty. Besides a marriage with the clan of Guardians will put to rest in the North any idea that Artúr will ever sit on the throne of Cwillan."

At his friend's words, a chill ran down Cullan's spine. *Or it will bring their wrath down on us all.*

"Your father is well pleased with you. Pleased that you have learned our ways so fast."

"Is it not all part of who I am? The learning?"

"There is nothing you cannot learn if you set your mind to it," Niall said. "Soon we will travel to Alibie to meet with Abbot Tadc. There you will be taught the things you need to know, but first you must meet Briana and the alliance between the clans will be sealed."

With reluctance, Cullan followed Niall. Rónán and Ciarán waited for them in the back hall. The introductions would take place up in the Ladies Bower. Cullan paused at the bottom of the stairs. He took down the torch from the bracket to look at the steps. The squares he had scratched into the bottom step were still there. He shuddered as he recalled the memory of a dark man looming over him. Sweat broke out on his forehead; he forced himself to calmness and replaced the torch and started up the stairs.

At the top, Niall stopped him. "Ciarán will go first, Rónán will come last."

The tall youths had to bend low to go through the small doorway. A single warrior could defend the entrance.

At the end of the bower, near the grape arbor, Cormac waited for his son. Athdar stood to his left and Aoife to his right.

"Welcome, Prince Cullan," Athdar said. He nodded to a servant, who turned and hurried inside.

From the inner chambers came a party of three. Bran, his wife, Síle, who was almost as tall as her husband. Cullan's attention went to the hooded young woman who walked between them. Head down, she studied the ground as she moved forward between her parents.

She looked like a person going to their doom, not to her betrothal.

Cullan waited by his father.

He had a dream about Medb during the night. What had become of her? No one had heard of the maid when he made inquiries. He had hoped to find her before this day. Now it was too late, his fate and Briana's would soon be sealed.

Bran stopped a few feet from Cormac. His wife and daughter stopped a pace behind him. "Prince Cullan, may it please you, this is my daughter Briana." He stepped aside, signaled for his daughter to move forward.

Only then did the girl look up; she pulled her hood back, let it slip across her shoulders to reveal her long red-gold hair. For a moment the two stood transfixed, unable to speak.

Briana broke the silence. "You!"

Not understanding what was wrong, Síle placed her hand on her daughter's arm. Briana gathered up her skirts, darted around her mother, managed to avoid her brother as well and ran back inside.

"My lord, I do not know what to say. I do not understand my daughter's reaction. She means no insult to the young prince," Bran said, his face red with embarrassed.

When Cormac spoke his tone was cold, unbending. "This marriage has been agreed to."

❦

Cullan sat down on the stone bench with a sigh. He leaned back against the sun-warmed wall, slipped the circlet off his head, and hung it on the grapevine that worked its way up the framework set against the inner wall.

Niall sat down next to him.

"You heard what I told my father," Cullan said. "She came to the stables below, told me her name was Medb. We met twice after the fire."

Rónán came out of the inner room. He came straight over to his friends. He scowled down at Cullan. "She will not speak to anyone, not even to our mother."

"Hear me. We have nothing to be ashamed of. We talked, nothing more."

Rónán sighed, "I expected nothing less from you, yet..."

"You wondered because of her strange behavior?"

"Yes," Rónán said. "Síle will talk some sense into her."

"Should that make me feel better? To have Briana forced to marry me."

All this time he had thought that Medb, Briana cared for him. Now he had to wonder. Had it been a cruel game after all?

CHAPTER ELEVEN

Cullan had to force himself to hide his disappointment when Niall and Rónán departed for Alibie. His friends would speak with Abbot Tadc. If accepted by the abbot, they would study there for twice the turning of a year.

When will it be my turn to ride to Alibie?

Cullans's days were busy, filled with affairs of state. Each new moon he listened to the judgments made by Maiú, the chief brehon who lived at the fortress. After that he talked with Tole, apprentice to Maiú, who hoped one day to become a brehon.

After his midday meal, taken with his father, Cullan practiced sword work with Ruadrí, the Master at Arms. Later he sparred with Ciarán. Always at the back of Cullan's mind, painful even after many mornings had passed, was Briana's rejection of him.

She told her father that she would join a holy order rather than marry.

It confused and saddened him.

Had he been wrong about her feeling for him?

One moon later, bored with sword work, he made an early escape. He climbed the steps from the practice field to find the main courtyard in chaos. Riders from the east had run into a war band from the north, two of the five were dead. Two horses stood nearby, he recognized Niall's dark gelding and Rónán's bay as a groom led them away.

He had to force his way through the crowd that had gathered around the two bodies stretched out on the ground. His heart began to beat faster. He recognized the design on the cloth spread over the bodies. It belonged to the Clan of Guardians.

No not my friends.

He knelt to check for himself.

The excited voices buzzed around him like angry bees. Cullan hesitated a moment before he pulled back the cloth. He felt relief when he did not recognize either man. Sadness too; tonight a mother, wife or sister would mourn, a father had lost his beloved son. He replaced the cloth over the dead men.

Behind him a woman screamed, a high-pitched blood chilling cry. He stood. She screamed again.

"Rónán, my God, no, not my brother," Briana cried.

Cullan tried to soothe her, to tell her that her brother still lived. She pulled away from him, looked him in the eye. For a second he thought she would strike him.

"This is all your fault, you and your kind will be the death of my family. Rónán!"

She called on the Father and Son, before she screamed a high-pitched hysterical wail that set his teeth on edge. She fisted her hands, began to pound on his chest. He grabbed her by the arms to hold her tight against him; she struggled, he held tighter.

He placed his face against her face, tried once more to soothe her.

The turmoil in Briana's mind filled his. She was running down a woodland path. Across a small glade, a man leaned against an oak tree. He neither waved nor acknowledged her presence. Only when she drew near did she see the second man who lay at his feet. Her heart beat faster with fear as she moved closer.

The first man was pinned to the tree with a spear. Both hands cut off. Blood was everywhere, staining the grass and meadow flowers. At his feet the second man had two spears through his chest. His sightless eyes looked up to the sky.

Both men in the vision looked familiar, though he was sure he had never met either of them. As she stared at the man pinned to the tree, he became the man with the spear through his chest and Ciarán lay at his feet.

Cullan broke his bond with Briana, but was afraid to release her. His heart raced with fear. What could cause such a horrible vision?

"Let me go!"

He hesitated, but did as Briana commanded.

She stepped back, her eyes fluttered. Cullan caught her as she slipped to the ground. He lifted her with ease. He had to force his way through the crowd gathered around them. Whispers followed him as he made his way to the fortress entrance. As they passed, men and women touched their forehead, then their chest.

He stopped a young servant girl. "Find Aoife, send her to me." The girl bowed, then hurried off. Two at a time Cullan took the stairs up to the first level. As he reached the top, Ciarán called to him and hurried to catch up.

"What has happened, lord?"

"She had some kind of spell. Do you know if Lord Bran and his lady are in their apartment?"

Ciarán shook his head.

Cullan was about to send Ciarán down to find them. He remembered in time that it would not look proper if they were alone. "Come with me, until they find Aoife."

The apartment used by Bran and Síle was empty. He took her into the first sleeping chamber. Ciarán helped him lay her on the bed.

Briana's pulse was weak but steady.

"You are an amadan to bring her here!" Aoife said from the doorway.

"I did not know where else to take her," Cullan mumbled.

She moved to the side of the bed to check Briana for herself. "If word gets around that you were in her chambers without kin present..."

"I needed a place to take her."

"Leave us. Go to your careless friends below."

Cullan backed out of the room as if he were a small child chastised by an older sister. Below he found a guard who explained that Niall and Rónán were with a healer.

"Where?" Cullan asked.

"Come," Ciarán said. "I know the way."

They went by the stairs to the kitchen and into another wing of the fortress. Cullan was surprised to find Mór with his two friends. Niall leaned against a wall, while Mór worked on Rónán. With careful stitches, she closed a wound just below his right cheekbone. There was blood everywhere. Cullan marveled that Rónán lay so still while she worked on him.

Cullan looked away from Mór and Rónán.

Niall moved over to stand beside him. There was blood spattered across his tunic.

"What happened?"

"We were set upon just a little east of here, as we were coming back. We made good account of ourselves. We lost two. We sent many more of them to their pagan gods."

"Briana thought..." Cullan started.

"What has happened? You look worse than Rónán."

"Briana thought it was Rónán that was killed. She..."

"She what?" Niall demanded.

"I am not sure what passed between us. Briana has this terrible memory. It came to me as I held her. I am not sure who the one man was, but the one on the ground was her kin."

"What else?"

Cullan shook his head. It did not make sense, any of it.

"What else, Cullan Og?"

Cullan closed his eyes, he hated being call by that name. As if he were still that small boy who witnessed a tragedy so many moons ago. Even with help, he could only remember a few bits of what happened at Carracán. He remembered nothing of the boy he had once been.

"What else?" Niall asked, this time in a low tone meant to soothe.

"Suddenly, I was pinned to the tree; Ciarán lay at my feet."

The blood drained from Niall's face, he bite his lower lip and looked away, before saying "The man pinned to the tree was my older brother." Sadness marked his words. "The one on the ground was Kleeta, her older brother."

"Why the hands? Why cut them off?"

"Because our enemy thinks that our power comes through the hands." Niall's voice was calm now. "Perhaps you have learned too fast. It is time you talked to the holy men."

"She stilled, then fainted. Did I hurt her?"

"You do not know how to gentle your touch. With your uncle or with Briana."

Cullan wanted to ask Niall an important question, but did not know how to put it to him. Instead, he looked over at Rónán. "Will he be all right?"

Niall seemed deep in thought. "Wounds to the face look worse than they really are. It is all so simple now. Yet no one saw the truth."

Mór stood up, her apron stained with blood.

"Come, Cullan. Help me with Rónán. I do not think he is in any condition to walk. He drank a whole crock of ale. We will talk in my apartment. Away from listening ears."

❧

Cullan watched his friend. When Niall did not respond to his question, he asked again. "Am I a witch?"

"Who put that idea into your head?"

"In Wyneth they said that there were men here who were witches."

"The holy men say that we came with the sons of Mil to a new and green land, from a place beyond the sea. Our clan was among the first to embrace the Father and Son as the true faith, brought to us by Pádraic. Later we were driven out of our green lands by an old enemy."

Cullan was not sure that Niall had answered his question.

"When my father hears of this fight," Niall said. "He will send his personal guard to take me home!"

"Is he still at Cwillan?"

"No, but bad news travels faster then a brush fire. I think we should go to Alibie before I am recalled to my father's holding. All your questions can be answered there."

"Your father does not like me."

"It is nothing personal. My father has lost one son. He takes the path that will keep what is left of his family alive. I will speak to Athdar, who will speak with Cormac. If the High King agrees, we leave for Alibie as soon as arrangements are made. I will also speak with Baltice, so Ciarán can join us. Make your farewells to Briana."

Chapter Twelve

The bench was hard; it was impossible for Cullan to find a comfortable position. Briana sat across from him. At the other end of the Ladies Bower, Aoife and Gila, Briana's companion, sat in the shade under the grape arbor.

Briana's father would not allow them to meet without Aoife or her companion with her.

Cullan smiled, she looked better than the afternoon he carried her up to her apartment. He leaned over, his words only for her. "I am sorry about your brother. I never knew until that moment when I held you."

Briana concentrated on a wicker cage, in which a small yellow bird sang. She turned to him. Tears stood in her eyes. "I was only nine summers when I found them." Briana blinked back tears. "My father was here earlier. He told me that the Ard Ri still wants me, us..." she stopped. "Now I wonder if you still want to go through with this...this?"

"Nothing has changed."

"I am surprised you can forgive me, for being an óinseach, a fool."

"There is nothing to forgive, a ghrá."

Satisfied that Aoife was busy with her needlework, Cullan moved over to sit next to Briana.

"Did you know Catháir?"

"Yes. All those with the gift are dead, murdered. Catháir was the last," she said. "When my brother told me that you were like him, I wanted nothing to do with you. To live in dread of the day when they would come and tell me that my husband was dead. I could not bear it."

"Even now knowing who I am?"

"Cullan, that makes it even worse."

He wished he had the words to comfort her.

"Artúr's uncle has sent one of his advisers to speak with my father. He wishes me to marry Selatin. It is an old request that Bran has no wish to fulfill. Before it was because I was too young. I do not know what he will tell him this time."

Cullan put a finger to her lips to stop this talk of a marriage with another. But quickly withdrew it, afraid he would bring on an unwanted memory.

"Perhaps he will tell him the truth; that your betrothal has already been set," Cullan said. "You see I have not changed my mind. I waited for you each morning at the ruins."

"I wanted to meet you. Somehow Aoife found out about my leaving the fortress alone. She sent me back to my father's holdings. There was no time to send a message to you."

Briana glanced over at Aoife, turned back to him. "I fancied you since the first time we met. I ask you on your honor; do you wish out of this arrangement? Think before you speak, lord."

"I need no time to think, Briana. Let us tell our families that we will wed when I return from Alibie."

She seemed to have trouble making up her mind.

"There will be times that I do not understand you, cannot understand you." Briana paused, "I do not think love will make things easier for us, but I will try."

Cullan turned to check on Aoife. She conferred with Gila over their needlework. He turned back to Briana, leaned over, and favored her with a brotherly kiss. She smiled, and gave him a real kiss. He gasped at the sweetness of her lips, far sweeter than any honey-ale he had ever tasted.

Early the next morning Cullan woke when Niall slipped into his room.

"Get your things together, we leave before sun rise."

Cullan stumbled out of bed. By the light of a single candle he dressed. He gathered his few personal belongings together. Out in the hall Cara waited. She pressed into his hands food wrapped in cloth.

"Take care, my lord."

Niall joined them at that moment. "Tell no one that we have left the fortress."

"Worry not, lord," Cara said. "I will tend the room as if the young prince still sleeps there. May the Father see you safe on your journey."

Cara bowed, then turned and left them standing in the drafty hall.

Their journey to Alibie took them half a moon. Niall stayed off the main roads, even forbade them the use of fire to heat their food at night. The four youths slept in the darkness, cold and lonely, each deep in their own thoughts.

Alibie stood on a much smaller plateau than Cwillan. The road to the front gate was in need of repair; it was pitted, rough, and uneven in places. At the gate, Rónán gave the rope hanging by the door a hard pull. After some time had passed the small square window set in the gate opened.

"Who disturbs the peace of Alibie?" asked a gruff voice.

"Prince Cullan and his Guardian, Lord Uaid's son Niall, and his Guardian. We wish an audience with Abbot Tadc," Rónán announced.

The window closed, metal grated on metal as the crossbar slid from its holders. The huge gates creaked open.

Upon entering Alibie, Cullan noticed the disrepair around him. The cloister looked as if at any moment it would fall down around the holy men. They dismounted in the large dusty courtyard. Apprentices hurried forward to see to their horses. As soon as the horses were led away, a tall, thin man stepped forward to speak with them.

"My name is Pól. There are no weapons in Alibie. You must leave yours here. They will be returned when you leave."

With reluctance, Niall handed over his sword. Both Rónán and Ciarán hesitated. Cullan handed his sword to Pól. He signaled to his friends to do the same. Like Niall, Cullan did not remove the dagger hidden in his boot.

"Your small weapons too."

Cullan knelt to remove the dagger. His friends followed suit.

They were escorted to rooms off a large courtyard. Water splashed out of the mouth of a face carved into the wall, down into a wide pool where golden fish moved silently through green water. Birds chirped unseen among the trees and bushes. Here and there bright flowers grew in half-barrels placed around the courtyard.

Fascinated, Cullan sat on the edge of the pool, and watched the bright fish dart in and out among the plant roots. He had never seen such beautiful fish before. As the day waned and the air grew cool he moved inside.

Pól brought them food and ale.

Before they had finished their meal the bells began to peal, calling the holy men to their evening offices.

Cullan sat in a low chair and dozed. The ale had made him sleepy. The breeze from the open door did little to cool the small hot room.

Four heads turned toward the door as someone knocked on it.

Niall called, "Enter."

Cullan sat up, rubbing the sleep from his eyes. He stood as two men entered the room.

Abbot Tadc was far older than any man Cullan had ever met before. His skin looked like old-yellowed parchment, almost transparent, with blue lines beneath it. Only a few wisps of hair remained on his head. His long white robe was clean, but too big for his frail body. On the third finger of his bony right hand, he wore a thick ring, with a spiral design worked into the gold.

Abbot Tadc walked over to Cullan. "I see your father in your face, and your mother too. May the Father be good to her. Welcome back young lords," he said to Niall and Rónán. I cannot name your father," he said turning to Ciarán."

"Ciarán is the son of Émer," Niall said. "A relative and member of my clan."

Abbot Tadc nodded and turned back to Cullan.

"Welcome, young prince. I understand you wish to become a Son of Déaglán. Few believe the old ways. You could still become Ard Ri and never learn of our past."

"I have heard," Cullan said, "that the only way to keep from repeating the errors of the past is to learn from them."

"Well said, Cullan. We will try to do our best by you. Pól will show you to your quarters. We will begin in the morning."

CHAPTER THIRTEEN

C ullan's tutor tested him often on his lessons. Only after a full moon was he allowed entry into the room that held the old books. Cullan walked down the row of leather-bound books and scrolls written by his forebears, and preserved by the holy men.

"These books tell our story, the story of the land we came from. How the tin ran out, forcing us to look for a new land. After a perilous trip by boat our forebears came to an island of rock and found a green and fertile land."

"This island, it is not this land, then?"

"No. We came here many years later," his tutor said.

"When will I start?"

"Tomorrow."

In the morning, his tutor placed one of the old books on the table in front of him. With care, his tutor turned the pages. The old language was different from the one spoken now in Cwillan; he had to learn it before attempting to read the books. Though different, he found it similar in many ways.

His tutor helped him work through the differences.

In the middle of reading one afternoon, the memory of his last meeting with Briana came to him. The memory so real that he felt again the sweetness of her lips on his.

His tutor coughed to get his attention back on his studies. Cullan stared down at the book, his face hot.

Even after several moons, Cullan had more questions then his tutor had answers for. The Power still puzzled him.

He saw his friends only at the evening meal. Felán, the novice assigned to help him, reassured him that his friends had their own studies to attend to.

In a strange, unsettling way he missed his father and the affairs of state. Above all, he longed for the day he would return to Cwillan and Briana.

Soon after his return they would be married.

He still felt too young to take on this new life of marriage.

Cullan learned the rules by which to conduct his life. He must never harm anyone. Simple, yet he was to learn that it meant so much more. To save one person he might have to harm another. His gift was never to be used to an evil end, also seemingly simple, yet good and evil meant different things to each man.

Abbot Tadc went over with Cullan what it meant to never harm someone. He told him that his conscience should be his guide in all matters of right and wrong. At times, he might have to do something outside the rules. To help someone he would be the one to make the final decision.

Samhain came, summer's end. The New Year brought cold to the land. The long, dry moons of winter dragged into spring. Still the cold clung to the land, refusing to give way.

"A bad omen," Felán said, "a winter without snow and cold so late into the spring."

Another said, "A green winter means a fat graveyard."

It was well into the month that should be warm when the winter released its grip on the land; the world around them turned green again. Flowers in a profusion of colors and sizes grew along the roadways and blanketed the meadows.

∾

In late spring, Pól brought the news to Abbot Tadc. Cullan had not been seen since the afternoon. He had missed his afternoon lessons and his evening meal with his friends.

On checking his room they found it empty.

"Check with the gatekeeper, send someone to the stable," Abbot Tadc told Pól.

Pól came running back to report that Cullan was not in the stable and that the gatekeeper said that no one had been in or out.

"Form groups of brothers, novices and Cullan's friends and search for him. Have them report back to me."

Each group came back to him to say they had not found Cullan. His friends continued to search for him.

There was only one place the boy might have gone to. Abbot Tadc told Pól to wait outside while he checked the King's Apartments. On entering he noticed that the folding doors to the courtyard stood open letting in the last of the day's sunlight.

He walked to the doors, was relieved to find the prince sitting on the edge of the pool watching the goldfish. "We are all wondering where you could have gone to."

"I needed time to think," Cullan said, without looking up.

Abbot Tadc sat down facing the boy. "How did the searchers miss you here?"

"I was in the sleeping chamber, they did not look in the alcove. I have never seen goldfish before, where do they come from?" he asked, as if this was a normal meeting.

"From Solaria, a small province south of here. It is actually a trading post. They were brought from there and given to one of your forebears."

"Trading post?"

"Like market day, but it goes from Samhain to Beltane. During the summer few people venture there because of the terrible heat."

"Who cares for the fish?"

Abbot Tadc cautioned himself to have patience. When Cullan ran out of questions he would say what was really on his mind."

"My son, Tuathall does. Someday I hope that he or his older brother will become Abbot here."

"I did not know that holy men could marry?"

"I was priested when I lived at Cwillan, I was married then. Marriage teaches you much, and helps to give advise about life. When your father made me abbot my wife came with me. When she died, may the Father and Son be good to her, I returned to a celibate life."

"Why is it that no one uses this apartment?"

"It is called the King's Apartment. Only one king ever used it. Once named, it stayed the King's Apartments. After that only the heir to the throne used it."

"The heir?" Cullan said, looking up. "Why was I not given these rooms?"

"If you will think back. I had you brought to these rooms on your arrival. This is a place for an arrogant, spoiled, and demanding prince. What I found when I met you was a young boy, living in a man's body, trying to live up to the life he was handed."

"Far too young to think of being heir to the throne, or to marry," Cullan said, for a second he smiled to himself.

"You are never too young to learn your duties as heir to the throne of Cwillan, nor to love someone. Wait here."

Abbot Tadc stood and went to speak with Pól.

"Brings us food and drink. Let his friends know Cullan is with me. Have my assistant do the evening offices."

"Yes, Father."

Abbot Tadc returned to the open doors.

"Come inside, it is getting cool, we can talk in here." Abbot Tadc lit two candles, placed one on the table and the other on the mantle-shelf.

They sat in silence.

Abbot Tadc waited. When Cullan remained silent he said, "Perhaps there is something you need to speak to me about, something I can help you with? Or something you would like to confess?"

"What would I have to confess?"

"All men have something in their life to confess."

"You could explain..." Cullan paused when a knock came at the door.

"Come," called Abbot Tadc.

Pól and a novice brought in food and drink.

"Do you want me to serve, Ab?" Pól asked.

"No. Cullan can serve."

After placing the food on the table Pól and the novice withdrew. Cullan served the meat and bread. Abbot Tadc noted that he gave him the best parts, keeping the smaller pieces for himself.

As they ate, Abbot Tadc asked, "Cullan, what can I help you with?"

"Explain the Father and Son to me. In Wyneth they have many gods."

"Pádraic brought the true faith to us from the east..."

"There is nothing beyond the great desert."

"Yes, I believe that is what they say across the river. But in truth there has to be something there. Do you think the world ends in nothingness?"

Cullan seemed to think about it.

"Well?"

"No, but..."

"There seems to always be a but with you. Our clan embraced the true faith long before Déaglán's time."

"Is he one god or two?"

Well, Abbot Tadc thought, this is going to be harder than I thought. He must have patience and remember that he was dealing with a boy of few summers, who was as tall as some men twice his age.

"What is important to you now is that the Father and Son created the world we live in, and the world we came from. When I say the east, I mean the land we came from. No one has traveled beyond the great desert here, thought there are those that say that there is a great body of water beyond the desert."

"Has anyone ever gone to look, to see this water?"

"Those that went into the great desert never returned. Déaglán's youngest son, Cuilin, was lost in the desert. This land was named after him. The entryway that Déaglán used to come here is somewhere in the desert."

"I have heard of the entryways."

"So you do know something about them?"

"Only something, Rónán said to me. Explain the Power to me."

Ah, so that is what is troubling him.

"Your tutor is very pleased with your grasp of the old language."

"It was easier than I thought it to be, I see similarities in both language, and some changes in some of the words and inflections."

"The Power has been in your line since the world was created," Abbot Tadc said. "Our ancestor, Déaglán, it is said, was the most powerful. That is how he brought us to safety, here to this fertile valley. It is a good place. But our success here has made those to the north envious. They would like to take this land from us. It is very important that we have a strong leader."

"But what is the Power?"

"The Power comes from within you. It is different in each man, and very different in a woman. Some men can read your mood, or understand your thoughts, even change your thoughts. Others can help you relax, ease your fears by touch." Abbot Tadc paused. How could he explain the Road of Life and Death to a young boy? "Some say you could even call someone back from the Road of Life and Death." There it was; he waited for Cullan to question his statement.

"My friend, Niall tried to explain the Road to me. Are we witches?"

Abbot Tadc caught himself before he showed his anger at the mention of being witches. It is what the church from the east had called them after Brian Mór was killed. The church turned on them forcing his people to travel to the west, to the end of the world, and then to here.

"We are not witches. We believe in the Father and Son, one God, and his son. We are men like all other men, we wish what is best for our wife and children, but all people have differences.

"Let me think on these things, Ab."

Abbot Tadc watched the light move down the colonnade as Cullan returned to his room. The light disappeared as he entered the stairs to the first level.

Funny, he thought, he could not see this tall boy on the throne of Cwillan. He shivered at that thought. What could it mean?

The insistent peal of the gate bell pulled Cullan away from his studies. His tutor opened the window shutters wide. They leaned out to see what was going on. Below in the courtyard the gatekeeper opened the small window in the gate. He stepped back with haste, and signaled for removal of the crossbar. The ancient gates creaked open.

The horse's hoofs clattered on the stone. The rider was dusty from a long journey, his horse lathered. An apprentice ran forward to take his horse. Without ceremony Pól led the rider away.

The excitement over, they returned to the their studies.

As Cullan washed and made ready to join his friends at the evening meal, he was surprised when someone knocked on his door. He called for them to enter.

Abbot Tadc entered, followed by his three friends.

"There is no use delaying; a messenger has come from Cwillan."

"From my father? Does he wish me to return to him?"

"Perhaps you should sit, young prince."

Cullan looked to Niall. Nothing showed on the youth's face. He moved over to his table and sat down and waited.

"The message is from your uncle. You are to return to Cwillan at once. Your father has taken ill. Lord Athdar thinks it is best that you attend him."

Cullan's mind raced; if he was being called back, his father must be very sick. He looked to Niall for help.

"We will accompany you back. We leave before first light. Just in case someone watches for our return."

"There is a back entrance; it is steep, but few know of it. If we are being watched, no one will know you have left," Abbot Tadc said. "Come, we will eat. Then you must rest. It is a long journey. Best to make haste, the less time on the road the better."

CHAPTER FOURTEEN

C ullan had just extinguished his candle when a soft knock came at his door.

Surprised he said, "Come."

The door opened on its oiled hinges. Felán entered with a candle held up to light his way. The apprentice placed his finger over his lips.

"You are wanted in the chapel."

Cullan pulled on his leggings and reached for his tunic.

"You are ready, we must go now."

"But..." Reluctantly, he followed Felán to the chapel. The apprentice held the door open for him to enter then took a seat on a bench at the back of the room.

Cullan looked around in astonishment. All the candles along both walls were lit, as well as those on the altar giving the usually austere chapel a festive look. The smell of tallow hung in the air, mixed with the sweet scent of incense.

Abbot Tadc, his assistant, and his tutor waited at the high altar. His tutor raised his hand and beckoned Cullan forward.

He walked forward to stand before the holy men. As the assistant chanted a prayer to the Father and Son, Cullan forgot about the cold stone floor beneath his bare feet, forgot that it was the dead of night, that he stood only in his leggings before the holy men.

When the chant was over the assistant stepped aside and Abbot Tadc moved forward to stand before Cullan.

"Child of Déaglán, do you you swear to uphold the beliefs of your forbears?"

When Abbot Tadc frowned at his hesitation, Cullan hurried to say, "I will do my duty."

"I hear a but in your voice. You need only to tell your children about Déaglán, so they can tell their children. You have the Power. If it is passed on to one of your sons, he will need to know our history."

"I will tell my children, Ab."

Abbot Tadc studied him, made up his mind, and motioned his assistant to come forward. The abbot's assistant held a tray. On a purple liner of the finest silk rested a gold ring with the same spiral workmanship as the abbot's, a silver cup, and an ancient book.

"Give me your right hand."

Cullan's hand trembled as he held it out toward the abbot. The ring felt cold on his skin as it slipped into place.

Next, he was handed the silver cup.

"Drink this, a symbol of the hardships of our people."

He took a sip, the drink was sweet and bitter at the same time, and very strong. When he finished it, Abbot Tadc took the empty cup and passed it to his assistant. Then he handed Cullan the book.

"This is for you to keep. When the time comes, you will know what to do with it. May the Father and Son bless you and keep you safe, Son of Déaglán."

The assistant stepped forward and sang a hymn in his high tenor voice. His tutor offered a prayer up to the Father and Son. When the short service was over, Felán came forward to escort Cullan back to his room.

❧

Ciarán woke Cullan just before first light.

"Niall says it is time for us to leave."

If his friends noticed the ring on his finger, they said nothing about it. It would be days before Niall would tell Cullan of his own journey to the chapel in the small hours of a new day.

On old rusty hinges the back gate closed with an ominous thud, sending chills down Cullan's spine. He looked over at Niall, wondering if he also felt that they would never return.

They started down the narrow winding track that was more suited for goats than horses. Cullan's feet slipped on the loose stones, causing more stones to break loose, gathering more and more as they rolled downward. He steadied himself by holding onto Warlord's bridle until he regained his balance.

"Are you all right, Cullan?" Niall asked.

"I am fine," Cullan said, with care he started downward again.

Once on flat ground, Niall set a fast pace, keeping off the main roads when possible. On the eighth morning after leaving Alibie, they passed into the lands that surrounded fortress of Cwillan.

Two mornings later they reached the fortress.

They rode through the silent village just as golden light in the eastern sky announced a new day.

"Open the gates," Niall called. His horse pranced, sensing his excitement to be back.

"Who wishes entry?" called a sleepy voice.

"Cullan, son of Cormac, and his retinue."

Metal grated as the crossbar was removed and the heavy gates were pulled open.

In silence they rode up to the fortress.

Cullan dismounted and threw Warlord's reins to a sleepy stable boy. Inside the fortress he made for his father's apartments. The guards at the entrance bowed and let him and his companions pass. He left his friends in the ante-room.

Without knocking, Cullan entered his father's sleeping chamber. The room was cold and damp despite the fire that roared on the hearth.

Aoife sat near the bed.

With a nod to Aoife, Cullan knelt down by his father. "Father, I have come..." words failed him.

Cormac opened his eyes. "Cullan Og, you have come," he said in a weak voice. "Thank the Father..." he coughed, lay still, before he tried to speak again. His voice was so weak that Cullan had to lean close to hear his words. "Be careful for I fear that there is one among us..." he coughed again, lay back and closed his eyes.

"Please," Aoife said, "your father is weak, let him rest."

Cullan wanted to tell Aoife that he needed to talk to his father now, that later might not come. Instead he stood up, a servant brought him a chair.

Cormac's life hung in the balance, between this world and the next. For Cullan the days dragged by, marked only by the servants putting new logs on the hearth, changing the candles. He found the nights were even worse. Aoife brought food for him, but he ate little, only sipped at the ale placed before him.

Niall came to him on the second day to speak with him. "I need a promise from you."

He was barely aware that his friend had joined him. "Cullan!"

Niall's insistent voice cut through his thoughts, he turned to his friend.

"You must promise me that you will not try to follow your father."

"Follow? I do not understand."

"You did not finish your training. The moment of death can be a very dangerous time. You must not look for your father...after."

"I do not understand, but I will promise."

Aoife came in at that moment.

As Niall passed her, he said, "If Cormac dies, send for me at once."

For five nights, Cormac, Ard Ri of Cwillan, lay in a deep sleep from which the healer found impossible to wake him. On the sixth he passed from sleep into death

❧

Behind the low cart that carried Cormac's body to its final resting place walked a warrior who led Meán Oiche, the High King's black stallion. Cullan and Aoife came next, behind them walked Ciarán. Niall and Rónán walked with the clan chieftains. The rest of the mourners followed in their wake.

The cortege made its way down through the tunnel. The slow procession moved down the forest road to the old burial grounds. Cormac would be laid next to his wife and children.

Men, women, and children from the surrounding farms lined the road. The children threw flowers, women keened, the men pulled their hats off and bowed their heads as the cortege passed. The service was short, presided over by Brother Seán, the priested holy man who lived in the lower village.

When it came time to place his father into the grave, Cullan found it impossible to watch. He walked back to the main aisle; he sat down under the winged statue. Only then did he remember that his father's sword had been left on the cart. When the cart rumbled past making for the gate, the sword was gone.

෧෨

Athdar brought the bad news.

"It was close; many, including Rónán's father, sided with you, Cullan. But with Artúr's army just outside the fortress many thought it best to accept him as king. Though it would be hard to take Cwillan by force, it would go hard for the surrounding farms."

Athdar left him with his three friends.

Cullan stood at the window looking out into the darkness. Cat sat on the window ledge next to him. Absently he rubbed the feline's head.

"I am not upset," Cullan said, turning to face his friends. "I never wanted to rule here. I suppose this means I cannot go back to Alibie."

"It would be best not to," Niall said.

"What of the pledge of marriage, between Briana and myself?"

"My father stands by his original pledge. There are those who say it should be broken. That she should marry Selatin. It will be brought before the brehon," Rónán said.

"When will Artúr arrive?"

"His army is camped two leagues north of Cwillan. A rider with a message for him to enter the fortress left as soon as they made their decision. Someone must have sent word to him when your father became ill. How else could he have arrived so fast," Niall said. "He could be here as soon as first light."

"I will miss you, my friends."

"What do you mean?" Ciarán asked.

"There is only exile for him now. Athdar told me earlier that if things went against Cullan that he would ride to King Owayn in Wyneth. He hopes to gain asylum for Cullan there."

"Here or in Wyneth, where Cullan goes, I go," Ciarán announced.

"Rónán and I discussed this also. We will go with you too. There is nothing left here for us. Artúr will be kinder to our families if all obstacles to a peaceful reign are removed."

Cullan started to protest his friend's decision.

Niall shook his head. "You will most likely be called before Artúr as soon as he is crowned king. We will be expected to swear fealty to him."

"So what do we do now?" Ciarán asked.

"We wait for our summons. Before that we must prepare to leave Cwillan with little notice, so no one knows when or where we have gone."

CHAPTER FIFTEEN

Cullan, and his friends, were summoned to Artúr, before the moon had waned, and a new moon took its place.

As Cullan approached the great hall the two guards at the door bowed to him; only the younger one, looked him in the eye. They pulled the heavy oak doors open.

He glanced over at Niall. His friend shrugged, puzzled also why the guards did not take their weapons.

The doors closed behind them with an ominous thud.

Artúr sat on the throne, waiting.

From a half round near the first bridge he had watched Artúr and his retinue enter the fortress. His uncle had identified each one as they passed.

Aoife sat to the right of Artúr. Darlisca, Artúr's uncle, and Selatin, his advisor, stood to his left and right. Newlyn, his father's reachtaire, was not in attendance. Arranged around the hall in order of their importance were the chieftains, their families and sept of each clan.

Through Cara, Cullan learned that Artúr would marry Aoife as soon as her twelve moons of mourning were over. Selatin had asked again to marry Briana. Bran had told him that the betrothal gifts had been exchanged. His daughter was honor bound to marry Cullan, son of Cormac.

Maiú, chief brehon upheld his position.

This would mark Bran and Maiú as enemies. How long would it take before Artúr replaced the brehon with his own man, or worse, disbanded the brehon throughout Cwillan.

Four feet from the dais Cullan stopped. His friends a step behind him would do the same. Something bright moved at the edge of his vision. He turned his head to follow the movement. On the huge overhead iron candleholder sat several birds.

Someone had set Aoife's birds free.

The small yellow bird flew to his left to land on the railing of the gallery. Several birds flew around the hall, before gathering on the candleholder. Cullan returned his attention to the yellow bird, feigning interest in the small bright creature. The torches were unlit in the gallery; barely discernible in the gloom stood armed warriors.

This is why they were allowed to keep their weapons. Artúr hoped they would try something, and had warriors ready to cut them down. Cullan glanced at Aoife and caught the slightest nod of her head.

"Lady Aoife, I see some amadan has let your birds loose."

"That is why the outer doors are closed."

Artúr signaled Selatin.

Selatin moved forward, at the edge of the dais he stopped, held up a scroll and read, "Do you, Cullan, son of Cormac, swear fealty to Artúr, High King of Cwillan?"

High King of Cwillan!

It would be so easy just to say yes.

Until this moment, Cullan was not sure what he would do; now he realized Artúr had taken what was rightfully his. What he did not want, he reminded himself. Still, how could he swear fealty to this man? He, Cullan, was the legal tanist here, even though he did not want to rule Cwillan.

"Lord Artúr," Cullan said. Artúr's eyes narrowed at being called lord, as if he were a mere chieftain. "I speak only for myself in my decline to swear fealty to you."

Behind Cullan, Niall began to speak. Darlisca moved forward, pulled the scroll from Selatin's hand. Artúr's advisor hurried to get out of his way, fearful of the older man's anger. Darlisca crumpled the scroll up and threw it on the stone floor.

"Think before you misspeak, Cullan," Artúr's uncle shouted at him.

At the sound of Darlisca's voice, Cullan's blood ran cold. Where had he heard the voice? Was it possible that he had met this man before?

'That fool in Cwillan will never realize whose hand has struck to his very heart.'

Darlisca stood at the edge of the dais dressed completely in black, waiting for Cullan's reply.

This is the man who haunts my dreams. Yes, they had met before. Long ago, in the back hall, where narrow steps went up to the Ladies Bower.

Cullan shut out the past, he needed to concentrate on the here and now.

"Well!" Darlisca demanded, his face red with anger.

"I need no time to think on this matter, lord."

"Then, let it be noted among all assembled here," Darlisca said, looking out over the assembly, "that Cullan, son of Cormac, is now an allúrach. Any that follow his folly will be marked the same. You have seven mornings, on the eighth morning if you are found within the gates of Cwillan or anywhere in *my* land you will be put to death."

Your land! No, Cullan thought, *this is my land.*

Silence reigned; not even a hushed whisper as every man and woman present waited. Darlisca scowled down at him, waiting for his response.

"I will leave the fortress on the seventh morning."

Around Cullan the room broke into whispers of astonishment, shocked voices rose in disbelief.

Lord Uaid stood, the look on his face told his feelings. His son, Niall, would follow Cullan. Still he hoped. His hope faded, the color drained from Uaid's face. He sank down on the bench and bowed his head, his wife tried to console him.

As Cullan turned to leave, the room behind him fell into silence. Then, a woman's voice among Artúr's retinue said, "I see why they call him Cullan, he is indeed a handsome hound."

When they approached the tall doors the guards pushed them open so they could pass through. He felt sadness, he was sure that it was the last time he would see Cwillan.

Early on the next morning, long before color came to the morning sky, he met his three companions at the stable. They tied thick cloth over their horses' hooves to muffle the sound. Single-file, they walked their horses slowly across the bridge and down the roadway. At the gate the Master at Arms, Ruadrí, his apprentice, and a servant waited.

"Where are the guards?" Cullan whispered.

"Some kindhearted person sent them a keg of ale for them to celebrate the new king. It will be awhile before they are able to return to their post."

Ruadrí s servant opened the small door set into the gate. It was just wide enough for a man to lead his horse through. Once out on the promenade, the servant pushed the door closed again. From inside came the sound of the lock turning with as little noise as possible.

They stood in the cold morning air, each deep in their own thoughts. Cullan hoped that Briana had been able to get out of the fortress.

Niall broke the silence. "Ruadrí and his apprentice have asked to join us."

So deep in his thoughts of Briana that Cullan had not noticed that the Master at Arms and his apprentice had their horses with them.

"Anyone who comes with me can never return."

"We go with our true king," both men answered.

They rode single-file down through the tunnel and past the burial grounds, taking the path that led to the old ruins. Niall paused only long enough to brush away any trace of their passing. From there they rode south. Seven mornings ride would bring them to the Wyneth River's narrowest point: a place called the Shallows.

From the safety of the trees a little south of the Shallows, Cullan and his small party watched a lone rider leave the forest and ride down to the riverbank. He dismounted and let his horse drink. When the horse had its fill, he checked his saddle.

"You still suspect a trap?" Cullan said.

Ruadrí nodded. "I don't like this. It is a good thing we circled around. I fear that there may be more men hiding up in the trees waiting for us."

"Even if we make it across the river, what will prevent Darlisca's men from following us across?" Ciarán asked.

"For now, I do not think that they will risk trouble with King Owayn. See that yew tree on the far bank, and the rock to the far right?"

"Yes, what do you have in mind?"

"There is a sand bar between those two points; ride across at that section of the river. Move up into the valley, there is a cottage there used at times by hunting parties."

Cullan turned from watching the riverbank. "And what will you be doing, my friend?"

"I'm going to ride south through the forest, then come back along the riverbank and have a talk with the rider. He is trying too hard to appear casual, but he keeps looking around. Perhaps looking for us."

"What do you want us to do?" Niall asked.

"If it is a trap I will lead them away. Cross the river, I will join you later."

"With that horse of yours," Niall said. "You will be caught within half a league. Let me go, my horse is fast."

Ruadrí looked at Niall, then at Cullan.

They were waiting for Cullan to make the decision.

"Have you ever hunted on the other side of the river?" Cullan asked Niall.

"No."

"That settles it. Niall will go down and see if it is a trap." Ruadrí started to protest. "We need your knowledge of Wyneth."

Ruadrí motioned to his apprentice, standing guard further up the hill, to join them.

The sun had barely moved in the sky when Niall came riding down the riverbank. The lone rider watched him approach. He turned toward the forest and made a pretense of brushing his shoulder.

Cullan told his friends to mount their horses.

Niall leaned over to talk to the man. The man lunged at the bridle. Wheeling his horse away from the man in a tight turn, Niall headed for the trees then turned his horse again heading north along the river.

Riders appeared from the trees to pursue him. The lone rider joined them in the chase.

"Come, my friends, this is our chance." Ruadrí said.

At the riverbank Cullan paused to see if Niall was in any danger. He signaled for everyone to cross.

Ciarán turned his horse and rode back to Cullan.

"See everyone to safety." When Ciarán hesitated. "That is an order. Now go."

Ciarán turned his horse and let it wade back across the river.

Cullan gave Warlord his head as he rode north.

When he closed the distance between himself and the last riders he began to shout at them. The rider turned, his look of surprise told Cullan it was time to slow his horse. Only half the riders turned to chase him. It was enough to give Niall a better chance to escape. He turned Warlord and headed south back toward the Shallows.

Ciarán waited for Cullan at the crossing. They rode across together with the enemy not far behind. Rónán waited with his companions, ready to take on the men if they dared to cross the river.

Darlisca's men followed them into the river. They stopped short of crossing into Wyneth, then turned and returned to Cwillan.

At the end of a narrow valley stood a large thatched cottage, Ruadrí called Hill Cottage. It had been built years earlier as a place for hunting parties from both sides of the river to use. Cullan dismounted at the small stable and walked with his friends to the cottage. As they approached, a young boy ran out onto the porch that ran the length of the cottage.

Cullan could not believe his eyes. With her close-cropped hair, Briana looked like a thin boy dressed in tunic and leggings. He ran to meet her, threw his arms around her, pulled her off her feet and swung her around with joy.

"Put me down," Briana, said, indignant at his behavior, but as pleased to see him as he was to see her.

He set her down and kissed her.

"I am overwhelmed with joy that you were able to get out of the fortress too."

Briana took him by the hand and led him into the cottage.

Hill Cottage consisted of a large hall with a high ceiling, hearth and kitchen and several small rooms on the ground level. Above was an open half level with rooms off a hall that ran along the back wall. The men would double up in the upstairs rooms. Briana would share a room with Gila, her companion, on the ground floor until they wed.

Briana showed him up to his room.

Once they were alone, he took her in his arms and kissed her again.

Three mornings after their arrival, Brother Seán, who had accompanied Briana, married them. The gifts traditionally exchanged at the betrothal were presented after the ceremony. Briana's family gave Cullan a large jeweled penannular brooch. He gave Briana a thick golden band, in the fashion of a torc with a horse's head at each end.

CHAPTER SIXTEEN

For a moon, life was wonderful for Cullan and Briana. Twenty-eight wonderful mornings and nights, each night seemed sweeter than the one before. Their love grew deeper with each new day. Cwillan lay behind them, the rest of their lives before them, life with its full tapestry of new delights.

Cullan went out with the hunting parties, or with Niall and his hounds. Played ficheall with Ciarán. After the evening meal his time was spent with Briana. When she announced that she was with child, he stayed closer to Hill Cottage.

Their lives changed in other ways.

It started with young men, just a few at first. Crossing the Shallows they came up the hill to join with the man they considered their king. Nothing to worry about, Cullan told himself. They would return home when they found that he did not intend to take the fight back to Artúr.

Near the end of Lúnasa, word reached them that Artúr's army had sacked and burned Alibie. The news shocked everyone at Hill Cottage and the encampment below. Only a handful of men had rallied to him so far. After the sacking of Alibie, it began in earnest.

As Samhain neared, it was not only young men, but also older men in groups of two and three. Soon whole families driving a few head of livestock before them crossed the river. All they owned they carried on their backs.

Artúr had the Western Bridge between Wyneth and Cwillan closed and guarded. Soon the Shallows on the Cwillan side were guarded too. Still, those who wanted to join him found a way to cross the river.

It puzzled Cullan.

He left Cwillan behind and all claims to the throne. Now Cwillan came to him. Land was cleared half a league from the river, and a rough village sprung up with thatched cottages, an alehouse, and a large enclosed area to the right for common grazing. On the riverside, a blacksmith and farrier built their dwellings just outside the village.

No matter what Cullan said to the men, they would not return to Cwillan. After speaking with Cullan, they moved down to the village to wait. Did they think he would change his mind? That he would come to his senses and return to Cwillan?

Athdar took two young men with him and rode to speak again with King Owayn.

As time passed, Briana looked far too thin for a woman with child. Gila stayed at her side. Cullan worried about Briana's health. He stayed close, never going down to the village for fear that she would need him.

In the late afternoon he climbed the hill to the right of the cottage, for a brief quiet time, he walked out to the point. From here, he could look across the river into Cwillan.

Coming from the north along the Wyneth side, he saw what looked like the hunting party that had left the village only one morning past. Their half horses were laden with heavy burdens. The distance was too great for him to tell what they were returning with.

Cullan ran down the path, called to Ciarán to see why the hunting party had returned so soon.

The sun had hardly moved in the sky before Ciarán returned with Eóghan, the leader. Behind him, he led several half horses. Cullan stood on the porch and watched their approach. Some inner sense told him that something terrible had happened.

Niall and Rónán joined him.

Eóghan tied the pack animals well back from the cottage, and came forward. Eóghan's tunic and leggings were stained with mud and a rust color that looked like blood.

Eóghan made to bow, caught himself, and said, "Lord." His gaze went to Briana who had just come out to stand beside her husband.

"What has happened?"

"My lord, perhaps we should talk in private," Eóghan stared at his feet.

A chill went down Cullan's spine at Eóghan's words.

"Briana, will you have the servants prepare a meal for the returning hunters."

"What is this?" Briana asked as she stepped from the porch. Eóghan made to stop her, thought better of it, and turned to appeal to Cullan.

"My lord, it is best she does not see this."

"Briana."

Briana halted halfway to the horses, placed her hand over her nose and mouth. Slowly she moved toward the first half horse; with difficulty she pulled back the covering that hid its burden. She stepped back and screamed. In several quick strides, Cullan was by her side. He caught her as she fainted. Before he turned he looked into the dead face of Bran. The stench of death was heavy around the eight wrapped bodies.

Cullan carried Briana back toward the cottage.

"Gila, see if there is someone in the village who is a healer, also bring Brother Seán.

When Cullan returned downstairs, he found his three friends and Eóghan sitting in a half circle around the hearth. Cullan moved to the hearth and leaned against the mantle-shelf, refusing the seat offered him.

"What happened?"

"We found them further north, on this side of the river. Bran, his sons, and warriors put up quite a fight. There were many of Artúr's men who died by their swords. In the end, they were overwhelmed. The women in the party were dishonored before they were put to the sword."

Rónán jumped to his feet. "When?"

"Not long; two, three mornings ago. They dragged the bodies back into a copse of trees and left them to the wild animals. We buried the servants and warriors on a low bluff by the river. We brought Bran, his family, and his personal guard for a proper burial. So a holy man can lay them to rest, to await the day the Father and Son return."

"Artúr does not have the fealty of all the lords," Niall said. "Bran was coming to join with us."

Cullan scowled at his friend, he wanted no talk of fealty, or who was the rightful Ard Ri of Cwillan.

"Are we going to sit here like old women and let Artúr rape and pillage our land and people?" Rónán shouted.

Before anyone could answer him, he stomped out of the cottage. The door slammed closed behind him. The sound echoed around the room.

"He needs time alone, this is a terrible blow to him," Niall said.

They buried Bran, his family, and personal guard on the high ground above Hill Cottage, in a small glade surrounded by tall trees. The whole village came to pay their respects to the fallen warriors and their women.

Briana had taken to her bed, did not attend the service performed by Tuathall, the abbot's son who had joined them after Lúnasa.

On Samhain eve, Briana went into early labor. Cullan stayed at her side. He tried to give her his strength. With each passing moment she seemed to grow weaker. The child was born and named Bri after her mother. Just before dawn, the child, only hours old, died in Cullan's arms. Briana slipped into a deep sleep and died quietly the next morning.

Heartbroken, Cullan sat by her bed.

He refused to allow Tuathall to attend to her. After a few days he finally came to his senses enough to allow them to bury Briana and the baby. Tuathall and a small group of men carried mother and child up the hill. They laid Briana next to her father; Bri was placed in her arms.

Cold settled over the land; soon the snow would fly. Each day Cullan sat on the hill near his beloved. Niall brought him food. At first he refused it. Rather than fight with his friend he took the food, only to pick at it. Each night Niall and Rónán had to force him to return to the warmth of the cottage.

Niall divided his time between keeping an eye on Cullan and getting news from the newcomers to the village. Some nights he sent Ciarán down to see what news he could get of Cwillan. Things were bleak in his homeland. Rumors came of more atrocities besides the burning of Alibie.

The weather turned colder as a bitter wind swept down on the land from the northwest.

Niall reached for his heavy wool cloak. Rónán stood to accompany his friend down to the village. Earlier, Ciarán had walked down to the village, but had not returned. Tonight Niall had persuaded Cullan to stay in his room. His friend was thin, his face drawn from no sleep, little food, and too much brooding on his loss.

Before Niall went down to the village, he told Gila to watch over Cullan.

Down in the village Niall and Rónán made their way over to the small thatched alehouse. Ciarán had no news, they were getting ready to leave, when the front door opened, cold air swirled around the room, making the fire and candlelight dance. Niall knew the tall man who entered. Peadar had worked for his father a few summers back. Perhaps he could get news of his family.

In a small, enclosed area at the back, they sat over mugs of ale.

"What news of my father?" Niall asked.

"Your father and mother are well."

"Is it true about Alibie?" Rónán asked.

The older man nodded, staring into his ale for a moment. "They burned all the old books and slaughtered the holy men. Your father, Niall, tried to stay Artúr's hand, but he only listens to his uncle. None escaped."

"Who among the clans would go against Alibie?" Ciarán said.

"The deed was done by Artúr's warriors, only a few of our people have joined with him, a small group, unhappy with how things were going for them."

"May they be condemned to the fires of damnation," Ciarán said. He stood and excused himself. "I have things to attend to."

"Another ale, Niall?" Peadar asked.

Niall and Rónán stood to follow Ciarán.

"Another ale sounds good," Niall said. "But we have things to attend to also. I will send back a mug to you. Are you going to stay long?"

"I will cross back tomorrow. I know a place a little further upriver; I act as a guide to those who want to join you. Do you not worry about the King of Wyneth? Perhaps he is nervous about all the people who have moved here from Cwillan?"

Niall was about to tell him that Athdar had taken a small retinue and had ridden west to speak with King Owayn. He changed his mind. Not sure why, but something told him to keep quiet.

"Thank you for news of home, friend. And the warning."

"Is Cullan Og, I mean Cullan, still here?"

Niall chose his words with care. "Only an amadan would sit here and wait for Artúr or his uncle to come and take him."

"Of course, of course."

Out in the main room, Niall had ale sent back to Peadar. As he moved toward the door he caught sight of Gila in a corner speaking to a young girl who served the men. Niall pushed his way through the crowded room.

"You were to stay with our lord."

Gila jumped up, surprised. "He was sleeping. I came down here for some supplies, I was about to go back."

Niall turned from the servant and hurried out the door. Outside he discovered that it was snowing. The white world around him looked peaceful.

Rónán caught up with him as he made his way up the hill. "What worries you?"

"Cullan barely sleeps these days. You know how he paces in the room he shared with Briana. Gila says he was asleep. Pray to the Father and Son, that this is true."

They met Ciarán as he hurried down the hill. "He is not in his room."

Gila caught up with them just as they made it to the cottage door. Niall went straight up to the first level to Cullan's room. The empty bed in the silent room mocked him. He searched through the other rooms while Rónán, Ciarán, and Gila made a search of the ground level.

Cullan was not in the cottage.

Niall pulled his cloak around himself. He lit two rush torches from the fire on the hearth. He handed one to Ciarán.

"Go to the stable. See if Warlord is still in his stall." Niall turned to the servant. "How long were you gone, Gila?"

"Not long, lord. Not long."

"He has to be here somewhere," Rónán said.

Rónán followed Niall outside.

The snow on the path up the hill was clean, untouched. Where else would Cullan go? They hurried up the hill. The snow in the burial place lay as untouched as the path.

Niall was disappointed to find the place where Cullan usually sat empty. He watched as the silent snow fell on the nine mounds. The only sound was the hiss as the snow hit the torch; the flame danced, casting strange shadows around them.

Gila joined them. "Is he here, lord?"

Briana's grave looked larger than the others; perhaps it was only a trick of the flickering light.

"Where do you think he has gone?" Rónán asked.

Niall shrugged. Indeed, where would he go.

Ciarán ran up the hill, his face red from running in the cold. "His horse is still in the stable."

"You are close to him. What do you think, Ciarán?"

"That he must be here."

"Here?" Rónán asked.

"We shall see my friends," Niall said. "Gila, go down and heat stones on the hearth. Be prepared for when we find Cullan."

Niall moved to the last burial mound. Ciarán and Rónán followed him. In the coming year the earth would settle. Now all the graves were mounds of white. Standing next to Briana's grave, Niall noted that this one was not only larger, but also wider at the center. The strange irregular pattern made by the snow puzzled him.

He handed the torch to Rónán and hurried to brush the snow from the mound. Instead of earth beneath the snow, he found a wool tunic.

Cullan lay unconscious across the grave.

Rónán helped Ciarán lift the young prince. He brushed the snow from his hair and clothing. Cullan's eyes fluttered open, then closed, his skin a bluish-white, his lips bloodless.

"How did you know?" Rónán asked, awe in his voice.

"He had to be here. This is the only place he comes to."

Across his shoulders Rónán carried Cullan down to the cottage.

Once they had Cullan back in bed, with heated stones placed around him, Niall sent for the woman in the village who had a little knowledge of healing. For six mornings Cullan went from cold to hot. The fever that raged through his weakened body threatened to take his life.

At those times Niall held his hand, gave him his strength. Then without warning, Cullan turned cold again and no amount of heated stones would warm him.

As the new moon came with little change, Niall dispatched Ciarán across the river to find a healer. When his kin did not return, he worried that Artúr had caught him.

CHAPTER
SEVENTEEN

Out of the fog of cold and heat, Cullan's mind drifted, a fish darting upward to light. There were voices also, there had never been voices before. He could even make out words. He listened for the one voice he needed to hear.

"Get that animal out of here," an angry woman's voice said.

That voice!

Aoife!

It was not the voice of his beloved. He tried to open his eyes when pressure told him that someone was sitting next to him. It took great effort for him to open his eyes; his lids were pasted together. His eyes watered when he finally managed to open them; he blinked to clear them.

They had moved his bed. He was now facing the window.

"How long has he been like this?"

"He had a fever, took a turn for the worse. He seemed to recover. Now he is worse again."

"Niall, how long?"

"Since early winter, he grows no stronger."

Aoife's soft hands cupped Cullan's face, she leaned closer, felt the texture of his skin, felt his pulse. She bent lower to listen to his heart. The fragrance of flowers filled the air around him. He tried to smile at her, but his lips were chapped, stiff and sore.

"Can he keep anything down?"

"Just gruel. Nothing that will give him strength."

She smiled down at Cullan.

"Aoife," he managed.

"It has been a long time. Worry not, Mór and I will take good care of you."

"I had a dream..."

Aoife looked up. "Rest now, lord."

Cullan had to know the truth. "Tell me, where is Briana, my baby?"

"I will not lie to you," Aoife said. "Briana and the baby died during the winter."

He closed his eyes. Better to sink back into nothingness then live without his wife and child. It was not the fog of cold and heat that awaited him, but a windswept road stretching into infinity. Men, women and children, old and young moved down the road.

"Cullan!"

Cullan walked toward the light. The voice spoke to him again, seeming to come from all around him. It told him to open his eyes.

"It is not your time."

The road dissolved into fog again; sometime later he was back in bed.

He opened his eyes. The dim light from the window told him it was late afternoon. Niall sat on the edge of his bed.

His friend smiled down at him. "Rest now."

Niall stood and moved out of his line of vision.

Cullan listened to the soft words spoken to Aoife. He had to concentrate on each word to get any meaning of what his friend was saying.

"You should not have told him the truth. One of these times I will not be able to call him back."

"Do you think I believe that he goes somewhere when he is unconscious?" Aoife asked. "It is better that he knows. Now to business, I will oversee his food."

"His servant sees to his food."

"He has a servant? Things are not as bad here as we were told in Cwillan."

"It is Gila, the companion Briana brought with her when she left the fortress."

"I know Gila. I will speak with her when I have time. When you go below, send Mór up. There is no time for her childish fancies. Keep your hounds out of here as well. Or I will take a broom to the beasts and to you too."

The door squeaked open.

"Aoife?"

"Yes, Niall."

"Why did you come? If Artúr finds out you helped us it will go hard for you."

"You sent Ciarán to me, asked for my help."

"We needed help, but I had no idea that Ciarán would go to you. So now I wonder why you came?"

"Artúr does not wish to see the young prince die."

"Really!" Niall said. His voice was hard with contempt. "If Cullan dies, then he becomes the legitimate heir to the throne. Do not tell me he wishes no harm to the prince."

"Send Mór to me, Niall."

"Tell the men that came with you that they can set up camp at the far end of the village. They are to stay there on penalty of death."

"As you wish."

The door shut with a thud that made the thin walls vibrate. Wood scraped on wood; Aoife sat down next to the bed.

"You can open your eyes, I know you are not asleep. Is there anything you can tell me, Cullan?"

He shook his head and turned away from her.

"Well then, when your friend can pull Mór away from Rónán we will see what we can do to bring you back to health."

~

Each day passed much the same as the day before for Cullan. Gila prepared special food for him, supervised by Aoife. Mór mixed herbs to give him strength.

Winter gave way to spring. The time of light returned to the land, the time for planting. Cullan kept to his bed, still too weak to stand without help. Niall's wolfhound bitch gave birth to three puppies. This only added to the noise below.

CHAPTER EIGHTEEN

Cat sunned herself on the window ledge across from Cullan's bed. She sat up, alert, as the bright notes of a bird filled the air. She stretched, but made no move to leave her post. By day she sat on the ledge, leaving only to eat. At night she slept on the end of his bed.

There was a tap on the door.

"I have your meal," Gila said.

The cat's head turned toward her, a low growl came from deep in her chest. Her golden eyes seemed to glare at the young woman. No matter how many times Gila shooed the cat from the room, she would return to find the cat on the window ledge again. When she tried to physically remove the cat she found herself confronted by an angry, spitting ball of fur. She still bore the teeth marks the cat made on her hand.

This puzzled Cullan, and it angered Gila.

"That cat should be made to leave the room. It is a bad omen. Cats bring evil spirits, not good for your health, lord."

"The cat stays, Gila. You of all people should understand; you helped Briana bring the cat here."

Gila did not answer him; she stepped over to a cabinet on the other side of the room. There came the sound of stirring. She moved back to the bed. "I wanted to make sure it was cool enough to eat, lord."

She sat on the edge of the bed. Took a spoonful of food and moved it to his mouth. Cullan smiled and opened his mouth to receive the food.

Below a loud bang shook the cottage walls, followed by the babble of angry voices.

"It is those puppies again. They get into everything. Aoife will yell at Niall. Or whomever she can find to vent her anger on."

Another loud bang downstairs made the cottage walls vibrate harder this time. There were shouts and the sound of bleating animals. Children and women shouted.

Aoife's angry voice rose above them all.

"Go down and see what is going on. I am well enough to finish on my own."

"Are you sure?"

"Yes." He lied.

Gila adjusted the pillow behind his back so he could sit up better. Cullan took the bowl and spoon from her. He took a small spoonful, chewed and swallowed.

"Your food has improved under Aoife's watchful eye."

Cullan waited until Gila closed the door. "Well, Cat, are you hungry?"

Cat's stare went from the door to him.

Downstairs everything quieted down. Gila had only been gone for a while when the door opened and Niall entered.

"Everything is under control. One of the children let the goats in. Gila will be back after she helps shoo them out of the cottage."

Before Cullan could ask Niall to stay he was gone.

Not really hungry, Cullan leaned back and closed his eyes. When the cat hissed he opened his eyes again to follow her gaze. One of Niall's puppies had wandered into the room when the door was open. The fat puppy ignored the cat and bound over to the bed.

This was the solution for what to do with the food. He leaned over and placed the bowl on the floor. Curious, the puppy moved over to the bowl and began to eat.

Later, when he glanced over the edge of the bed; the bowl and puppy were gone.

Cullan listened for Gila's return, not sure what he would tell her. He closed his eyes, too tired to worry.

❧

With effort Cullan pushed himself into a sitting position, surprised to find it was morning. It was early but someone would come to check on him. He felt better than he had in weeks. His sleep after his midday meal had refreshed him.

There was a soft knock on the door and Mór entered. She gave him a pleased smile when she saw that he was awake. "You must be hungry; when Gila came up with your meal last night you were sound asleep."

"Sorry, I was very tired."

"So it seems. Did Gila bring up the small bowl yesterday, the one with the blue band around the edge?"

Should he tell her that he had not eaten all his food?

"I set the bowl on the floor. Perhaps it was pushed underneath the bed," he said without guile.

Mór knelt, felt around beneath the bed with her right hand. She gave a squeak of surprise. Mór sat back, holding the bowl before her; a puzzled look had replaced her usual calm expression. She lowered herself to the floor again and peered under the bed, she sat up and stared at him for a minute, a look of anger on her face.

To his surprise she placed the bowl on the floor, took his hands in hers.

"Forgive me, lord."

He did not understand what she meant. Without a word she began to examine his hands, paying careful attention to his nails. Her mumbled words made no sense to him.

She kept saying over and over, "Right before our eyes, yet not one of us saw the truth."

Mór stood and hurried out of the room, leaving the door open. She called to her brother below. Light footsteps sounded on the stairs. Mór pulled her brother into the room.

"You must find Gila, send her up into the hills. She has to gather all the small white starflowers she can find this time of year. Send one of the young women with her to help." Without giving her brother a chance to speak, she went on, "Then bring Aoife and your friends."

Confused, Ciarán stared at his friend. Cullan shrugged, not understanding what was going on.

"Ciarán, do as I say. It is very important. Do not, hear me, bring Niall and Aoife up here until Gila is away."

Her brother hesitated. "But why such urgency? Cullan looks better then he has in a long time."

"Yes, but let Gila think he is worse and anyone who asks. Do not let on to the truth. On the fealty you swore, do this for your lord."

With another glance at Cullan, Ciarán nodded, turned and hurried from the room. Mór waited with the door open.

From below came Ciarán's voice as he called for Gila.

Then other voices joined in, asking why he needed the servant girl. Then Gila's voice joined the others.

"Good," Mór said as she closed the door. "Now we wait for your friends."

It was not long before the heavy tread of footsteps sounded on the stairs. Niall came into the room breathing hard, as if he had run all the way from the village. He stood in the doorway and stared at Cullan.

"One of the house servants came down to the river, he told me that Gila had been sent up into the hills. He said that Cullan had taken a turn for the worse, that..." Niall stopped. "What is going on?"

Aoife arrived at that moment in a more sedate manner. She looked at Cullan and sighed in relief. Next to enter was Athdar, who was also relieved to find his nephew sitting up.

"Did you find the missing puppy, Niall?" Mór asked.

"What does the puppy have to do with you suddenly taking charge above your elders?" Aoife asked.

"It has been before us all this time. Yet not one of us saw the truth." Mór sat down on the chair by the bed. "I will not ask you, lord, to relive that day Briana and your child died. But you Niall, do you remember anything strange about that day?"

Mór had the full attention of everyone in the room.

"Carrying the child was hard on Briana. After her family was slaughtered, she took to her bed. Early labor began, she went into a deep sleep after the child died, and never woke up again. What are you getting at?"

At Niall's words, Cullan had to fight back the horror that threatened to drag him into a place he would never find his way back from. His dark mood dispelled when the door flew open to bang against the wall. Rónán filled the small doorway.

"What is going on here?" Rónán asked, looking from Cullan to his friends. Ciarán followed Rónán into the room and closed the door.

"Now that we are all here, go on," Aoife said. "Mór is one of the best healers I have ever trained. She could teach the holy men a thing or two. So what have we missed, child?"

"You did not eat all your meal yesterday?"

Cullan nodded, puzzled at what that had to do with what was going on. "I placed the bowl on the floor. The puppy got into it, he must have pushed it back against the wall."

"The puppy is still there."

With quick strides Niall moved over to the bed, he knelt down, felt around and pulled the puppy from beneath the bed. The small shaggy animal looked like a child's toy. He stood, leaving the dead puppy on the floor.

"I think Briana and the child were poisoned. If you doubt me, look at Cullan's fingernails."

Aoife examined his hands.

When she was done, Cullan stared at his hands, noted the strange color his nails had turned along the cuticles. He blinked, no longer his long hands before him, but the aged hands of his father, with the same telltale nails.

His wife and child poisoned, right before his own eyes. His father also; now they had begun to poison him as well. Who hated his family enough to do this horrendous deed?

"They were poisoned? By the one person we all trusted," Mór said.

"Now I see why we were allowed to come here. We were to witness your death," Aoife said.

"Traitors are put to death. First, we must find out if it is really Gila behind this. Is there anything she does each time when she would bring your food up to you?" Niall asked.

"Gila always set the tray somewhere behind me. She wanted to make sure it was not too hot to eat."

Niall stepped over to the cabinet set against the wall. It was nothing more than a small wooden table top with a rough cabinet added above and sides and doors added below. He pulled open the top door to reveal bedding. He pulled open the two small doors below. Nothing, he was about to close them again, when he leaned forward and felt along the inner edge. He stood and opened the top door again. He ran his hand under the bedding along the inner edges, then at the back.

"There is something at the back." Niall pulled out two small, narrow earthenware jars. He handed the jars to Aoife. She examined the jars, worked one stopper out with her nails.

"No ordinary jar, the stopper has a wax coating on the inside. Though I doubt the contents would seep through."

She sniffed at the jar and handed it to Mór. She opened the second jar and inserted the tip of her small finger inside. "It has a bitter taste."

Mór took a taste and wrinkled her nose. "Angel root, a woman's weapon, makes a person sick. But when given long enough or in a large dose it can kill even a strong man or..."

"Or a woman with child," Cullan finished for her. He lay back, exhausted. "Or an old man."

"Come, Rónán," Niall said. "We will meet Gila before she returns to the cottage."

❦

Gila sat in a chair in the center of the room. She told the story of how she poisoned Briana as if she were relating to them her latest trip down to the village. Cullan listened in horror as she said the baby only required a small amount to put her to sleep.

"Who else?" Niall asked. He stood behind her, his hand resting on her shoulder, his fingers touching her neck, as if he were encouraging her to speak.

She told how Peadar, her partner, made friends with a girl in the kitchen. The kitchen help soon grew accustomed to him hanging about. He managed to put poison in the food for the Ard Ri.

"They wanted him dead before you returned from Alibie," Gila said. "Your meddling uncle sent a messenger to you. Our men watched the gate for days. Somehow you were warned and escaped our trap. It was so simple in the end. Briana took me, her trusted companion and servant, with her."

Gila smiled at her good fortune.

"How can she be so calm about what happened?" Cullan asked.

"To her way of thinking she has not committed a crime."

The half smile on Gila's plain face looked out of place. She seemed unaware that what she told them would condemn her to death.

"When will Peadar return?" Niall asked.

"He comes after each new moon. Brings a few who are in need of a guide with him as a cover and gives me instructions. When they learned that Briana was with child, Artúr signed her death warrant. It would be a simple matter for me to carry it out. It amazed me that she carried the child as long as she did. Such a lovely girl, it is a shame. She bought it on herself; she should have married Selatin."

"Does Artúr hate me that much that he stoops to a woman's method to kill those I love?" Cullan asked.

Gila did not answer Cullan.

"Answer his question, Gila," Niall said.

"As long as an heir with close ties to the throne lives, Artúr will never be sure of his hold on Cwillan. So once you and Niall are removed, he could hold the throne by force if necessary."

"What of my father?" Rónán asked.

"Answer Rónán's question."

"I know nothing of the matter concerning Lord Bran."

"How long can you control her?" Cullan asked.

"Gila is under my power forever. The bond between us is now complete," Niall said, as he removed his hand from her neck.

"Rather than dispose of her, let us use her."

Niall smiled at Cullan. "You are right. How many warriors do you think we have in the village?"

"Not enough to give Artúr a fight for the throne," Gila answered. "Is it not strange, no matter what they do to stop your people, they still find a way to get across the river."

"Your people? You are one of us, are you not?"

"My father is of northern blood. They are my people."

"Look at me, Gila," Niall commanded. She glanced up, waited. "Tell Peadar when he returns that there has been talk of a spy in the village, that it isn't safe for him anymore. In the future meet with him north of here at the small rinn." When she didn't agree he added, "The small peninsula north of here."

"Yes, lord."

Amazed, Cullan said, "Niall, can you teach me how to do that?"

"I can help you understand it." Niall turned back to Gila, "Something else. You will tell Peadar that Cullan is very sick and may not last the summer."

"As you wish."

"Could you make her do anything?" Ciarán asked.

"Yes," Niall said. "Anything."

CHAPTER NINETEEN

Each day Cullan grew stronger. He was eager to return to a normal life, to ride again, to feel the sun on his face, the wind in his hair. Niall cautioned him to keep to his room to lend truth to the rumor that he would not last the summer.

Gila still came to his room with food, though now a young man from Cullan's clan called Rogan came with her.

Word reached them that Artúr had gathered an army to take Boweayn. Flann, a minor chieftain under Uaid, had his lands confiscated by Artúr and given to Selatin. Flann killed the men who came to take over his holding. When Artúr sent armed men to take him, Flann, his family and warriors took refuge at Boweayn.

Uaid refused to turn Flann over to Artúr.

The siege of Boweayn began.

Tempers ran high in the village.

Eóghan came up to Hill Cottage to report that the men wanted to cross the river and ride to the aid of Boweayn.

How long, Cullan thought, *will I be able to keep these men here.*

Even Niall, usually level headed, wanted to ride immediately to his father's aid.

Cullan studied his friends. He did not want war. However, Artúr had forced his hand. He looked around at his small band of seven, his three friends, Ruadrí, his apprentice Pól, Eóghan, and Fionbharr, who had joined them in the spring.

"The false information we fed Artúr through Peadar is working. He feels safe enough to start to steal our lands and take on my father," Niall said. "I will tell Gila that we are divided on the matter of Boweayn. If we do agree, it will soon be Samhain. Far too late to take the fight to Artúr."

"Artúr will think he is safe," Fionbharr added. "That spring is the earliest we could reach Boweayn."

Cullan stood and moved over to the hearth to stare into flames.

"Will you excuse us," Niall said. "I need to speak with Cullan."

When they were alone Niall moved to stand beside him. "What is the problem, Cullan?"

"I do not want this power forced upon me at the cost of the lives of brave men."

"We will not be able to hold the men in the village much longer. Would you rather they go on their own and die? For die they will if they do not get training and have someone to lead them."

Cullan turned and paced the room.

Niall moved to the sideboard, picked up a long cloth-wrapped bundle he had placed there earlier. With care, he unwrapped the cloth to revel a long wooden case. He undid the latches and let the top fold back flat, then removed the inner packing.

Cullan looked on with a mixture of surprise and wonder. "How did you come by my father's swords?"

"We removed the case when the Ard Ri died. Ciarán saw to the removal of the broadsword from the cart after your father was laid to rest."

Cullan removed the sword from its niche. Metal grated on metal as he slid the scabbard off. Never had he seen anything so beautiful, yet so deadly, as this sword passed down through generations of his forebears. Light from the rush torches reflected off the blade, making it appear to be a weapon of flame instead of metal.

"All your warriors will recognize your father's sword. Not that there is any question whether they would follow you into battle," Niall said. "I also have this."

From a pouch made of velvet, Niall pulled Cullan's gold circlet.

"You left it on the vine up in the Ladies Bower."

Cullan took the circlet from him and sank down on the bench near the table.

"War has come. Will you lead your people to victory?"

"Do I have a choice?" Cullan asked. "I can lead them, or someone else can. Perhaps I will be better at looking out for their welfare."

Cullan was surprised when he learned that Ruadrí and Eóghan had been training the men over the summer. Now they would make plans in earnest. Once started Cullan would have to go all the way. First Boweayn, then they would see to retaking the fortress of Cwillan.

Why, had that which he thought he had left behind come to him again?

He did not have an answer.

Fionbharr, though no older then Niall, had ridden with the army Cormac sent to drive their enemy back across the northern border. He was the closest they had to someone who had recent battle experience. Ruadrí had not fought in a battle for many years; he would go through their army and pick the men that would make the best leaders.

Word spread across the river, and their ranks swelled with more men. All the warriors needed time to train. Time was against them, they would have to leave soon or find themselves on the road during winter.

As soon as they crossed the river, Artúr would know they were coming. It would be a long march to Boweayn.

After less than a full summer of training, the warriors were broken up into smaller groups of thirty to fifty men. Each group would march north for a league, then return to the river to cross on flatboats by night. The groups would gather again at Realin, a valley to the east of Boweayn.

༄

"Will you walk with me, lord?"

Cullan smiled at Aoife.

On this warm night many would find it hard to sleep. Perhaps a walk in the nearby woods would calm his nerves enough to catch a little sleep before morning and his duties began again.

Ciarán joined them, but kept back a few paces. In the woods a pale golden light marked where someone had set up a tent. Mór waited for them at the entrance.

"Lord." Mór bowed and held the flap back for him to enter.

Inside he found a table and benches and a rough bed of blankets and pillows on the ground.

"Do not get the wrong idea, lord." Aoife said as she motioned to him to sit at the table. "Soon you will leave for Boweayn. We must talk."

Mór placed two pitchers and a trencher with meat and bread before him. Then slipped out of the tent.

"What do you need of me?"

"It is for Mór, not myself."

"I know about Mór and Rónán."

"You have decreed that only wives may travel behind the army."

"If I could, I would leave the wives here as well. We will have need of them to help with the wounded, but a young unwed maid..." Cullan shook his head.

"Is it fair to her?" she said, as she poured out a mug of ale for him and water for herself.

Cullan took a sip. The ale, chilled and sweetened with honey, tasted finer than anything he had drunk in a long time. How could he solve this problem? It came to him, so simple, why had he not thought of it sooner?

"I will speak with Tuathall in the morning. See if he will marry any of the couples that wish to do so."

"For Rónán or for Mór?"

"Mór is a healer. She will be needed."

Aoife poured more ale into his cup.

"It is not just for Mór, it is for myself that I would speak to you."

With his dagger, Cullan speared a piece of meat, placed it on a piece of flat bread and began to carve it into smaller pieces. "Speak then, what can I do for you?"

He almost choked on the meat when she said, "I also wish to go with you."

"I cannot say no to one, then break the rules for you, Aoife."

"You forget, I am a healer too. Tuathall will need my help. I could travel with him."

It was a possibility he had not thought of.

"I will speak with our abbot. What else, there is more? I can see it in your eyes."

"I thought you might find the peace here more restful."

"Indeed?" he said as he studied her beautiful face. "Would I be alone?"

Aoife's face flushed crimson.

Cullan stood to leave. Did she not realize he was still in mourning for Briana?

"Wait!" She took his hand, placed it against her cheek. "They say you can read thoughts. What do you read there? I do not want you to think I am merely changing sides or worse, that I was..."

Love. Aoife loved him.

He felt affection for her. Did he love her as he had loved Briana? He did not think he would ever feel that way about another woman. Through her he recalled the day they met at the birdcage. By then, his thoughts were only of Briana.

There was more. He pulled his hand away. The bond between them ended.

"Under Brehon Law, the Ard Ri could take another wife, or even one of a lesser degree, with no claim to the throne. I was never your father's wife of any degree. He took me in when my parents died. We were very close, like father and daughter, nothing else."

Cullan watched her, not sure what to say.

"No one would find fault with you if..."

"You let the birds out to warn me and you came here to help. I thought you stayed because..."

"I wanted to," she finished for him. "Some of us had little choice in the matter, there was no way out after the chieftains turned against you."

"Many of them will live to regret it."

"By then it will be too late for them. How much does a dead man learn? How much will Darlisca learn when you kill him."

"Dead men learn nothing; it is a warning to the living. Perhaps I will not have to kill Darlisca."

Aoife shook her head sadly. "You know it will come to that. Do you think he will give up so easy the lands he has coveted for so long? Can you afford to let him return to his lands only to bide his time? Watch for a weakness and return to claim our land."

She was right. In the end, it would be between Darlisca and himself. Artúr was only the tool to gain the lands that his uncle wanted. Artúr was his kinsman. What would he do with him?

Aoife was beautiful and was as tall as Briana, but rounder, with creamy skin, light eyes, a little older perhaps. He leaned over, and kissed her. She held herself stiff to his touch.

"Will you abide by the rules I have set down for the other women?"

"Yes," she answered him, her voice husky with fear, or perhaps anticipation.

In the morning, he might regret this night's weakness, but for now there was only the pleasure between a man and a woman.

๑

On the march to Boweayn, Cullan hoped to move through the countryside without notice. Right from the start, he found it would not be possible. He kept his army of two hundred handpicked warriors out of the villages, only to find that the villagers and farmers would wait for them at the crossroads with gifts of food. Young girls decked their horses with wreaths of flowers.

Young men asked to join him. If the young men were of age, or close, he put them under tutelage of an older warrior. There was not a chance in the world that they could get to Boweayn without word of their coming reaching Artúr.

CHAPTER TWENTY

Cullan moved to the edge of the trees. He used the thick boles as a cover. Below at the end of the long valley stood the fortress of Boweayn with its back to the rocky foothills of the western mountains. There was only one entrance and exit to the valley. What were they thinking building in a place without a way to escape? Halfway down the valley Artúr's army camped, effectively cutting off Uaid's clan.

It was late, the day's fighting over.

There was only one place Artúr could set up a trap to catch Cullan's army. Not far from the entrance to the valley, on the right side, were huge rocks and bushes that narrowed down the approach to Boweayn for half a league. From here the enemy had a place to strike at them. Above that, just below the valley rim, were flat rocks. This is where Cullan would place his best archers.

Their journey here had been too easy. Surely word had reached Artúr that he had assembled an army to stop his siege on Boweayn.

As the wind blew through the trees it made a mournful sound. The wind died and the world fell into silence. When the caw of a Raven in the branches above his head broke the silence, his blood ran cold.

Carrion birds; a bad omen.

Cullan hurried back through the trees to the place he left Ciarán with the horses.

Tomorrow it would start.

∾

In the half-light just before true dawn, Tuathall waited for the signal to start the benediction. Cullan nodded to Ciarán. His guardian held up his hand to get the assembled warriors' attention. Most of the warriors dismounted, many knelt before the holy man as he moved along the line. Tuathall stopped every five paces to bless the men who would shortly go into battle.

Cullan dismounted, waited as Tuathall made his slow way toward him. When the abbot was before him, he knelt. Ciarán remained on his feet, his hand on the hilt of his sword. His Guardian would watch Tuathall's every move.

"May the enemy fall before you as grain before a scythe," Tuathall intoned. Before moving on he placed his hand on Cullan's head. "Go with the blessing of the Father, Son of Déaglán."

Before mounting Warlord, Cullan watched Tuathall continue down the line. After the holy man was done here, he would bless the main army hidden inside the forest behind them.

More to himself then his Guardian, Cullan said, "Why did the good abbot think I would stop him from blessing the warriors?"

"Tuathall was visiting family on that horrible day, he is one of the few holy men to escape the slaughter at Alibie. By your decree he is now our abbot. I think he is still unsure of himself."

Athdar was in charge of the defense of their camp in case they lost the day. His warriors were older men, young boys not of age yet and camp followers. To ask for Artúr's mercy meant they would forfeit their lives and die by his hand. Better to die as true sons and daughters of Déaglán than be slaughtered like sheep.

Two older men picked by Ruadrí stepped forward. They could still ride, but were beyond fighting; they would beat the war-drums. Both men bowed to Cullan, unmindful that this displeased him.

"A slow beat at first," Cullan said. "Once we are through the narrow place in the valley, I want the beat to pick up. Once we engage Artúr's army, take a position near the entrance. It is your duty to warn the camp if we fail this day."

"As you wish, lord," the taller of the drummers said.

Both men bowed again before they stepped back to mount their horses.

Angered, Cullan turned to Ciarán. "I thought you talked to our men?"

"Old customs die hard. It is a show of respect for you, nothing more."

Perhaps his friend was right. Cullan mounted Warlord. Ciarán mounted Achill, his dun gelding. Cullan's gift to him when he became his Guardian.

"Do you think Artúr has a trap set to spring on us?" Ciarán asked.

"By now Artúr knows we are here. The narrow place near the valley entrance, that is where he will set his trap."

From the forest behind them rode Niall. "Have you reconsidered staying back with us?"

Cullan shook his head. "I cannot ask my men to do what I would not do myself."

"Take my hounds with you."

"Keep the hounds as an added defense of our camp."

Niall, was not pleased with his answer, but nodded.

"It is time to look to our men," Cullan said. He looked to the east; the sky was a pale blue now. "The sun is up, it will come over the mountain soon. It is the best time to ride into the valley. Artúr's warriors will have to look right into the morning sun."

"You still fear a trap?" Niall asked.

"It is best to be prepared."

"Take good care of him."

Before Ciarán could answer Niall, he turned his horse and rode back toward the main army. Rónán rode out of the forest to meet him. Together they disappeared into the trees.

Ciarán gave the signal for the horsemen to mount up, to get ready for the charge. Cullan looked at his men. All of them had volunteered to be the bait for

Artúr's army. To a man, they wore saffron tunics with a blue band on the sleeves, over light armor. This way they hoped to tell friend from foe in the heat of battle.

Cullan nodded at the drummers.

With Ciarán to his left and Eóghan, his standard-bearer, to his right, Cullan raised his hand. The morning breeze caught his standard; the running white horse on a field of blue and saffron seemed alive, galloping into battle. He dropped his hand, drew his sword and lifted it high. Around him, the sound of a hundred swords being drawn echoed in the morning air. He let Warlord move forward at a walk. Soon the most dangerous part of their plan would be upon them, riding through the narrow section of the valley.

Warlord danced to the side, pulling on the bit, eager to run. Cullan reined in the tall horse. He studied the slope inside the valley. Nothing stirred among the rocks and bushes.

He turned to Ciarán. "Pass it back. They are to ride no more than three across, stay to the left until they are through the narrow section. We must stay together. I will give the signal where we make our stand."

Ciarán turned and told the warriors behind him and to the side.

They waited while they order was passed back.

When the sun stood well over the eastern mountains, Cullan gave the signal, urged his stallion forward at a canter. The sunlight crept forward as they rode into the valley. The rhythm of the drums came faster, a living heartbeat, echoing the beating of Cullan's heart.

From the rocks a man ran down to stop Cullan. Seeing so few mounted warriors, the amadan had left his place of concealment. The man keeled over, an arrow in his back. More men ran down the sides toward the small band of warriors. Cullan did not check his horse. Those who moved into open ground would fall to arrows from the archers above.

Artúr's army was ready for them; they stood with their backs to Boweayn, waiting for the oncoming army. At less than half a league, Cullan turned his horse and rode along the enemy's line. He reined in Warlord, turned to the enemy, and beat his sword on his shield, taunting them.

The valley echoed with the din made by the Sons of Déaglán. Darlisca's archers moved to the front and a rain of arrows hissed down on them, some plunging into the grass while others struck shields. Nearby a horse screamed in pain.

Cullan waited.

His plan to draw Artúr's men into breaking ranks seemed destined to failure. Just as he thought his plan would not work, a single warrior burst from the ranks, a berserker. He shouted at his men and pointed his sword at the enemy. The whole line broke, surged forward to catch Cullan and his small band before they could escape.

Cullan turned Warlord to face Artúr's army. He would let them come to him. Over the sound of oncoming horses and screaming men the rhythm of the drums quicken.

Outnumbered ten to one, their only hope was that Niall would be in time to save them. Fionbharr at the head of a third band of warriors would keep his men in reserve to help where needed.

"We make our stand here!" Cullan cried.

Eóghan leaned forward, planted the end of the standard pole into the ground and drew his sword. Cullan waited with Ciarán at his side, and a dozen men who were to stay with him during the battle.

The two armies came together with a horrendous crash, the war cry of men, screaming horses, and the clang of metal on metal. The sound echoed down the valley.

Horns sounded somewhere in the distance. Cullan did not have the time to wonder what it meant.

Artúr's main army converged on the ground that Cullan and his men held. If their assault failed, there would be no escape. Cullan's warriors fought a desperate battle to stop them. The enemy army encircled them, overwhelming their small band.

Cullan lay back on the makeshift palette. He closed his eyes, tried to shut out the horror around him. He opened them again; nothing could shut out what had happened this day. The once green valley ran red with blood. The dead and injured warriors from both armies littered the ground for as far as he could see.

The stench of death made him sick. Overhead, carrion birds gathered to feast on the dead.

Niall knelt and pulled back the blanket to examine the wound. "It will leave a scar. You will be able to show it to your children's children and tell them about the great battle of Boweayn."

"Was our camp spared?"

"Lie easy, your uncle stood well, our camp was not overrun."

Cullan tried to rise. "No looting."

Niall frowned at him, as he forced him to lie down again.

"As you wish, the order has gone out. Artúr would not be so kind. They are looking for him among the dead.

Ruadrí sent a band after the survivors, to make sure that the enemy does not try to pillage the villages on their journey back to Cwillan."

"I heard a horn much earlier. What did it mean?"

"Lord Uaid and Flann joined us in the battle. As soon as we move you into the fortress, my father wishes to speak with you."

To the left a horse screamed. Cullan turned his head to see what was going on, fearful it was Warlord.

"Lie easy, lord. They are putting the horses to the sword that are too badly injured. Tuathall and the women are seeing to the injured men."

"Have you seen Ciarán?"

"I am here, lord." Ciarán knelt down on his other side. His Guardian wore a cloth tied around his upper right arm; blood had seeped through to soil it. His face and clothing were spattered with blood.

"And Eóghan?"

Ciarán shook his head. "He put your standard through the warrior who attacked you. Was cut down from behind by another."

"Those who have a chance at life are being moved into the fortress," Niall said.

"Dig a pit for the dead. They must be buried as soon as possible."

"Tuathall said as much, and has given the order. Rest easy now, Cullan."

CHAPTER TWENTY-ONE

Twelve times the moon had waxed and waned. Harvest was over and it would soon be Samhain.

Cullan had a new worry. He dismounted as soon as Riga and Teague moved out of the dark forest on the far side of the Dubh River. He moved down the steep bank to the water's edge. Ciarán waited with the horses.

On this side of the river the ground went from flat meadowland to rocky soil cut back by spring floods forming a high ridge over the riverbed.

Both trackers ran down to the water, lopped easily in the shallow river, sending up sprays of water. Near the center they were forced to slow. At this point the river ran deep. As they neared the west bank the water became shallow again.

Riga reached Cullan first.

"Lord, we lost their trail on the far side of the Dubh Valley."

Teague joined them. He stood next to his father.

"Get some food and rest. We cross the Dubh in two mornings."

Teague spoke for the first time. "We will go out again, at first light."

Cullan shook his head. Riga nodded. Father and son moved up the path.

Cullan's fear for Aoife's safety had pushed everything else of his head. Something important nagged at the back of his mind.

"Riga, did you see signs of Artúr's army?"

Riga waited for Cullan to join him on the ridge. "We saw signs of an army, perhaps Artúr's or Darlisca's."

"Where?"

"This side of the Dark Valley," Riga said. "Closer to the river we saw signs where riders passed through, twenty riders, perhaps more. They rode single-file to hide their numbers. I would say five to six mornings ago. In the same area, we also saw the tracks of a lone rider. He or she was in a hurry and made no effort to hide their tracks."

"Which way?"

"North, upriver." Riga answered Cullan's unasked question. "Not Aoife, she headed east."

Cullan mounted Warlord. Before turning the stallion to head back to their camp, he stared across the river, a slight break in the trees marked the trail they would soon take. From there they would cross the Dubh Valley and head back to Faolán, where they would spend the winter.

He turned Warlord. "Why would she leave me?".

"Women are strange creatures at best," Ciarán said "May the Father and Son be with you, Aoife, on this journey you have undertaken." Cullan touched his forehead, then his chest, before he rode back to his camp.

⌒๏

Two mornings later, Cullan woke to find their camp in a state of organized chaos. As soon as a wagon was loaded, it started its slow trek to the river. This was the only place shallow enough for them to bring the wagons through. He had men at the river working on a ramp to allow the wagons to reach the riverbed.

After breaking his fast with Ciarán and his personal guard, Cullan moved among his men, helping where he could, and giving words of encouragement to those who needed it. Ciarán followed him, ready to help where needed. Most of his men smiled, grateful for his help. Only Taydan seemed displeased to see him.

Cullan would have to speak to his second-oldest chieftain. Taydan wanted to be more than a chieftain, perhaps Ard Ri. Cullan was pulled out of his thoughts by the plaintive blare of a horn.

Men began to run toward the sound.

Cullan moved to the center of their camp, from here he had a clear view up the valley to the west. Riding at breakneck speed the rider blew on his horn, a clear warning in the crisp morning air. Without waiting to see what the problem was, Cullan ran back to his tent. Rogan had Warlord and Achill saddled.

When Cullan rode to the edge of the camp, he found Taydan giving orders.

"How many?"

"We don't know yet, I'll send men into the woods to see."

"Wait for our sentry, perhaps he can tell us what is going on."

Taydan watched Cullan, his eyes dark slits, his hands so tight on the reins his knuckles were white. "If we wait, our enemy will have gained an advantage."

"It is better we see what is going on, then we can decide what to do. Those who enter the woods might never return."

Cullan did not have time to debate procedure with Taydan. With Ciarán and his personal guard behind him, he rode along the edge of the camp, shouting to his men to form a shield wall, until mounted men took their place. Half a dozen riders burst from the trees, too far behind the sentry to stop him. Cullan watched as the warriors advanced toward his camp. How many men are hidden back in the trees?

Niall joined him. "Do you think it is a full-scale attack?"

"It is hard to tell. Move up the hounds."

Niall shouted to the men that handled the hounds.

Cullan called to a warrior running by to have the sentry report to him first. His warriors formed a line to protect their camp. His personal guard waited with him. He turned to Ciarán. "Ride to the river, let them know what is happening here. Have them post sentries. We do not want to be caught between two armies. I'll join you there."

The sentry told Cullan that he saw a dozen or more armed men making their way through the woods.

Two men ran forward with the leads to a pair of hounds held in each hand. They had trouble controlling the beasts. Like his men, the hounds were eager for battle. Once out in front of the mounted warriors the handlers waited, ready to release the hounds on command.

"Release the hounds."

Scolán, larger than most wolfhounds, shot forward; working in pairs, the hounds circled around the riders jumping and snapping at the horses' flanks, always mindful to stay away from the dangerous hoofs. Scolán picked his target, dropped back and came around on the rider's unprotected side. For several paces he matched stride for stride with the horse. Waited. Then jumped, his momentum unseating the rider.

They went down in a tangle of arms and legs. Scolán's powerful jaws found the rider's throat. The next rider tried to run the hound down, Scolán dodged aside and around to take out this rider as well.

Niall would keep the hounds out only as long as they had the advantage.

Cullan turned his horse, his personal guard followed. They were forced to ride along the edge of the camp. Men and women who had suffered when Artúr's army passed their way milled around. Some with nothing but the clothes they stood in turned and began to run. Fear would drive them toward the river crossing.

Tuathall emerged from his makeshift chapel, shouted to get Cullan's attention. Cullan slowed his horse, waiting for the abbot to make his way through the throng of men and women.

"I received word earlier. One of the wagons has broken down. It will be awhile before they can fix the wheel."

"I'm headed for the river now. Try to see if you can calm our people."

"It would be easier to stop the sun in the sky, but I will see what I can do."

Cullan turned his horse, stopped, turned back. "Tuathall, last night you were telling me what a dry summer we had."

"Yes, lord. Dryer than most."

"Does that mean that there might be a place to cross farther upstream?"

"Do you think this is how they have come up behind us?"

"Yes. The real question is why?"

Why attack now?

When they could have come earlier, caught everyone still in their beds. It did not make sense.

What were Artúr and Darlisca up to?

At the river he found that the lead wagon had been unloaded to make it easier to repair the broken wheel. It would be some time before it was fixed. The ramp was ready to pull down to the water's edge.

He rode to the edge of the ridge above the dark waters of the Dubh River. On the other side the forest looked peaceful in the early morning light. He was about to go and see if he could help with the wagon when a flock of birds rose out of the trees on the left side of the trail, then a second flock followed on the right. He watched as the birds circled over the trees, waiting for them to settle down again.

When they flew up river he had his answer.

Those who enter the woods might never return.

Cullan turned Warlord around so fast the warrior behind him was forced to wheel his horse out of the way.

The first of the frightened camp followers had reached the wagons. They hesitated for only a moment, before hurrying on toward the river. Cullan dismounted, knowing that to turn the throng of frightened men and women was hopeless. The leaders dodged around him. He caught a woman dragging a small child with her.

"Would you risk the life of your child? The river is too deep for a child to cross."

"Then I will carry him."

"I cannot let you cross."

She screamed curses at him; her hands clawed at his tunic. She tried to claw his face. Before she could do any damage, Ciarán caught her from behind. Her child beat at him with his small fists.

Cullan stepped forward. He hated to do this, but he had to stop her. He placed his hand along her neck. Her mind was filled with fear. Her family farm had been sacked and burned by Artúr's army, both partents, her sister, and brother-in-law murdered.

He hit her, effective, but a much more primitive solution than what he could have done. Ciarán caught her.

"Place her and the child near the wagon." To the rest of his men he said, "Try to stop as many as you can."

Rónán rode up, dismounted and hurried to Cullan.

"More warriors are riding out of the woods."

"Have they confronted our men yet?"

"That is the funny thing, that is why Niall thought you should know. They seem only to want to scare us."

Dubh meant "dark" and also "evil".

"They want to drive us across the river," Cullan said more to himself, "we need to stop our people from crossing."

Niall's Guardian did not question him, Rónán looked around, a look of puzzlement on his broad face. Cullan's personal guard were having little success in stopping the frightened men and women. Rónán motioned for the lead wagoner to join them. Ailill hurried over to them. The leader of Cullan's personal guard joined them.

"You know this area, Ailill," Rónán said. "Is there anywhere we can go and avoid crossing the Dubh?"

Ailill scratched the wisps of gray hair on his ample chin. "The ole 'utter rood."

Ailill's accent was thick, hard to understand. Cullan listened to Rónán explanation.

"The old Butter road, I have never head of it. Where is it?"

"There used to be a holding south of here, near the river bank," Rónán said. "It was abandoned in my grandfather's time."

"Where?"

"Just beyond those young trees along the river. The Butter road runs along the river bank."

Cullan told the leader of his personal guard to take several men and find the road, see if we can shelter in the ruins. Clear any trees in the way."

With axes in hand they headed toward the river.

Cullan turned to Ailill. "If the road is too narrow, you might have to leave your wagon here."

Ailill looked at him as if he were crazy. "I will no 'eave me 'orses."

Cullan heard something about the horses. "Then unhitch the teams and move them into the trees." He turned to Rónán, "Go back, tell Niall to take the fight to Artúr. Let us see what they will do. I will join you presently."

❧

Wind off the river chilled everyone to the bone. Cullan refused go into what was left of the old fortress, what everyone referred to as the Butter Fortress, or to let Ciarán build a fire. Camp followers huddled around him; old men and women and those with children were allowed to shelter in what was left of the great hall.

All he could think of was Aoife. Was she a prisoner of Artúr or Darlisca?

Overhead the moon took its nightly ride from east to west. Across the water came the eerie cry of some tormented soul being put to the sword. Cullan, whisptered a prayer for those caught on the road that morning, tourch his forehead, then his chest. "Please, Father, see Aoife to safety."

Niall sat down next to him. His friend ran his fingers down his long mustache, the ends curled upward.

"Where is your cloak, Cullan?"

"I gave it to a woman with two small children."

Another cry came from the other side of the river.

"They know we are over here, but not sure of where. And they want to keep us from our rest, dispirit us by putting the men and women they caught on the forest road to death."

"He is making good work of it," Cullan said.

"He will keep his men awake as well. It is only a matter of time before we catch him."

"In the meantime, more of our people will die."

"What do you think Artúr would do if he caught us?" Niall said, changing the subject.

Cullan did not answer him. Another cry echoed on the night air, sending shivers down his spine.

"I think, he would drag us through the roads of Cwillan, then take us north to his fortress."

"Probably, I can see Darlisca being dragged behind Warlord, stripped to the waist and barefoot. Artúr is another matter, he is kin."

"You must not forget that at Boweayn, he tried to kill you," Ciarán said, sitting down next to his friends.

"Come," Niall said. "I found a place up on the first level where we can try to get some rest."

CHAPTER
TWENTY-TWO

Cullan shivered; the war was not going against
them, but it was not ending either. Pulling his
fur-lined cloak tighter around him he sat down next
to Niall.

They were here today to try to negotiate with they
enemy.

Above, unseen behind thick gray clouds, the sun
rose in the sky. It would be Samhain in three nights. It
was far too late in the year for negotiations.

Still they waited.

Niall sat back against the rocks, his head bent forward. His hood pulled down so that not even the tip of
his nose was visible. Riga brought horn cups with hot
water steeped with rose hips. He handed Cullan a cup,
moved to give Niall one, hesitated, thought better of
disturbing him, gave Rónán a cup before he returned
to the small fire.

Cullan let the heat from the cup warm his hands before taking a sip. He was surprised at the taste; he wondered where Riga had found honey. Rogan, of course, his steward thought of everything.

Rónán moved over to Cullan, knelt down next to him. "Do you think he is all right?"

He understood his friend's concern, his fear for what Niall was trying to do.

"He knows what he is doing. If I sense any danger I will stop him."

As the light waned, the wind became bitter.

Niall moved with a jerk, as if he had woken from sleep. "We must go. Now! Riga can you guide us across the moors?"

"Yes, lord," Riga said, standing.

They hurried down the hill to the place they left their horses. They mounted and followed Riga to the east. Single-file they rode across craggy land. As the ground grew marshy they slowed, careful to avoid the areas that could suck down man or beast.

When they came to what looked more like a shallow loch than moorland. Riga signaled for them to halt. He studied the ground before taking out a long strand of leather and held it before him. At the end hung a thin piece of metal with a pointed end like a small spear. It swung back and forth in the light breeze, turned to point to their left, as if an invisible hand had moved it in that direction.

Riga beckoned for them to follow him. "Keep close behind me, single file."

Midway across the bog, Teague, at the back, called to his father. They stopped and turned in their saddles. He pointed back the way they had come. Riders were approaching the edge of the moor.

Cullan felt a chill go up his spine. It would be full dark soon. Without knowing the correct path, these men would get lost.

As if reading his thoughts, Riga said. "If they follow us, they will die here."

Riga turned forward and signaled for them to follow. It was dark when they returned to the fortress of Faolán. All the chieftains gathered around their small party to hear if the war was over.

"The emissary did not show," Cullan told them.

All around him he heard groans and muttered words of disappointment. He was disappointed as well.

Cullan led his friends up to his apartment. Rónán had servants bring them food and ale. After their meal, he threw another log on the hearth. They moved their benches closer to the fire.

"So tell us what happened. We were to meet an emissary from the north to put an end to this war," Cullan said.

Niall stared into the fire. "I do not think there was an emissary, or perhaps he was betrayed."

"Betrayed," Ciarán said. "By whom?"

"It was strange, I fell into a light sleep. Then I stood in the great hall at Cwillan. Darlisca sat at the end of a long table, Artúr to his right and another man to his left. All of a sudden Darlisca looked up, as if he sensed my presence and smiled that wolf-like toothy smile of his. It was time to leave."

"This other man, did you know him?" Ciarán asked.

"No. He never turned so I could see his face."

"My chieftains will return to their holdings. I will winter here at Faolán," Cullan said. "Will you return to Boweayn, Niall?"

"I will leave right after Samhain."

CHAPTER
TWENTY-THREE

Guards on the north tower sent word that riders were coming around the loch. Overhead the sun moved out from behind a cloud bathing the loch and forest in sunlight, warming the air. Three riders made their way along the edge of Loch Faolán, avoiding the small village half a league from the fortress.

"Who do you think it is?" Ciarán asked, as they hurried up the steps to the curtain wall on the lakeside of Faolán.

"Hopefully someone with news."

"Not Niall or Lord Uaid. It looks like a man, a woman, and a boy or young man. Strange the boy stays well back from the other two riders."

Cullan hoped that it was Aoife, returning at last. Some inner sense told him that he would never see her again.

Not in this life.

When the riders were close enough for him to make out the lead horse, he smiled at his Guardian. "It looks like Abbot Tuathall is paying us a visit."

Below, Rónán hurried across the courtyard, his reachtaire behind him. When he learned it was Abbot Tuathall he called for the gates to be opened.

With Tuathall still in the lead, the riders entered the courtyard. The young boy hung back, staying well away from the abbot and his companion.

After they dismounted, the boy moved away to stand near the wall. The woman kept the hood of her cape pulled forward, casting a shadow across her face.

Rónán listened to the abbot, nodded once or twice, and called up to Cullan. "Our good abbot has brought you a message."

With Ciarán at his heels, Cullan moved down the stairs to the courtyard.

"I will have rooms prepared for you and your companions," Rónán said. "Come and break bread with us when you are done talking with our lord."

Tuathall waited until Rónán and his steward went inside. "Cullan, I will give you first that which they sent with the message."

He motioned to the boy.

The boy picked up the leather satchel he had laid on the ground at his feet and moved forward.

Tuathall put his hand over his lower face. "Open the satchel," he told the boy, then stepped back.

As soon as the boy was a pace away from him, Cullan caught the stench of death. When the boy opened the satchel, by sheer will, he kept himself from being sick as he looked into the dead face of Selatin, dead a half moon or more, his face bloated, almost unrecognizable.

Cullan turned his head away. Behind him Tuathall told the boy to take the head and bury it in the woods.

"And the message?"

Tuathall nodded to the woman, who stepped forward and pulled her hood back. Cullan was surprised that it was Cara. When she heard voices coming their way she pulled the hood back into place.

"Perhaps we should go inside."

"Is there somewhere we can talk in private?" Tuathall asked.

Cullan nodded and asked them to follow him to his apartments.

Rogan saw to the fire, poured hot water steeped with rose hips and honey for their guests, he withdrew, leaving them to talk in private.

Cullan motioned for his quests to take seats near the hearth. "So tell me, is this a petition from Artúr to put an end to the war."

"No," Cara said. "But some of his minor lords wish it over. They are tired of supplying Artúr and Darlisca with men and weapons. That is why they sent you the head of Selatin."

"Did you know about this?"

Tuathall nodded.

"To end the war will be very costly."

"How costly?"

"I want Darlisca, Artúr, and the seven lords under them." Cullan corrected himself, "Six lords."

"And if they can not do that?" Cara asked.

"Artúr and his uncle only hold the lands around Cwillan, and a little to the north. We can sit back, bide our time, and pick them off one at a time. It is their choice."

"I will take your message to the man who contacted me," Cara said as she stood. She turned to the abbot, "We should return."

"Cara, first tell me why they picked you."

"They knew that I was a friend. They needed someone they could trust. Last fómhar, the person they picked betrayed them. Some of them were put to the sword."

"Can the boy be trusted?"

"Cullan, the boy is my apprentice. May the Father and Son protect us if I cannot trust him. Rónán will expect us to break bread with him. Perhaps it would be better if we leave at first light."

"It is best that I am not seen here." She took a sip of her drink. "Have your steward bring food up here for the boy and myself."

Cullan turned to Ciarán, "I need you ride to Boweayn, tell Lord Uaid to take his men north as soon as possible."

"You want to cut off any chance of Artúr and Darlisca crossing back into their own lands."

Cullan nodded.

CHAPTER TWENTY-FOUR

Darkness was almost upon them when Cullan set up his camp in the ruins of Carracán.

Rogan brought him food and ale.

Niall burst into the room shouting, "They are coming with Darlisca and Artúr."

"Good. Now we can put an end to this insanity."

"A rider just came in," Rogan said, hurrying into the room. He wishes an audience with you. He rode to Faolán, then here."

"Send him in."

The rider hurried forward, pulled off his hat and gave a half bow. "Lord, I was to deliver this to you at Faolán. It was urgent that I reach you as soon as possible. As soon as I heard you were here, I came straight away."

"You are one of my people."

"Yes, lord. Darlisca directed me to put this in your hands. He gifted me with a fast horse, he said it was very important."

All eyes were on the package as Cullan unwrapped a small wicker cage. Inside was a small yellow bird, its tiny feet curled up in death.

"Perhaps the bird was dead when Darlisca gave it over to my hands."

Cullan felt a chill. Darlisca had Aoife.

Would he dare use her as a bargaining piece? He had declared his plans for their enemy, it was too late to change now. The thought of Darlisca putting Aoife to the sword sadden Cullan. Her blood would be on his hands? As much as he hated this new turn of events, no matter how much his heart said bargain with his enemy, for the sake of his people he had to go on with his plan.

"This will not change what will take place this day. Rogan, see to this man and the bird."

Donal released Cynthia, they were back on the island in real time. Cynthia leaned against him and sighed.

"That was so real. I can't get over how young you were,"

"Yes, very young."

"How old are you now?"

"Will it matter if I am younger than you, Cyn?"

"Not at all." Cynthia sat up and kissed him. "You look to be in your mid to late twenties."

"I do not know my true age." He smiled at her, "We better get back to town. It's getting late."

CHAPTER
TWENTY-FIVE

Donal turned over in the king-sized bed. Happy he was back in real time, in their suite at the Prescott hotel. He wanted to go back to sleep. The strong aroma of coffee and bacon made it impossible for him to drift off again. His stomach growled, his last meal had been noon yesterday, out on the island.

"Get up sleepyhead," Cynthia said.

He stretched, sighed, and sat up. In the living room a waiter was busy setting up a table. When that was done, he placed covered dishes on the sideboard.

Cynthia stepped back into the living room. When the waiter was done, she gave him a tip and closed and locked the door behind him.

Donal glanced at the clock by the bed. "You should not have let me sleep so long."

"You needed the rest, you were dead on your feet last night when we returned."

"I'll take a quick shower and join you."

When he checked out the dishes on the sideboard he was astounded at how much food Cynthia had ordered.

"We could feed a small army on this."

"Yes, I suppose we could."

Something in her voice made him turn around to face her.

"What's wrong?"

"I was thinking about Peter Og."

"Peter Og?"

You've told me everything else. Scottie told me about Zelda and Ted. Remember Roseita's message. I'd like to know about Peter Og?"

Donal served himself a large portion of scrambled eggs and several slices of bacon and added two pieces of toast. He sat down across from Cynthia. She poured him tea, moved the sugar and cream over to his side.

"Peter Og is the youngest son of Carlos Hernandez. He was a typical eight-year-old, never quiet, never still; he was always into trouble. No matter what his father said to him, he would climb up into the loft and jump off into the hay."

Donal hesitated, before he went on.

"He misjudged the jump one day, striking his head on the railing below. Carlos was sure he was dead. If I could hold him until an ambulance came he would live."

"You saved the boy's life?"

"I gave him my strength, kept him here."

"Here?"

"Kept him awake, so he didn't pass into a coma." He didn't want to get into the Road of Life and Death. Not now, perhaps never. "Only Carlos was afraid of me after that; when he thought I wasn't looking, he would make the sign of the cross. As if to ward off evil."

"I had a feeling that there was something he didn't want to talk about. The key is the island, right?"

"Yes. The entryway is on the island. It is a portal between your world and mine. How Déaglán found it, I don't know."

"You can go back and forth?"

"Yes, but it is only open certain times of the year. From this point of view, it makes more sense. The belief of our Celtic ancestors that at Samhain, the shields between the worlds were thin, that the dead could pass through into our world."

"Only it wasn't the dead that passed through," Cynthia added for him.

"Who knows, at one time they might have known the truth. Maybe that knowledge was lost over the years."

"Don't you want your son here with you?"

He told Cynthia about the promise he had sworn on his father's sword. He would send his son to rule Cwillan and each of his friends would send one of their sons to him for fostering.

He had given this a lot of thought. Cwillan needed his son more than he needed him here. He wished it otherwise, but for now his son belonged there. When he grew to manhood, he could make the decision for himself.

"My son belongs in Cwillan, not here. Niall will look after him."

"And his mother?"

In his mind he saw again the small wicker cage with a small yellow bird inside. He didn't want to talk about Aoife. His son would grow up without a mother or father, like he had.

"She died."

"I'm sorry...I know you loved her." Cynthia smiled at him, she looked unsure how to go on. "Aren't you afraid of causing a paradox?"

"A what?"

"Some people believe that if you could travel from one time to another that you would change history. Create a paradox. Since you weren't born here, our world now has one more person than it should."

Donal thought about it.

"I'm not sure. I am not going from one time to another, rather from one place to another. I'm not sure the same rules apply here. How many people die every minute, how many are born? How many things are changed by just taking a different path, by passing their destiny?"

Cynthia Tolan stood and came around to his side of the table. He pushed his chair back. She sat down sideways on his lap and threw her arms around him. She hugged him with all her might, buried her head against his neck.

The smell of her floral perfume pleased him.

CHAPTER
TWENTY-SIX

Before moving to Prescott, Donal decided to keep his clients. It would be easy for him to continue being their consultant, meeting with them over a cyber video-link. He would work out everything with his father-in-law.

Part of his personal portfolio he cashed in to start work on the building that would include Cyn's studio on the first floor. Which would include a small apartment for them to live in until the main house was built. On the ground level would be his office, storage, and several small rooms.

"We are going to need a cook," Cynthia announced one afternoon.

Surprised, Donal turned from his computer to face his wife.

"You're busy all day with the crew working on the studio building and your clients in the evening.

I am busy with my paintings. I'm not much of a cook anyway."

"Do we place an ad in the Prescott or Peoria Times or go through an agency?"

Cynthia Tolan smiled at him, pleased that he agreed with her. "All three."

"You know what kind of person you want, and what we can afford, so perhaps you should call the newspapers to place the ad. Let a local agency know what qualifications you are looking for in a cook."

Donal wondered where the new cook would sleep.

As if reading his mind Cynthia said, "You're wondering where we'll put her?"

"I am."

He waited, knowing she already had it figured out.

"My studio and our apartment will be on the second floor. Why do you call the second floor the first floor?" she asked.

"Because it is the first floor, or level. What you call the first floor is the ground floor to me."

"Okay. Downstairs will be your office until the main house is built." Cynthia turned over a piece of paper. She drew out a diagram of the floor plan. "Here is your office, the storage area, there are four other rooms. We could put in plumbing and make them into bedrooms. Until the house is done she could use one of those rooms."

They really didn't need a cook. The main house would be started a year or two after they moved into the studio building. It might even be longer than that. There had to be more to this than she was telling him.

"You've completed your end of the bargain," Cynthia said. "Soon your friends will complete their end. Where do you plan to put the boys? Those extra rooms will be ready for them when they come. Besides, when we move out of this apartment, I'll need someone to help me."

Puzzled, Donal stood, "What is it? Are you sick..."

"No." Cynthia gave him a radiant smile. "I'm pregnant."

Donal enfolded her in his arms, kissed the top of her head. For the moment she seemed content to let him hold her. He didn't have the words to express to her how happy he was.

"I hope it's a boy," Cynthia said.

"Boy or girl, Cyn. As long as the baby is healthy." He was both surprised and pleased. Later, they would learn that she was going to have twins.

The ad ran in the Springfield Journal-Register, the Chicago Sun-Times and Tribune, and the local cyber newspapers. There were a number of inquires about the job.

Cynthia encouraged him to sit in on the interviews. Most of the women were older, set in their ways. From their expressions, the idea of living out in the middle of nowhere didn't please them. Several came right out and said that they would never find someone. The isolation, in addition to low wages, was a deterrent to taking the job.

They gave up after a month, they had interviewed a dozen or more women who didn't like the location, the wages, didn't want to live in, or wanted more time off. It was always something. The employment agency she called wasn't much help either.

For the time being, they gave up looking for a cook.

Three months later the agency called. They had a young woman looking for a position. She was young, but had experience as a cook as well as with children. Not expecting this interview to go any different from the others, they made an appointment to meet Sally Brown the next afternoon.

Cynthia brought Sally Brown back to Donal's office.

Sally stood in the doorway looking nervous. She was far younger than most of the women they interviewed.

Cynthia made the introductions.

Donal held out his hand. Sally hesitated, with a self-conscious movement she shook hands with him. In an instant flash of emotion, he felt her fear, her need. She was drowning in the responsibilities forced on her.

Cynthia's phone chimes sounded, she excused herself and stepped out of the room.

He gave Sally a reassuring smile. "Please sit down."

Donal took the chair opposite. Sally looked around his small office with a look of wonder on her face. "You have a cyber video-link?"

"Yes, I need to keep in touch with my clients."

"Oh."

He wasn't sure what "oh" meant.

"Our twins will be born in less then six months. We need someone to cook and help Cynthia."

"Here? In this apartment?"

"No. We are building a place out in the country. I've never been keen on living in the city."

"Oh."

"The life will be pretty isolated, well away from everything."

"The country will be good for the babies."

Donal liked Sally Brown. He didn't feel that she was too young to join them as a cook and later to help with the twins.

Cynthia joined them at that moment. Donal moved back to his desk, to let Cynthia finish the interview. As she talked to Sally, the tension began to leave her and she relaxed.

"Perhaps some tea would be good," Donal suggested.

Sally jumped to her feet. "I'll make it."

"That won't be necessary," Cynthia said. "Come into the kitchen. I'll make it and we can talk."

Before leaving his office, Cynthia looked back at Donal. In her brief glance she conveyed her pity for the girl, then shook her head just a tiny bit.

After Sally left, they sat together in their small kitchen discussing whether they should hire her.

"She's nice, but so young."

If they didn't hire Sally, what would become of her? She was in a bad situation. Her mother had re-married, a man with five small children. Her stepfather expected her to care for them, while he and her mother drank.

"She has experience with cooking, she would be a lot of help with the twins."

"Honey, we can't take in every stray we find."

"Of course, you're right."

"You want to hire her?"

"Yes." Donal wondered if Cynthia would go along with his idea. "There is that small back bedroom. It's empty, we could furnish it, Sally could move in, take over the cooking and washing now."

"That's a great idea. That way before we move we'll know if she is going with us."

Donal never told Sally Brown she was on probation. Something told him that she would work out. He paid Sally's fees to the employment agency, so that she was free and clear of them. When they made the move into the studio building Sally moved with them.

Their twins Robert Niall and Donald Ciarán were born there. Their names were shortened to Rob and Don.

Contact with Liam and Mánus was limited to a Christmas card that year.

CHAPTER
TWENTY-SEVEN

At one o'clock Donal entered the Tuscan Grille. The maitre d' looked him over. It was clear he didn't like what he saw before him.

He thinks I don't belong here. He's probably right, Donal thought, amused.

"May I help you?" the maitre d' asked stiffly.

"I'm here to meet Mr. Long."

At the mention of Robert Long's name, Donal's worth went up in the man's eyes.

"This way, sir," the man said politely. He led Donal down the main hallway, passing crowded rooms with tables covered with expensive linen, silverware, china plates, and crystal. Where men and women ate the best meats, drank vintage wines and whiskeys. These people lived better than his father, might not have as much power, but they lived better.

At the end of the hall a flight of stairs gave access to the exclusive upper level. Before Donal started up the stairs, a familiar voice called out to him.

"It has been a long time, Donal."

He turned to find Liam O'Brien, Mánus Scanlon, and another man, perhaps ten years older than Donal, with a young boy. From their looks, he guessed them to be Liam's son and grandson.

Liam made the introductions.

Donal liked Cathal, Liam's oldest son, a quiet, serious young man. His grandson Alvin, like most young boys his age, was antsy, impatient to go. When it looked like there would be a delay, his attention turned to a small table by the stairs where silverware and several napkin rings lay.

"I was going to call you, this is better," Liam said.

What would Cynthia say when he told her that he had run into Liam and Mánus. Would she think it was a setup? Impossible, when Robert Long called him last night, they made plans for lunch today.

"We were just leaving, but perhaps we could have a drink and talk?"

"I'm meeting Robert Long for lunch."

The maitre d' told Donal to go up when he was ready. Mr. Long had a table at the back and excused himself.

"Before you go and sign yourself to the devil, perhaps we should talk."

Donal liked Liam and Mánus, but they lived in a world that was very different than the one he lived in.

"My father-in-law is waiting, perhaps another time."

"Let me give you this," Mánus said. From his inside suit pocket he produced a folded color brochure with a business card attached. "You might consider something like this, living so far out of town."

"Thank you."

Before heading up the stairs, he glanced at the brochure. It was for a home security company. The business card: MSS Security Agency, Liam O'Brien, with a telephone number and email address. Interesting. Were Liam and Mánus going into a legitimate business?

Two waiters at the table near the stairs quietly argued. Donal glanced in their direction, and saw the problem immediately. The silver napkin rings were gone.

Liam and Mánus weren't common thieves. They wouldn't like it when they found out what Alvin had done. Not my problem, he told himself, and started up the stairs.

∾

Donal found Cynthia painting in her studio. She had four tall panels against the outside wall. He examined each of the dozen sketches she had made of his three friends and himself. She caught each subject in a different pose; she hadn't decided which to use on the panels for the Four Horsemen. Each panel would hold one of the horsemen; when done they would form one large painting.

"I should make you grow your mustache out, so I can use you for a model. You were so handsome when you wore it long and full." When he didn't answer her, she asked, "Do you like it?"

"It is nothing like anything you've done before," he smiled at her. "I love it."

Donal followed her into the small kitchen. He sat down while she cleaned her brushes. Only when she had laid them out to dry, and put away her paints and supplies, would she relaxed and talk to him.

"How did the lunch go?"

"Fine."

Cynthia studied him. "So what did father want?"

"He wants to open an office in Chicago."

"And you to manage it, right?"

"Yes. It would mean a lot of commuting. I told him to have John Stills do it, or one of the senior agents."

"Is he still coming for dinner on Friday night?"

"Yes. He will try to get you to persuade me to take his offer."

"Well, you are going to have to do something."

Donal was surprised; Cynthia usually took his side. He didn't want a life of sitting in an office from nine to five.

"It will be a few years before you can get the horse farm up and running. You won't touch my money. You'll need something. Four children can be very expensive."

It took him a minute before he realized what Cynthia had just said. He stepped over to the sink and took her in his arms.

"When?"

"I just found out this morning," she said, excitement in her voice. "I didn't want to say anything until I was sure, so last time I was in town I bought an EPA test. It showed positive."

They sat down at the antique Formica and aluminum kitchen table. The table with matching chairs still with the original covering in good condition was a find. Donal wanted his whole house to be done up in antiques.

The first of their foster children would join them in the spring. Two children of his own, one on the way, and his foster son made four children to feed, clothe, and educate. Should he take the offer and work for his father-in-law full time?

"I ran into Liam and Mánus today."

"Really, where?"

"At the Tuscan Grille."

"I'm surprised that they even know it exists."

"Be fair. They aren't as bad as that." Before she asked him what Liam and Mánus were doing in Prescott he said, "Liam thinks we might be interested in a security system for the house, that's all."

"Are you sure?"

Cynthia was right. Liam and Mánus wanted him for a partner. Robert Long wanted him to manage his new office. Of the two, who would be the best to work with?

Before they could discuss it further, the downstairs door opened with a loud bang. High-pitched voices echoed up the stairwell to them. Minutes later the door closed again with a thud. Sounding like a heard of cattle the twins ran up the stairs. Who would be first? Rob would win, he always did.

Sally Brown followed the twins into the kitchen, her face pink from being outside in the cool weather.

"Now, now, boys. Your parents are busy."

Rob and Don noticed the empty table and turned to Sally with pleading cries for an afternoon snack.

"Is it okay to give them a snack?" Sally asked.

"Grilled cheese, please" Don pleaded.

"PB and J," Rob said.

"PB and J," Cynthia said, turning back to Donal.

He wondered if she realized how often she sided with Rob. How he was used to always getting his way.

"See what they have to say."

Surprised, Donal said, "Okay."

"Then later we can invite them out here for dinner."

❧

On Friday, Rob and Don were busy showing their grandfather the different sketches of the Four Horsemen.

Robert Long studied each one.

"This one looks familiar, though I don't know why."

Rob glanced over at Donal setting the table and smiled.

Donal winked at his son.

Cynthia came into the room.

"Time for bed boys." She smiled at her father. "Would you like to do the honors, Dad."

Robert Long followed his grandsons into their bedroom.

When they were alone Cynthia said, "Have you had a chance to speak to my father?"

"No. Can you delay dinner for about fifteen minutes. I'll talk to him as soon as he puts the twins to bed."

"I'll let Sally know." She started to go back into the kitchen, stopped and turned back to Donal. "Are you sure about this?"

"I think it is the only fair thing to do. It helps us both."

"Good luck."

Donal finished setting the table. It was a task he enjoyed, it took him back to his time in Arizona when he worked for Scottie. His friend had met a woman he would marry in the spring. Together they planned to open a restaurant in Phoenix.

From the cabinet near the bedrooms, Donal took out a bottle of champagne. He was easing it down into a bucket of ice when Robert Long came into the room.

"Are we celebrating something?" Robert Long asked, puzzled.

"Perhaps. Take a seat. I have something to run by you. Can I get you something to drink, coffee, a beer?"

"I'm fine," Robert sat down across from Donal. "I don't know what you would want to talk to me about. You told me the other day you don't want to help me."

Donal heard the disappointment in Robert's voice. Perhaps it was anger at not getting his way.

"I want to go over the info on the office in Chicago again."

"Why?"

"Because, I want to help you get it set up."

Robert Long gave him a look that said he was both surprised and pleased. "Okay, let's hear your ideas."

It took longer than fifteen minutes to go over all his ideas with his father-in-law. Sally would keep the food warm until they were ready to eat. When he was done, Robert Long frowned at him. "Why the change of heart?"

"Because it is good for you and good for me. Pick a location and we can go from there."

"You've given this a lot of thought."

"I have."

"Let me think it over first. I'll call you later in the week."

"There is no hurry. Take your time."

Sally, with Cynthia's help, brought in the dinner.

CHAPTER TWENTY-EIGHT

Donal entered the Fourth Street Pub. He liked the feel of the place. It was very different from the Tuscan Grille, darker, older, with wooden floors. It was relaxed and comfortable, like a familiar pair of jeans. The large room was divided into smaller sections of tables and booths. A huge C-shaped bar dominated the back of the room. On each side, stairs led to the second floor.

There was a rumor going around that the pub owner was looking for a buyer. Donal wondered what it would be like to be a restaurateur.

The hostess, dressed in tight jeans and a skimpy top, came over to him.

"Can I help you?"

"I'm meeting Mr. O'Brien and Mr. Scanlon."

"They haven't arrived yet, they reserved a booth in the back."

She picked up four menus and escorted him to the back, to a large private booth that would seat eight people comfortably.

"Can I bring you something to drink while you wait?"

"Yes. I'll have a Guinness."

"Pint or glass?"

Liam, his son, Cathal, and Mánus joined him at that moment.

"Make it a pint," Liam said. "In fact we'll all have a pint."

Mánus took off his tinted glasses, folded them and placed them in his breast pocket.

The hostess smiled at Mánus, "I'll have them right over."

Mánus slipped into the booth, Liam sat next to him. Cathal sat down beside Donal.

"How is your lovely wife?" Liam asked.

"She is doing very well. We are expecting our third child."

"Good to hear," Liam said. "Your call certainly came as a surprise. Decided to take us up about the security system, then?"

There meeting had nothing to do with a security system. Donal would wait until Liam was ready to get down to business.

After lunch, they ordered another round. It was time to get down to why they were here. Cathal explained the video surveillance system. On a napkin, he drew a square representing the house. With dotted lines, he showed how much area each camera covered.

"We place a camera at each corner. If you have a porch in the front, we place another one angled out from the front door. Also around any outbuildings, garages, things like that. There are no blind spots."

"So many cameras?" Donal said.

"That is just the start. We can place them in the halls. Our clients with au pairs like to have one in the nursery. With our software you can access information from a central camera room or your office computer, or even from an outbuilding."

Like the studio, Donal thought. "Who heads up the MSS Agency?"

"Mr. Monaghan, for now. You've met Dominic haven't you?" Liam asked.

Donal remembered Dominic Xavier Monaghan. So he had been right, Dominic was a friend of Liam and Mánus.

"Dominic, Cathal and sometime in the future Seán Scanlon will join them. Son, did you bring the contract?"

Cathal checked through his paperwork, "Damn, I left everything in the car. I'll be right back."

"I'll walk out with you, son."

Donal faced Mánus across the table.

"Surprised? Because you will deal with me?"

"Yes. I thought that Liam was the boss and you his backup."

"That is the beauty of the whole thing. People never take me seriously, just another pretty face. It gives me an advantage."

"Why make Cathal head of a security company?"

"You don't approve? Because he forgot some paperwork?"

"We both know the paperwork was left in the car on purpose. What do you want?"

Mánus laughed and shook his head.

"Is this about forming a partnership?"

"We, Liam and I, thought you could use a security system living away from the city."

Did he jump to the wrong conclusion?

"What kind of deal did your father-in-law offer you?"

"What makes you think he offered me something?"

"It isn't every day that Robert Long comes out here, so I figure he wanted something."

Donal went over the offer and the money Robert Long offered as a signing bonus. He also told Mánus about his counter offer.

Mánus looked impressed. "What you left behind will come to you again. The choice is not yours to make. You cannot run from it. What is to be, will be."

"You talked to Brid."

"Yes. We found her by accident. She helps me from time to time. She was pleased to find out you were well. All she told us is you came from a long distance, which told us nothing."

"I haven't the slightest idea what she meant."

Mánus watched him, his eyes unreadable. "I guess we have nothing to talk about then." He sat back. "Your father-in-law's offer is a good one, your counter-offer is even better. I imagine he accepted your offer. Enjoy working for Robert Long."

Angry at his dismissal, Donal slipped out of the booth and left without a word. Liam and Cathal sat at the bar. As Donal approached, Cathal stood up as if he planned to try to stop him. Liam put a hand on his son's arm. Both men watched him as he passed.

As Donal walked along the busy street he passed a disheveled man begging. The old man reminded him of Fred Tolan. Without Fred's help, he wouldn't have made it in this world. In return, he tried to do everything he could to help Fred in his time of need.

Donal stopped and waited for the light to change. By the time he reached the second corner he found himself more confused than angry. He moved along with the crowd on the street. Coming toward him a beautiful young girl smiled and winked at him as she passed. Donal's face grew warm. Now if he were good-looking like Mánus he could understand someone winking at him.

At the third corner he stopped for a red light.

You are the special one, the one who will unite all our people.

Simple words, but what did they mean?

Sometimes, late at night, after Cynthia was asleep, he lay awake. In his mind he heard Niall's words, 'You are the special one, the one who will unite all our people.' Simple words, but what did they mean? His son, Feargus had taken his place in Cwillan. Did he still owe his friends and son something?

Where is my place?

Was his place here?

What you left behind will come to you again. The choice is not yours to make. You cannot run from it. What is to be, will be.

Was it true, that he had no say in the matter.

No one can show you the way. You have to find your own path. In all matters let your conscience be your guide.

Donal didn't want to work from nine to five in an office for Robert Long. Yet, he had signed on to set up an office in Chicago. He figured it would take a year or longer to get it running. His thoughts turned to Cathal. He would do what Mánus and his father told him to do and do it well. But his heart would never be in it.

The answer came to him in a flash, an epiphany of understanding. Mánus wouldn't force him into anything. He had to make the choice himself. Find his own path, as Abbot Tadc had told him so long ago.

Angry people pushed past him. Startled out of his reverie, he realized the light had turned green. Instead of crossing the street he turned to walk back to the pub, parting the pedestrians like a ship parting water. The men and women muttered and swore as they moved out of his way.

Back at the beggar, he took out his money clip, pulled off several bills and handed them to him.

Always let your conscience be your guide.

As their fingers touched, mentally he told the old man to go to St. Anthony's shelter on Catherine Street. They would help him there.

The old man gave him a gap-tooth smile. "Bless you, son."

When he reached the Fourth Street Pub, he found a Cadillac parked at the curb. The driver's door was just closing. Donal walked over to the car. Through the dark glass nothing was visible.

He was sure it was Mánus's car.

The car started to ease out into traffic. Donal stepped back. He was too late. Would he look back on this day with regret? Halfway out of the parking space the car stopped and eased back against the curb. The driver waiting for the space laid on his horn in anger. The passenger window slid down; the driver leaned over and shouted abusive words.

The Cadillac driver's door opened and Cathal stepped out. "Do you have a problem?"

The driver took one look at Cathal's size, didn't bother to close the window or check traffic. He barely missed a car as he pulled into traffic. Horns blared and brakes screeched as drivers tried to avoid a collision.

Cathal came around and opened the passenger door. Mánus stepped out. Liam moved over to watch through the open door.

"Changed your mind, have you, lad?"

"A three-way partnership. I'm the boss. I want to buy this restaurant for a start or one like it."

"Sounds reasonable, lad. And the Robert Long Agency?"

"When they find a location in Chicago, I'll work it in. One more thing, I want Cathal to work with me."

Without giving it any thought, Mánus held out his hand. "Done!"

They shook on the new partnership.

CHAPTER
TWENTY-NINE

At the right-hand end of the C-shaped bar, on the kitchen side, Donal sat in the afternoon. He liked to sit there and work on his laptop, loved the hustle and bustle of the busy pub. He never used his dark and overcrowded office upstairs that doubled as storage space.

It was Wednesday. The day the Prescott Herald ran its restaurant review. He keyed in the address that would take him to their review. With a keen sense of pride, he read the report about the Fourth Street Pub, now renamed Tommy O'Flaherty's. They received two and a half stars out of a possible four.

Not bad for a new place.

Mánus and he had met with Ted Dowling, the owner. Ted confessed that he had bought the pub on a whim. Over the years he had lost interest in it, letting John Reiley manage the place for him.

Donal sent a copy of the books with the contract to Pete Learner, an attorney recommended by Robert Long. Two weeks later, over dinner, Pete told them that he wasn't comfortable with what he had seen in the books. He seemed displeased with the whole deal. When he was done, he advised Donal to pass on the pub.

Bottom line, the price was high and the profit line low.

Donal turned to Mánus. His partner had been quiet during dinner. He had an unusual look, almost a self-satisfied expression on his handsome face.

"What do you think, Mánus?"

"Buy the place and fire the barman."

"I gave you my best advice. Take it or leave it," Pete Learner said. He thanked them for dinner and stood to leave. "Give my regards to Robert Long when you talk to him."

Mánus smiled at Donal when they were alone. "He'll call your father-in-law as soon as he can and say that your partner is a most unreasonable man. Robert Long in turn will wonder if you have made a big mistake."

"I think he already feels that way."

"Next time we'll use Dominic Monaghan. How is the Chicago office coming?"

"Robert gave up on a location downtown. He's looking in the suburbs. So what do you think about this deal?"

"Buy the pub."

"You know something?"

Mánus shrugged. "Remember, I used to be on the other side. I thought of several ways to skim money off the top. Hire your own auditor to go over the books."

His first act as the new owner, after changing the name, was to hire an auditor. He found that he didn't have to fire the barman. John Reiley quit. The auditor couldn't prove anything; the cost for liquor and food was high, too high even for a pub as big as O'Flaherty's.

Donal had the staff change from their casual sexy dress to a style similar to what they wore in Ireland in the last century, a floor-length black apron over black slacks or a long skirt with long sleeved white shirts and blouses. Sometime in the future he hoped to change the menu. He wanted his pub to be more than McDonald's with beer. He also made a rule that after the busboys cleaned a table; they had to wash their hands before setting it up for the next customers.

The week after John Reiley left, two waitresses quit; the next week a waitress and both young men who helped in the kitchen left.

Cathal O'Brien took over ordering and helped tend bar with two college students who agreed to work part-time until Donal found full-time replacements. He helped by waiting on tables. When would the next person leave? His grand plan for the pub seemed destined to failure. He didn't get one response from the ad he placed in the local paper. It was almost as if the word was out not to apply for a job with the new owner.

Four weeks after Donal officially took over the pub, Cynthia brought the twins in for a visit. By the time Donal drove home at night the twins were in bed. Peggy Joyce, Cathal's wife, and Sally Brown came in with her. When a customer grumbled about the slow service, Peggy Joyce told Donal not to worry. "I worked as a waitress my first year of college."

She asked the hostess to get her an apron, and took over the section, and offered the patrons a complimentary drink for having to wait so long.

Cynthia and Sally helped by busing tables and delivering orders.

Donal hadn't seen the twins for a while. As he passed Cynthia on his way to a table with food, he asked her where they were. She smiled and told him Cathal had them behind the bar.

The usually active twins were sitting on overturned milk crates, out of Cathal's way. They each had a tall plastic glass with scoops of ice cream and soda pop. Instead of using the straw, both preferred the long spoon and had ice cream all over their face and clothing. The twins waved at him. It was the first time he had seen them quiet for more then five minutes.

As soon as things quieted down Donal encouraged Cynthia to take the twins home. She was just beginning to show her pregnancy; he worried about her being on her feet for too long. Sally Brown accompanied her home.

Peggy Joyce stayed to help.

Late that night as they were getting ready to lock up Donal asked Peggy Joyce how Cathal got the twins to behave.

"He is very good with children. Of course, the floats helped."

Did most children include Cathal's son Alvin?

"You must miss your children?"

"I do. Teddy, Cathal's brother, is taking care of them. Is it true that as soon as things settle down we will be going home and Cathal will finish his degree?"

"Hopefully Cathal will be able to start the summer term."

He wondered why they added her single surname to her married name? Surely not to show that she was neither an O'Brien or Scanlon. Perhaps to show she also came from a proud Irish family.

"Thanks for the help, Peggy, you saved the day."

"Saved the day?" She stacked the tray on the counter. "Isn't it me that should be after thanking you?"

Donal smiled at the way she talked, she must have picked it up from Liam. "I don't understand."

"Your man out there is happier than he has been in years."

Your man referred to someone not present, but known to both of them. That she was talking about her husband.

"And you, how do you feel?"

"Mánus was a late-in-life child," Peggy Joyce said. "Old Séamus was desperate to have an heir. Even before his wife died, he took up with a woman forty years younger then himself. Séamus died before Mánus was two years old. He never talks about his mother. Liam raised him with his children."

Donal waited.

"Did they tell you their great-grandparents immigrated to Canada during the famine years?"

"No, they didn't."

"Their family friendship goes back generations. Ask Cathal about it sometime."

"I'll do that." Donal had to repress a smile at what she said next.

"Some of our ways will be hard to understand for an educated man like yourself. When the old one died, Mánus became The Scanlon and him being only a baby. Do you know what that means?"

Donal did. It was a concept from the past, still honored in Cwillan, but not in Ireland since the breakup of the old Gaelic system.

"Mánus became your chieftain."

"Liam took care of things until Mánus graduated from M.I.T. You're thinking it is a very archaic way to do things. You might think that you entered into just a partnership. But Mánus says that you are our new chieftain and much more than that." She finished what she was doing. "I'd better make sure the tables are all done." At the kitchen door she stopped. "I think we have nothing to worry about. You will make a fine chieftain."

Before Donal could respond, she pushed the door open and stepped into the pub.

After weeks of just getting by, Donal hired two more waitresses. Peggy Joyce would stay on until it was time to go home.

❧

Donal didn't get a chance to talk to Cathal about his family and their history until his last night at Forest Lake. Cathal and Peggy would be flying home in the morning. He wasn't sure how to start up the conversation. Cathal was a man of few words.

In his office, he poured Midleton into two tumblers and handed one to Cathal.

"How is everyone taking the change?" Donal asked.

"You mean the partnership and everything?"

"Yes."

Cathal sat down on the couch, Donal sat down across from him.

"There have been no regrets, at all."

"How did Mánus come to lead both families? He seems a bit young."

"It is a long sad story."

"We have time."

Donal had read about the different risings in Ireland. The famine years and the events that led to the Proclamation of Independence, the Irish Free State, and finally the Republic of Ireland.

Listening to Cathal tell the story of the two families with the history of Ireland as a backdrop gave it a whole new meaning for Donal. He envisioned the bodies along the roads, dead from green mouth. The horrors of the coffin ships, no family untouched by famine fever on the long voyage to the New World, with a loss of one-third of the passengers in many cases on the small, overcrowded ships.

As if he were a bard of old, a seanchaí, Cathal told the history of the two families. Stories handed down from one generation to the next, he told as if he had been there

Liam O'Brien's great great grandfather died on a ship bound for Canada, leaving behind a wife who would follow him in less then a week, two small boys, and a thirteen-year-old girl. The youngest boy died on Grosse Isle in Quebec, where the fever victims were shipped.

Tomás Scanlon, now the oldest, had lost his wife in 1846, became head of the two families. Liam had his dogs shipped on a British ship leaving Queenstown. Out of the four dogs shipped, Tomás only received two of the puppies, the ones the ship's captain considered ugly. He didn't realize they were Irish Wolfhounds of the Kilbane line.

Tomás worked two jobs to feed Liam's two children and his son Seámus. The families moved to the United States in 1904.

"No one understands just how bad it was."

"England sent corn and built roads?" Donal said, quietly.

"Oh yes, but the government didn't stop exporting food to England. Most of the corn never made it to the people. Speculators exported it back and forth across the Irish Sea.

"Our families worked hard all their lives. When it seemed as if there would be another rising, they sent every dollar they could spare through Clan na Gael to support it, bought bonds to help the Irish Free State."

"Your family went back."

"Yes, Donal. When it became a Republic our families went home. Then old Seámus Michael, Mánus' father, decided to move back to the United States."

"Still, Mánus is your leader. You never wanted to change that?

"Was Donal. We all accept you as our new leader. Mánus has never been wrong about things before. Do you think it is time to get beyond the past?"

"Perhaps," Donal said.

He wasn't sure what to tell Cathal. It was hard to hold on to the old ways without the past. You learned from the past. Are we more civilized now? Would world governments make better decisions the next famine? He doubted it. Their track record in modern times wasn't any better than before.

"It is part of your history and the history of Ireland, horrible as it was. We need to remember the past and learn from it."

Chapter Thirty

The real turning point for Donal in running O'Flaherty's came when he hired Matthew Brody. He was older than most of the college students who applied for the position of bartender, or barman as Mánus always referred to him. Most of the students were looking for short-term employment. Donal wanted someone in for the long haul, someone willing to stake his or her future on working at Tommy O'Flaherty's.

Donal liked Matt from the first interview and hired him without waiting for the report from the MSS Agency.

"I need a small sherry," Jenny said.

"Is it Wednesday already?" Matt asked, as he poured the drink.

After Jenny left, Donal asked him, "What was that about?"

"Poor woman sits out in the waiting area as if she expects someone to join her. Only no one ever does."

"So you invited her in?"

"Well...yes. She sits at the table in the left-front window waiting. God only knows for who or what. I hope you don't mind, Mr. Tolan?"

"It isn't a problem."

Matt looked relieved.

"Do you have children?"

Mánus told Donal that Matt lived with his wife and his nephew, James Madison, on King Street just off West Main, on the Middleton side of the river, in a house built early in the last century.

He also knew about Matt's previous jobs.

"No, Mr. Tolan. Not of my own. We took my nephew in when his mother died. His father left them years ago. Tina and I were never lucky enough to have any of our own."

"How old is your nephew?"

"James, he likes to be called Jimmy, is six. Wants to become a musician."

"When he is ready, tell him he can start here."

"Thank you, sir."

"My third is due next month."

"Congratulations, sir."

"What I was getting at. I'm going to take some time off to be with my wife when she brings the baby home."

"Will the big fellow be coming back then, or your pretty-boy partner? The waitresses would like that."

"Cathal will do some training here. As well as manage the place for awhile."

Donal ignored the reference to Mánus. He didn't think Matt was even aware of how he phrased it.

"You know Cathal would make a good bouncer."

Donal smiled.

"Not to say anything against you, sir. Cathal has a no-nonsense look about him."

"Do you think we need a bouncer?"

"John Reiley wasn't a big man. He kept a Louisville Slugger under the bar. Something to think about."

"I'll do that. I need to hire an assistant manager. I was wondering if you would consider the position?"

Matt looked pleased, then frowned. "I think I should tell you something first. Then you can decide if you still want me, sir."

"Fair enough. But if it is about not charging for the sherry, you have nothing to worry about."

"No, though there is that too. I..." Matt hesitated. "I spent some time in a readjustment center. That is why I happen to be out of work."

Mánus had given Donal all the information about the incident that landed Matt into court and a readjustment center for a short time. Matt's lawyer managed to get the decision overturned. His former employer didn't take him back.

Matt explained to Donal what had happened.

"The decision was overturned, Matt, don't worry about it, there really isn't a problem."

Donal held out his hand. Matt dried his hands on his apron first before they shook on his new position. Hiring Matthew Brody was a lucky break for both of them.

"I'll make the change in your salary as of today. You know, Matt?"

"Sir?"

"The odd sandwich wouldn't hurt."

"Yes, sir. There she is now."

Donal watched as the lady walked along the bar on the way to the mna, the ladies room. She was far younger than he expected. She couldn't be more than in her mid-to-late twenties. Pretty if she would do something with her hair and clothes. Her dress and jacket hadn't been new for a long time.

In that brief look, a shiver went up Donal's spine; he would never forget the lost look in her eyes. No, not lost, haunted.

"Have you lived in Middleton long?"

"About five years, sir."

Matt calling him "sir" was beginning to annoy Donal. He would have to speak to Matt about calling him by his first name.

"See what you can find out about her."

"Yes, sir."

"How is Ben doing?"

"Not bad. He is still staying out at St. Anthony's. They are looking for a place for him to live."

"See what he can do with the upstairs room. I'd like to make a couple of small private rooms up there, snugs as my partners calls them."

Donal turned off his computer. Time to go home.

০৲

Donal watched the woman who sat at the front window table. She came in every Wednesday. She ordered tea, a scone and a small sherry. He noted how thin she looked. Could this be the only food she ate all week? She usually wore the same dress and jacket. Clean but well worn. Perhaps something she found at a thrift store.

Now why did he think that?

"Her name is Sandra Murphy," Matt said. "She rents a room over on Sycamore Street. I haven't been able to find out anything else."

"Thanks, Matt."

Donal opened his laptop, placed his right thumb on the track-pad, typed in his partner's name. Mánus appeared on the screen a minute later.

"Good afternoon."

Mánus was seated in the makeshift office at the building site of his new house. He was dressed in a suit and tie. Donal felt underdressed in his black slacks and white shirt. He gave Mánus the information on Sandra Murphy.

"I'll get Cathal right on it. As soon as I know something, I'll get back with you."

"How is the house coming?"

"Fine. As soon as we move in we'll throw a big party. How is Cynthia?"

"A little tired, nothing serious."

"Grand. Oh, Donal, Cathal is excited about the new position you outlined for him."

"I'm glad he feels that way. I know he is going to be a little older than his classmates. I was worried he would turn me down. Did he give you the details?"

"A bit. After the baby comes and things settle down here as well, Mary Catherine and I will drive over and spend some time with you. You can explain the whole thing to me."

Donal turned off his laptop.

The position he offered to Cathal hinged on finishing his education and putting a year in at the pub. It looked like he had been right about the oldest of Liam's sons.

I'm a very lucky man, he told himself. He felt uneasy; he had never considered himself particularly lucky.

Thoughts of Briana and his daughter came to mind; the pain now softened by time didn't send his thoughts into a tailspin. At other times he thought about poor little Banba, her innocent life cut short by a man's greed.

Sometimes late at night he lay awake and worried. Things were going along well, why worry, he asked himself.

Because things were going too good, that's why.

CHAPTER THIRTY-ONE

Several weeks after the anniversary of forming
Tolan, O'Brien and Scanlon Enterprise, shortened
to TOSE. Rob and Don pulled Donal out of a sound
sleep. The twins never knocked on the door; they
would charge into the bedroom, drag a chair over to
the bed, climb up onto the four-poster and shake him
until he was awake. On one occasion Rob pulled up
an eyelid to see if he was awake.

This morning they yelled at Donal to get up.

Cynthia stood smiling in the doorway, she held
little Rónán in her arms.

Donal groaned, glanced over at the clock. It wasn't
even eight. He noticed that Cynthia and the boys were
dressed already.

"You better get up, sleepyhead," Cynthia said.
"There's a truck at the gate."

"Were we expecting a delivery?"

"Some more of your antiques, I'm sure."

෨

Paulie Hewson looked through the ornate wrought-iron gate at the three-story mansion at the end of a long drive. Three steps led up to a porch that ran the length of the house. Decorative white metal patio furniture on the porch added a homey feel to the place.

Beyond, in a low valley, the tops of several outbuildings with blue and red slate roofs, showed among the trees.

"Grand place."

"Impressive, isn't it. There's a pool in the back," added the driver through the open truck window.

Though Mánus had assured him, Paulie still had doubts. Now if Mr. Tolan was as nice as he had been told, then he would leave her with no worries.

"Are they home?" asked the truck driver, suddenly inpatient to get back to Chicago.

"We were told they would be," Paulie said as he rang the bell to the right of the gate.

෨

Donal dressed in a hurry.

Down in his office he turned on his computer, keyed in the gate cameras. A man stood clipboard in hand at the gate. He waited a minute, before he rang the bell again. The camera in the woods across from the gate showed only the white sides of the large truck.

Donal spoke into the speaker, "I'll be right down."

He told the twins to stay on the porch with Cynthia and Sally. He walked across the grass, instead of taking the long walk down the asphalt drive to the gate. His old companion, Cat, ran ahead him. As he approached the gate, the man pulled off his hat.

"Good morning, Mr. Tolan. We have a delivery for you."

The man slipped the clipboard through the bars of the righthand gate. Donal checked the paperwork. They were at the correct address. It was the antique sleigh bed for the front bedroom. But the salesman had told him not to expect delivery until next week.

Donal stepped back, called Cat over, and pointed a small remote at the gate. The ornate gates opened on well-oiled hinges. The truck drove up the drive to the front of the house.

Sally opened the front door.

The driver jumped down from the cab and helped the older man roll up the back door, pull out the ramp, and lower it to the ground.

Before going inside the truck Paulie said, "You can close the front door. I don't think you will want this beauty in your front parlor."

Puzzled, Sally hurried over to close the door.

Donal looked at Cynthia surprised.

Paulie Hewson disappeared into the truck to appear a moment later leading a beautiful bay mare with a white blaze on her forehead. The twins squealed with delight and jumped up and down, wanting to ride the pony.

Rónán in Sally's arms pointed at the horse and said, "Dawg."

Donal didn't know what to say. He ran his hands over the beautiful mare. He stepped back to admire the fine lines of the animal. What he wouldn't give to own a horse like this.

Finally he came to his senses. "There must be some mistake here."

"You are Donal C. Tolan, right."

"Yes."

"Donegal Lass is the finest horse in all of Ireland."

"I can see that. I still don't understand...Mr..."

"Hewson, Paulie Hewson" the man said, held out his hand.

Donal shook the hand offered and introduced his wife and family.

"'Tis a gift from your partners, Mr. Scanlon and Mr. O'Brien. If that is a laptop your good wife has yonder, you best take it up with them."

Donal stepped up onto the porch. Cynthia had placed a laptop on the glass-topped wrought-iron table; she pressed several keys and turned it toward Donal. On the screen Mánus sat at his makeshift desk smiling at him.

"Good morning."

Even at this early hour his partner was dressed in a suit and tie, and wore blue-tinted glasses. In the background, the house framework was a silhouette against the sky.

"I don't understand?"

"You said you were going to get your stallion soon. You'll need a mare to get your horse farm up and running," Mánus said.

"I don't know how to thank you."

"No thanks necessary. The stocks you advised me and the lads on are grand."

"I could give you my first foal," Donal said.

"Och! And me never near a horse in me life." Mánus smiled at him. "It's a gift. How is the new lad?"

Donal swung the laptop around so that he could see Rónán Og. Rob and Don moved over to wave and call hellos to their Uncle Mánus.

Rónán pointed his pudgy hand at the computer and said, "Dawg."

"Sorry, it's his favorite word."

"Looks like his father," Mánus said. In the background came the sound of raised voices. "I'm glad you like the mare. I have to go, there seems to be a problem. Talk to you later."

The screen went blank. Donal looked over at Cynthia.

"You knew?"

"Yes."

The twins straddled the mare's back for the short ride down to the stable. Donal kept a tight grip on the bridle, Paulie Hewson on the other side did the same.

CHAPTER
THIRTY-TWO

"No matter how sound the economy, the restaurant business is the toughest in the world," Jeff Lewis said.

Jeff's ideas were sound. Though Donal didn't want to get into a long-term coupon deal with him, but liked the idea of the extra advertising. Let people know the pub was under new management, get them to try the new place.

Hopefully they would come back.

He agreed to a short-term contract with Jeff's company. After all the paperwork was done, Donal walked Jeff out to the front.

As they passed the bar, Jeff said, "I see Clancy is visiting you."

Donal looked at the man at the bar. In the back mirror he made out a well-built man, in his late twenties, thin with dark hair and a pronounced nose.

"He bought Stan's Roadhouse. The historical society is all over him to keep the place as it is. Stan's is the last of the vintage roadhouses on the Old Chicago road. I'll introduce you."

After Jeff made the introductions, Donal invited them to a drink in one of the back booths. Jeff declined, said he had two more clients to see.

Clancy accepted the offer.

"What's your pleasure?"

"I'll have a Sam Adams."

Donal asked Matt to bring a Sam Adams and a Jameson Cooler to the back.

Over drinks they talked about the restaurant business, and about how they both were new to it. Clancy played for the Chicago Bears, retired early due to an injury. Thought he would try his hand at running a roadhouse.

"I have to admit," Clancy said. "My name is only a nickname."

"What is your full name?"

"Charles Atkins Willis."

"That is a far cry from Clancy. There must be a story behind it."

"Yes there is. My great-grandfather lived in a small town in Maine. His family, was the only English family in the area, everyone else was Irish. One of my great aunts married a Clancy. The name has come down through the years as a nickname."

"But not for the good."

"Well, it is usually given to someone who is a black sheep."

Donal smiled; he liked Clancy, or Charles. It didn't matter to him, Gael or Saxon. All the Troubles had been a long time ago.

After Clancy left, Donal sat down at his usual place at the end of the bar.

"Good afternoon, sir."

Donal glanced up and smiled at the mailman who delivered in the downtown area. He handed Donal a bundle of mail held together with a thick rubber band.

"Nothing to go out today," Donal said. "Stop by when you are off duty."

The mailman turned, and smiled, "Will do."

Donal pulled off the rubber band and sorted through the mail. Most were advertising, addressed to O'Flaherty's. Near the bottom he found an envelope address to him personally. He slit it open and pulled out a single sheet of folded paper.

He stared at the page, shocked at what it said. Small squares of paper cut from newspapers and magazines had been glued to the page. He read the message a second time: We know who you are! Go back to where you came from! Punctuation had been added by hand.

Donal folded the letter and put it back into the envelope. He folded the envelope over double and placed it in his inside pocket. Once he was home he would contact Mánus.

CHAPTER
THIRTY-THREE

"I **hear** the pub is doing so great that you might be opening a second one," Joan Cyrus said.

"Yes. Donal is thinking of opening one in Chicago."

"I have the catalogue right here." Joan pulled a catalogue from under the counter. She opened it to the section she had marked with a card. "There are several chairs to pick from."

Cynthia took the catalogue. The first chair was close to what she was looking for. However, it was from England. She really wanted something from Ireland. Three pages over she found the exact chair she wanted. It was a reproduction from the Rock of Cashal. The high-backed chair had a dark plush seat and back with scrolled arms and legs, with finials on the top at the back. It was solid oak and very pricey.

"How long will it take?"

"About six weeks."

Cynthia took out her gold Amex card and paid for the full amount, including shipping. It would be a surprise for Donal. She wanted it delivered to Forest Lake.

"Do you realize how lucky you are?"

"Yes, I do," Cynthia said.

Out on the street Cynthia walked to her small personal van. It was really a medium-sized truck; inside she had built-in racks to hold completed artwork and canvases, and drawers for supplies. As she unlocked the door, she thought about how lucky she was, a wonderful husband and four sons. Little Rónán would be two years old next month.

Martainnrinn, the first of Donal's foster children, had joined them in the spring. She loved him like one of her own. The serious boy watched over the twins and the baby even though they had Sally to care for them.

Donal shortened his name to Martin Rinn, which became his legal name; he didn't seem to mind.

Cynthia pulled out her estate-linc, opened it, and pushed the phone button. This was one of Mánus' gadgets. Donal had been right about Mánus, he wasn't as bad as she had first thought. His wife, Mary Catherine, was a kind, generous woman.

She pressed the number that would reach Donal's office.

"Forest Lake," said the voice she loved.

"I'm done shopping. I'll be home in forty-five minutes."

"I'll let Sally know, Cyn."

In the background Rónán chattered and the twins fought about something. She smiled to herself. Yes, she was very lucky.

At Fifth and Chandler the light tuned red; she stopped the van. When the light turned green, she stepped on the gas. Out of the corner of her eye she saw the blue-white headlights of a fast-moving vehicle on Fifth. The vehicle seemed to be moving too fast for town driving.

Cynthia heard the high-pitched squeal of the anti-collision warning system in her van and the pickup truck. The heavy truck caught the lighter van, pushing it across the road and into a tree.

Her last thoughts were of Donal.

༄

Upset or not, Donal didn't want to wait for Jamie Ryan to come out to Forest Lake, then drive him back to Prescott General on the west side of town. So he drove into town. At the hospital he ran across the parking lot to emergency. Breathless, heart pounding, he inquired at the desk about his wife.

The nurse escorted Donal to a small waiting room. "Please wait here. Dr. Tamara is with your wife. He will be right in to speak to you. He'll let you know when you can see her."

Like a caged tiger, Donal paced the small room. The waiting was driving him crazy. What was taking the doctor so long? When the door opened and the doctor entered, his heart went cold. Something in the man's demeanor frightened him.

"I'm sorry, Mr. Tolan."

Doctor Tamara was brisk, but also gave a feeling of his sincere compassion for Donal's loss. He explained to Donal that Cynthia had died minutes after the ambulance reached the hospital. The world around Donal turned cold and gray. His anchor was gone, he was drifting in a bleak lifeless world of anger and incomprehensible grief.

Mánus and Liam took care of the arrangements for the funeral. In a state of stunned disbelief Donal agreed to everything they suggested. The graveside service, the wake, even talking to Robert and Mary Long seemed to be happening to someone else.

The days he sat in the courtroom for the trial were a blur.

He didn't really understand what was going on.

The teenage driver admitted that he had been drinking the night of the accident, and threw himself on the mercy of the court. The judge revoked his driving license and sentenced him to four years in a readjustment center.

Even if Donal had understood, it wouldn't have mattered; nothing would bring Cynthia back. Forest Lake, only one person short, now seemed empty to him. He retreated to his office, took out a bottle of Jameson. For the first time in his life, he intended to finish it.

❧

"He's getting worse," Sally said.

"Did something set him off?"

"It's that chair. Cynthia must have ordered it before she had the accident. It came over the weekend."

"Where is he?"

"He's back in his office. I hope I did the right thing calling you?"

"You did right," Mánus said, smiled to reassure her. Sally relaxed. "Will you see to a bit of food for Carl?"

Sally looked over the thin, dark boy.

"Of course. Please tell Martin I have his dinner for him."

"Carl will need a place to sleep, he can help with the horses."

"I suppose he can sleep down in the studio building."

"I knew you would understand." Mánus flashed her another radiant smile. She relaxed even more, even offered him a small smile.

Mánus walked back to Donal's office. When he didn't get an answer to his knock, he opened the door. The room was dark, the curtains drawn. It took him a minute to find the light switch. The overhead light went on.

Donal sat on the couch staring off into space. Martin sat across from him. On the coffee table next to an open bottle of Jameson sat Cat.

"Martin, lad, Sally has your dinner."

The boy looked over at Donal, then back at him and shook his head.

"Lad, I'll take care of the Taoiseach."

Reluctantly Martin stood and stretched. He glanced at Donal before leaving the room. Martin was tall for his age, at this rate he would be well over six feet as an adult. Only eight years old, going on twenty-eight.

Mánus moved over to sit across from Donal.

Jaysus, he thought, *Donal looked like he had been on a month-long drunk.*

His partner hadn't shaved in days, eyes bloodshot from lack of sleep or too much of the drink taken. He didn't seem to notice what was going on around him.

He would have to be careful what he said to Donal. He reached over and let his friend's grief wash over him. Not only grief, but also the emptiness of his world without Cynthia.

"We have always believed, that in the midst of death there is life..."

Donal focused on Mánus, as if seeing him for the first time, and pulled away.

"I never had a chance to tell her I loved her, to say goodbye."

"She knew you loved her, lad. You have four sons to care for. Those boys need you. Their grief is no less than yours."

"I could have called her back. Kept her here with our sons."

Mánus wasn't sure what Donal meant by calling her back. Their beliefs went back to a time before Christianity, before they traveled to Ireland. He wondered if Donal was talking about the Road of Life and Death. Did it really exist? If it did, was it possible to call someone back from there?

"Rónán is only two years old. He'll grow up like me, never knowing his mother. Live his life with only a few memories of her. It isn't..." Donal choked up, leaned forward and buried his face in his hands.

"Fair." Mánus finished for him and shook his head. "Lad, who told you life was fair? You have to hold onto the good times. Not one of us knows when it will be our last."

Had life been fair to Donal's mother and father? Had it been fair to Briana or his baby daughter? Had life been fair to his own father, Old Seámus, to give him a son, then take his life? To give me a mother who was only interested in money?

Mánus leaned forward, he wanted to take Donal's hand. His friend needed to let go, to let all the grief out.

"Don't try to force me. I won't let you."

"I couldn't force you if I wanted to. Please, let me help you."

"Nothing can help me now. Nothing."

CHAPTER THIRTY-FOUR

C at jumped off the bed to scratch at the bedroom door.

Donal woke up, the sound grated on his nerves. He rolled over to face the windows. When the noise went on, he rolled over again. His head began to ache, he tried to say something to the cat. Only a harsh croaking sound came out of his parched throat. He needed a drink. With trembling fingers he reached for the light switch, he fumbled with it for a minute before he finally turned the switch and the light came on.

Cat ran to the bed and yowled at him, then returned to scratch at the door.

With difficulty Donal sat up and lowered his feet to the floor. An empty bottle and tumbler sat on the nightstand. Damn. He would have to go downstairs and get another bottle. He glanced around the unfamiliar room wondering where he had put his clothes, only to find that he was dressed. He had passed out on the bed with his clothes on, including his boots.

Cat stopped to look at him, then returned to her scratching at the door.

"What's wrong, Cat?"

She turned to stare at him, ran over to the bed and yowled up at him, and ran back to the door.

Cat wanted out.

Donal couldn't ignore her any longer. On shaky legs he stood. He had to grab the edge of the dresser to keep from falling. Out in the hall he paused, confused. Why was he on the second floor?

Cat, tail held high, ran down the hall. In the distance he heard Rónán crying.

Where was Sally? Why didn't she come to see what was wrong. Martin would find her. Donal didn't want to go and see what was wrong. His sons reminded him of Cynthia. Even the paintings hanging on the walls reminded him of his loss. Everything in the house reminded him that Cynthia had died, that he would never hold her in his arms again.

Rónán went on screaming.

Cat stopped at the door to Rónán's room, turned, and yowled at him. On unsteady legs he moved down the hall and paused at the door. He sighed, and pushed it open.

Donal's whiskey numbed brain took in the scene before him. The twins were huddled together on the love seat in the corner. Martin was trying to soothe Rónán, who stood in his crib, red-faced, screaming. When the baby saw him he held out his pudgy arms.

"Da, Da," Rónán cried. His small fists opening and closing.

Only a short time ago Cynthia and he had been delighted when he learned to say Da.

Donal stared at Martin, then at Rónán. He wanted more than anything to pull the door closed, go downstairs, find a bottle of Jameson and numb his brain to the pain of his loss. Instead he stepped over to the crib and picked up his youngest son. Rónán stopped crying, sniffed several times and laid his head on Donal's shoulder. His pudgy thumb found its way to his mouth.

Without thinking, Donal began to rock back and forth to soothe his son.

Sally hurried into the room. "Come on boys...Oh! You're up. I tried to wake you earlier..."

What Sally Brown was saying to Donal barely registered. His attention was on the small ornate mirror over the crib. Who was that man staring back at him? His hair stuck out at strange angles, eyes bloodshot, with several weeks of stubble covering his face.

"When was Mánus here last?" Donal asked, as he stared at his reflection in the mirror.

"About two weeks ago. He stayed here for a week, but had to go home on family business, Mr. Tolan."

It was the first time in years that Sally addressed him as Mr. Tolan. Rónán shifted. His hand went to his son's neck to steady him. In a flash the problem came to him. His son was sick, very sick.

"Have you called the doctor?"

"The amadan said we have to check his temperature every hour and bring him into emergency if it goes too high."

"Sally, come with me."

Donal pulled the comforter from the crib and wrapped it around his son.

"What are you going to do?" Sally Brown asked, worry in her voice.

"We need to take him into the hospital. Martin, please stay with the twins. You'll have to drive, Sally."

At the bottom of the stairs, Donal paused. He still needed a drink. All he had to do was go into the solarium or into his office. If he did, he was sure he would never get to hospital.

Sally's voice broke into his thoughts. "Are you all right?"

Donal looked at her and nodded.

The worst was over. Donal caught the expression on Sally's face. Almost smiled, he looked a sight. With his left hand he tried to pat down his hair. "All the gossips in town will have something to talk about. Come on."

"The car is out front, I brought it around earlier."

Four days later Donal brought Rónán Og home to Forest Lake and began to put his life back together, a step at a time. He was surprised to find a young boy by the name of Carl taking care of the horses.

CHAPTER
THIRTY-FIVE

Donal cut his time down to two days at the new pub in Chicago. He didn't have to worry about O'Flaherty's in Prescott. Matt had everything there under control. There weren't enough hours in a day to get everything done. Fortunately, the Robert Long office in Chicago was up and running. John Stills was promoted to manager of the new location. Unless something came up where his help was needed, Donal left him on his own.

Besides the pubs and his clients, he had a house and stable to run. Sally Brown took on the running of the house.

Carl, Martin and the twins wanted to help with the horses. Donal had a strict rule. They could only help on weekends; during the week he wanted them to concentrate on their schoolwork.

Donal sat at his usual place at the end of the bar sipping a Jameson cooler.

Jenny picked up the tray of drinks. "I'll need a sherry, Matt."

"Does Sandra Murphy still come in?" Donal asked.

"She quit for awhile," Matt said. "Right after she had the row with her family about going back to Chicago with them. About two weeks ago she started coming in again."

Donal stared at the glass of sherry; an idea began to take form. When Jenny came back for the sherry, he told her he would take it over. He also told her if he wasn't back in ten minutes to bring over scones and all the fixings, plus a pot of tea.

"Be careful. Since the incident with her family she is very nervous."

Donal paused at the entrance to the left-hand window tables. Sandra sat at the same table where Ted Murphy had proposed to her, where he had told her a year later that he would ship out to the Middle East at the end of the month. They had shared their last meal on a Sunday afternoon, in the window of O'Flaherty's.

Sensing his presence Sandra looked up. She reminded him of a frightened deer. So nervous that at any minute she might run from him. He flashed her his best smile as he stepped up into the window section.

"Your sherry," he said as he placed it on the table. "May I join you?"

"You're the owner."

Donal nodded.

Sandra seemed to think about him for a moment, before she said, "My condolences."

"Thank you."

Jenny brought the tea and scones.

Cynthia would have said he was picking up another stray. She would have been right.

Donal wanted to help Sandra. He had held onto his grief too long in his own life. No one should choose that way to live. He put his hand out to her; she would have to meet him halfway. When she took his hand he helped her get beyond the pain of her grief, to move on with her life. Her family in Chicago would be pleased when she called them.

Later he would find a job for her, perhaps even here at the pub.

❦

Donal stared at the letter. Like the first one he received, this one didn't have a return address.

He read again the message, "I guess you didn't understand my message. Go back to where you came from. If not, suffer the consequences."

The first letter ended up as a dead end. He didn't think they would find out who sent this one either. He folded the letter over double and shoved it into his pocket.

It was late afternoon. The lunch crowd had given way to late afternoon diners.

Tabitha Ryan, the hostess, came over to talk to Donal.

"There is a young lady asking for you. I told her I would check to see if you were still here."

"I wasn't expecting anyone."

"She gave the name Barbara Sedgwich. She wasn't sure if you would remember her. I put her in number twenty in the side room. She has a friend with her."

Tabitha waited.

Donal smiled, his photographic memory was legendary at O'Flaherty's. He remembered Miss Sedgwich from the time Rónán had been in the hospital. She was an intern at Prescott General. They had met in the cafeteria.

That was over nine months ago. What did Ms. Sedgwich want?

"Tell her I'll be over."

Matt came over, "Don't look so worried. It won't hurt for you to talk to her."

"I know, Matt. It is just..."

"Cynthia would want you to get on with your life."

After some soul searching Donal finished his drink and walked into the side room.

"Good afternoon, ladies."

Barbara introduced him to Amelia, a fellow intern. They insisted that he join them.

"How is your son, little Rónán, doing?"

He was impressed. She had remembered his sons name.

"Fine. He chases his two brothers around the house."

When the waitress brought their food, he ordered another Jameson cooler.

Over the next hour, while Barbara and Amelia ate their late lunch, Donal nursed his drink. They talked about the hospital, the election coming up and the latest video-film.

"Do you have to spend a lot of time here?" Amelia asked.

"One day here, and two over at the pub in Chicago. I don't know what I will do when we open the new pub in Boston. It won't be as simple as a commute to Chicago."

"Find someone you trust to run it," Barbara suggested.

Donal had given it a lot of thought. He hadn't asked Matt yet. He hoped he would consider becoming the manager at the Boston pub. He would have to find someone to run this place. For the time being he could run it with Tabitha Ryan's help. If things worked out, he would offer her the manager position. The senior waitress would have the option to move up to hostess.

"I'll work on that idea," Donal said and smiled at Barbara. She wasn't exactly pretty. On the other hand, she wasn't homely either with her honey-brown hair, nice features and slim figure. There was something about her that he liked.

After lunch, he ordered two special drinks for them and a Sprite for himself. When he had brought Rónán home from the hospital, he promised himself he would never have more than two drinks at a time.

"So, what is so special about these drinks."

"Our specialty is Irish coffee. A friend in Ireland sent me the original recipe they used on the transcontinental flight that started the whole thing."

It was a pleasant afternoon. Donal wasn't interested in starting a relationship at this time, perhaps sometime in the future, but not now, it was too soon.

Four months later Donal received an invitation for a formal dinner put on by the Chamber of Commerce of Prescott and Middleton. Barbara came to mind. He wondered if he had waited too long to get back with her.

Donal left a message for her at the hospital. That evening she called him back. He read nothing in her voice to say that his call had surprised her. They talked about different things before he came to the point of his call.

"I would love to accompany you to the dinner."

"Wonderful. Give me your address. I'll pick you up at seven-thirty on the tenth."

"I have mid-afternoon hours that day. Pick me up at the hospital, at the main entrance."

"Seven-thirty at the main entrance."

It seemed strange that she wasn't going home first. He thought about it overnight. The next morning he contacted Mánus. His partner would be happy to see what he could find out about Barbara Sedgwich.

Donal put thoughts of what Mánus might come up with out of his mind. He was looking forward to the dinner with Barbara.

Two days before the tenth his laptop beeped. He opened it and placed his right thumb on the track-pad.

Mánus came on the screen.

"I have the information you wanted. Sorry it took so long. We had to do some extra digging. Not about Barbara, about her mother, Margaret.

"Barbara Ann Sedgwich lives with her mother, Margaret Wilson Sedgwich, on the west side of Prescott, in a huge Victorian house that is far too big for the two of them. No servants, has a cleaning lady come in twice a week. She belongs to the Prescott Country Club. Lives well beyond her means, which by the way is a small pension from her late husband, Colonel James Sedgwich."

"I don't understand? Why the extra digging?"

"Margaret Sedgwich claims to be related to the House of Windsor. If England still had the monarchy, she claims she would be in line for the throne."

"Is that the truth?"

"That's how Mrs. Sedgwich tells it. In reality, she is a distant cousin. They aren't as blue-blooded as she likes to make out."

"I see."

"I don't think you do at all, Donal. The old lady is a loyalist. She isn't going to want an Irish Catholic in her family."

"Mánus," Donal tried to keep his comment light. "The Anglo-Irish war happened a long time ago. Surely you don't think that they…"

"Hardly long enough for some people. My grandfather used to say, 'We never forget a friend or an enemy.' It is a mere thirty years since Ireland was united."

"I'm sure it won't make a difference."

"Take care, lad."

Donal told himself that it wouldn't make a difference. At the back of his mind the fact that he wasn't picking Barbara up at home nagged at him.

After their second date, Donal and Barbara settled into a pattern of seeing each other when she had time off. Kept their relationship casual, just good friends. Donal didn't want to rush things.

He waited until they had been dating for a few months before he brought Barbara back to Forest Lake for a visit.

They rode out to the lake and had a picnic with his boys. Rob really liked her. Donal would always look back at the picnic as the turning point in their relationship. Barbara still hadn't introduced him to her mother. As time went by, he began to wonder why.

When Barbara moved to her own apartment, she bought a large wall-mounted video-screen and took out an entertainment subscription. They would watch the latest video-film or theater production from Chicago and New York on it. Now and then they made dinner together, or went out to eat at a local restaurant, nothing like the Tuscan Grille, just nice places with good food.

Time passed and slowly Donal grew very found of Barbara. Was it love? Perhaps. She would make a good mother for his boys.

Later, he would ask himself if he really loved her, or was it the need to have someone mother his boys.

"How long have we been going out together?" Donal asked. He wanted to see what Barbara would say.

Donal sat up and moved over so Barbara could sit down on the edge of the bed.

"We've been going out a while."

"You don't think there is anything funny about it?"

"Funny? No, darling. Is something wrong?"

"You leased this apartment after we started dating."

A frown pulled at the corners of her mouth. "No big mystery. It was time for me to move out on my own. What are you getting at?"

"I find it strange that I have never met your mother."

"My mother is so busy, it is hard to pin her down..."

Mánus words came back to him, *"The old lady is a loyalist."*

"She doesn't approve of me?"

"It's not that..."

Donal slipped off the other side of the bed. Barbara tried to stop him. "I have to leave early, school night. I need to check on my boys. Think about it, Barbara. Don't you think I should meet her before we get married?"

CHAPTER THIRTY-SIX

The next day Barbara called Donal.

"I thought Friday night we could swing by mother's house and you could meet her."

Margaret Sedgwich turned out to be a beautiful, trim, silver-haired woman, younger than he thought she would be. She was elegantly dressed in a black cocktail-length dress. Her only jewelry was a double strand of pearls and matching ear studs.

She shook his hand. "So I finally get to meet the young man that has been taking up so much of my daughter's time." Was there a hint of asperity in her voice. "Tolan? Is that a Welsh name?"

"It is a Donegal name."

"We, young man, belong to the House of Windsor. If those fools hadn't done away with the monarchy, my daughter would have been a princess."

"And you would be Queen," Donal said.

"Exactly, young man," Margaret Sedgwich said. "I think we understand each other."

Barbara laughed, "Don't take mother serious, darling. It is a family joke, nothing more."

Donal wasn't so sure. Would she believe him if he told her he had given up being a king. Not a good idea he told himself.

"I guess England's loss is my gain."

"Yes," Mrs. Sedgwich said dryly. "I understand you have a chauffeur?"

"Well, not really a chauffeur. Martin, my foster son, drive sometimes. He's too young to drive without an adult in the car. My other foster son, Carl, has an interest in horses. I hope to send him to Michigan State to become a veterinarian."

Donal wasn't sure what to make of Margaret Sedgwich. Should he take her serious? Barbara didn't seem to think he should. Still, worry nagged at the back of his mind.

After that night they visited Mrs. Sedgwich now and then, usually at her home.

In the autumn, the Prescott Country Club Margaret and Barbara belonged to held a Harvest Ball. Barbara invited him as her guest. The country club scene didn't interest Donal; still if he married Barbara Sedgwich he would be obligated to join.

Mánus reminded him it would be good for business.

Barbara had an emergency at the hospital on the afternoon of the ball. She called him to say she would meet him at the country club.

Just before seven-thirty he parked his Land Rover in the side lot and walked to the main entrance. Many of the members had chauffeurs. The young lady at the door checked his name on a list attached to a clipboard.

"You're assigned to table ten, right on the dance floor. Some of the members are gathered in the lounge for a pre-ball drink, Mr. Tolan."

No one was sitting at table ten. Donal decided to see about a drink in the lounge. As he entered he spotted Margaret Sedgwich and headed in her direction. She was holding court with several couples.

"My daughter only dates him to annoy me," Margaret said. "It will be a very amusing evening. He is nothing but a common bar owner, lives off his late wife's estate."

Her words stopped Donal in his tracks. His jaw tightened.

"What's he like? My daughter says he is quite handsome," asked the woman to her right.

"He's a dumb Mick. Has a black son. His horses are huge creatures that should be pulling carts."

The man to her left noticed Donal, coughed several times to warn Margaret.

"What is the matter with you, Charles?"

Charles put his hand on her arm and nodded in Donal's direction.

Margaret turned and looked Donal in the eye. Instead of looking embarrassed, a smug self-satisfied look came over her face.

The woman to her right tried to smooth things over, "We were just talking about a cousin."

"I would put one of my horses up against any horse you could come up with," Donal said.

"Really," Charles said. "If you are so confident, care to make a small wager. Perhaps ten grand."

Donal never gambled; still, he had thrown down the gauntlet. He had to follow through or look the amadan.

"Make it twenty and we have a bet."

"Twenty it is."

Donal put out his hand to shake on the wager.

Charles stared at him. "My word is good."

"Set it up and call me at my pub."

Barbara was just coming in, cream satin and lace. "Where are you going, darling?"

Angry at Mrs. Sedgwich words, he wanted to calm down, take the edge off his anger before he discussed it with Barbara. He loved her. She loved him, or did she?

"What is going on?"

"Talk to your mother. I'll be at the pub."

Half an hour later Barbara called him. Asked him to meet her later at her apartment. He pulled up in front of her apartment at ten.

"It was a joke on my mother's part, darling. She saw you coming in."

"Just answer me, Barbara. Do you date me to get back at your mother?"

"I'm hurt, that you would even think that that is true."

"Let's get married."

"Why ruin a wonderful relation by getting married."

"Because I want you to live with me at Forest Lake."

"On your late wife's estate?"

Donal had to fight down his anger. Why did people always assume that it was Cynthia Long's estate?

"The money from my wife's estate went into a trust for our sons. Is it because I am nothing more than a bar owner, a common publican?"

"It's not that. It's too far out of town. I don't want to commute."

"I make the trip several times a week," Donal said. He didn't like this at all. "Do you want to marry me?"

"Yes. But not now."

"Not now? Or do you mean never?"

"Darling." Barbara sat down next to him and tried to kiss him. He pulled away. "I'm all my mother has, eventually she will agree to the marriage. We just need to go slow."

Donal stood to leave.

"Darling, please, you don't understand."

"But I do."

CHAPTER
THIRTY-SEVEN

Donal fought the urge to drive down to Stan's and have a few drinks. Clancy would smile and ask as a joke if he was slumming.

Remembering his promise to himself to have no more than two drinks, he headed home. He put the car away in the garage.

About to go up the stairs, he noticed that there was a light on in the first stable. He crossed the stable yard and entered the side door and walked back toward the office.

Grey Ghost stuck his head over the half-door and whinnied. Donal stopped to pat the light gray stallion. His first stallion, Warlord, had been put out to pasture. Ghost carried all the attributes of his sire.

"How are you tonight, old friend?"

"Is that you, Donal?" Martin stood in the office doorway, a dark silhouette against the light.

"You're up late."

When Donal entered the office, he found Carl sitting at the desk. Carl closed the book he was reading and stood to leave.

"Next month is your birthday. Is there anything special you would like, Carl?"

Carl stopped at the door and turned to Donal. Under the overhead lights his eyes looked more green then brown. You never noticed his darker skin tone until he stood next to one of his sons, or Martin.

"Dinner at O'Flaherty's would be nice, I mean..."

Carl had an unusual position at Forest Lake. He wasn't family, an employee, or a servant. Donal treated him as if he were family. Carl had to be the son of someone in the clan. He didn't know the boy's history. It didn't matter one way or the other. He would give Carl a good education.

"Main dining room, or one of the snugs upstairs?" Donal asked.

"Not sure," he glanced at Martin for help.

"The side room is nice," Martin offered.

"The side, yes. I..."

"Anything you want, just name it, Carl."

"Do you think Mánus would come?"

"I don't see why he wouldn't. I can invite him, or you can."

Did Carl think that Mánus was his father? He had none of the Scanlon good looks. More likely he was an O'Brien or Ryan.

"Thank you, Donal."

After Martin and Carl left. Donal sat down at the desk. Carl had been going through his book of photographs of Warlord, Donegal Lass, and their offspring.

"Are you all right?"

Donal looked up to find Martin standing in the doorway.

"I thought you were going to bed, young man."

"I forgot my notebook." Martin picked up his book from table by the window. "Are you all right?"

"Things change in life. Sometimes it isn't what you wanted at all."

His foster son looked puzzled. "I'll say good night then, sir."

Before Martin left Donal asked him, "Do you miss your family?"

"Being fostered by you is an honor. But sometimes, yes. I have my sketches of them in my book."

"I didn't know. Your father never told me what he sent in that last package."

Martin stepped over to the desk and opened the notebook. Inside, protected in clear plastic sleeves, he had three sketches. One was of Lord Rónán, his father. Martin looked a lot like his father. The second sketch was of his two younger brothers. The third was of Mór and Moya, his mother and aunt. Moya was really a second cousin once removed, but Martin had always called her his aunt.

Moya reminded Donal of Briana in a way. The nose was different though.

"She likes you, you know."

"Moya?"

Martin nodded.

"She reminds me of your aunt, the one who died long before you were born."

"Moya says when she grows up she will marry you."

Donal smiled at Martin. His foster son never noticed the big difference in their ages. Neither did Moya. How old was she now, fourteen, perhaps fifteen?

"Next time we go into town, let's have those sketches framed. You could put them on the wall in your room."

"I'd like that. Are you sure you are all right?"

"Yes. Why?"

"You only talk to Grey Ghost in English when you're upset about something."

"Martin if you were to run a horse race tomorrow, who would you pick?"

"For speed or endurance?"

"I think a little of both."

"Who will be the jockey?"

"Me."

"You're too big to be a jockey. You wouldn't make the weight, even under the new rules."

Donal was surprised that Martin had heard about the weight changes for jockeys.

"Then you must be thinking of riding Ghost. Fast and strong."

"I might have made one of the biggest mistakes in my life tonight. Do you think he would be up to a race with a thoroughbred?"

"Ghost is a thoroughbred, Donal, and yes, if you ask him to."

"Thanks. I'll be fine."

Chapter Thirty-Eight

"I wouldn't believe it if I hadn't heard it myself."

Startled, Donal stopped currying Grey Ghost and turned to the stranger that had appeared out of nowhere. Ghost snorted and tossed his head at the intruder and stomped his huge hoofs. Battle-trained like his sire, he was ready to take on the intruder. Donal reached for his bridle.

"What were you singing to him?" the stranger asked.

"Who are you?"

"Do you always answer a question with a question?"

"This is a private building," Donal said. "So I'm wondering who you are and how you found us."

"It isn't important who I am, not now. If you win, then it might be very important to both of us," the stranger answered.

"No comment," Donal said and threw the curry brush onto the small table next to the bed of straw he had made for himself.

"You're not superstitious?"

"Why should I be?"

"I was thinking about the last match race, Ruffian and Foolish Pleasure."

In Donal's mind's eye he saw again the tall dark bay filly, Ruffian, on an old tape Liam had found of the last official match race in the United States. The crowd was cheering wildly as Ruffian edged ahead of Foolish Pleasure. It looked like the filly would beat the colt when tragedy struck; at the mile marker Ruffian broke her leg.

Both jockeys said later that they heard a sound like a board being broken.

This match race wasn't sanctioned by the Illinois Racing Commission, though it would be run at Pendleton racetrack. It would be run before the official opening of the racing season.

"No comment," Donal said again.

"I'm not a reporter."

"Why are you interested in us?"

"I wanted to see the cart horse that is going to run against Dawn Lightning, the next Triple Crown winner."

The stranger moved closer Ghost, he let out a long whistle. Grey Ghost's ears pricked forward. "This is anything but a cart horse. Nice lines. Big, strong, now if he can run, the people backing this race might be in for a big surprise."

"We'll win," Donal said, with more confidence than he had.

"So what were you singing to the horse?"

"A cradle song, a lullaby." Briana had taught him the song.

"I couldn't make out the language."

"It's Irish."

"That's right, you're from Ireland. Good luck on race day, Mr. Tolan." Without a backward glance the man walked down the row of empty stalls and out the front entrance.

A few minutes later, Cathal ran back to him. "Are you okay, Donal?"

"I'm fine."

"Who was that man?"

"I don't know. See if we can put a guard at the back."

"Yes, sir."

᷉

Later, Mánus joined him.

"I heard you had a visitor."

"I don't have the slightest idea who he was. Perhaps a spy from the other side?"

"I'll have someone at each end. Do you want someone in here until after the race?"

"Just Martin."

"Having second thoughts?"

"Stay out of my head, Mánus. I was thinking about something else."

"About Barbara. If you care for her so much, take care of Mrs. Sedgwich."

"It isn't that easy. I like Barbara, but I'm not sure if we're destined to marry. Did you take care of Mary Catherine's parents?"

"No."

"Putting a spell on someone is against everything I believe in."

"In truth, I never had to. If Mary Catherine's parents had not agreed to our marriage, she would have married me anyway."

Donal sat down on a bale of hay.

"Barbara doesn't love me enough to marry me against her mother's wishes. Do you think I am weak not to change things?"

"I think Abbot Tadc and Niall taught you well. I try not to let my conscience get in the way, lad. I am not above leveling the playing field in life or a race to give us the advantage."

Mánus wasn't talking about Barbara any more.

"I could take care of their jockey for you."

"You would do it if I asked you to?"

"But you won't ask me to. This is important event for the future of your horse farm. After the race I plan to invite the country club group to the party at the Prescott Hotel. They can settle up their bets with us there."

"Bets?"

"Your bet and the ones I made with Charles Blesstin and John Tillman. Also a bet I put in for your friend

Clancy over at Stan's Roadhouse. I wouldn't have minded a bet with Margaret Sedgwich."

"We win and Margaret goes bankrupt over a horse race."

"It would teach her a lesson. Don't look so surprised. When she insulted you, she insulted all of us."

"I want this race fair."

"No problem," Mánus said. "I have a friend coming who will look good on your arm at the party."

"I don't..."

"You wouldn't want to hurt the feelings of the poor cailín, now would you?" Mánus smiled at him. "On the home front, Sally has enlisted the help of Cathal's wife to keep an eye on the twins and the little one. They keep getting away from Sally. I had to pull the three of them out of the fountain in the hotel lobby this morning."

Donal laughed. What would the twins be like when they were in their teens. He immediately felt depressed; the time would fly by and too soon his sons would be young men. It would be good to have this race behind them and settle down to a normal life again.

"They just wanted to see how far they can go with their Uncle Mánus."

❧

Early the next morning, Donal mounted Grey Ghost. Liam O'Brien walked with them down the row of stables to the track for their first morning workout. Donal wished they had a lead pony; Ghost could follow the pony around the track several times. There would be no problem with him catching Dawn Lightning on the day of the race. The problem would be to get him to pass the horse without a challenge.

Everyone turned to watch him; some made uncomplimentary comments about horse and rider. Others laughed as they passed by.

"You're too big to be a jockey even on that huge animal," one man yelled at them.

"Don't let them upset you, lad," Liam said.

Donal had to fight Grey Ghost to keep the stallion's mind on running. He seemed more interested in the other horses getting their morning workout. Since the track wouldn't open until later in the month, there weren't that many horses on the track that morning.

Ghost had no problem catching the horse ahead of him. The problem came when they caught up; Ghost would cut over, anticipating a fight. The other jockey would yell at him to keep his horse back, forcing Donal to pull his horse to the outside.

After an hour, Donal gave up for the morning. He would try again later, after the horses getting ready for the opening of the racing season were back in their stalls.

The next day went the same. Grey Ghost would catch the horse ahead of him, still expecting a fight. Toward the end of their evening workout Ghost seemed to understand what Donal wanted of him.

During their last circuit Liam would time them. Donal let Ghost take the bit and run. After six furlongs, he had a fight on his hands when he tried to slow the stallion down. He had to run his hand along his neck to calm him. At a canter he rode back to the railing where Liam waited.

"Were you able to get a time?"

Liam smiled at Donal. "They won't be laughing at you now. Not a track record. Fast enough to make those men up on clubhouse porch begin to worry."

Donal glanced over at the clubhouse. Several men leaned against the porch railing watching through binoculars.

"Let's cool down Ghost and make some plans. Too bad we only have two weeks to get this together," Liam said. "Do you mind if I call a friend in to help?"

"Not at all. We can use all the help we can get."

"Good. I called her this afternoon, she should be here in the morning."

Donal dismounted so he could walk alongside Liam.

"I want a fair race."

"No problem, don't worry about Mánus's offer of help."

"How much did he bet?"

"We all went together, Mánus, Cathal, and me, for a bet of forty grand. Clancy put up another ten."

Donal stopped. "That is a lot of money! And if Grey Ghost and I lose?"

"Not to worry, lad, you aren't going to lose."

CHAPTER
THIRTY-NINE

Terri Leahy, Liam's friend, arrived at three the next afternoon. She turned out to be a woman in her mid-to-late thirties. She wore her blonde hair pulled back in a frizzy bun and looked out at the world through faded blue eyes. Her ample mouth pulled down in a permanent frown.

Liam introduced Terri to Donal.

She looked over Grey Ghost from a safe distance. "God almighty!"

This didn't sound like a good beginning.

"Pardon?" Donal asked.

"I have never seen the likes of that fancy bridle and saddle. Are those inlays real gold and silver?" Terri circled Ghost. "God almighty, do you ride him in parades?"

"I've never ridden him in a parade in my life," Donal shot back at her.

Terri shook her head. "You didn't think this out, did you?"

"I guess not." Disappointed Donal said, "So you think it is hopeless."

"Hopeless is putting it mildly. In a match race the horse that gets the jump on the other horse usually wins. Another thing, they won't give you a break on the impost, the weight your horse will carry." She shook her head. "You don't need a trainer, you need a god-damned miracle worker."

Terri stumped off. Liam hurried after her, trying to catch up.

An hour later Liam returned.

"Don't let Terri upset you. She has a few rough edges. She is going to help us; first light we start your first official workout."

"What is in this for her? And by the way, who is she?" Donal asked, still upset by her comments.

"Second cousin once removed, fallen on hard times. Has experience training horses down in Florida."

"Cousin. Every time I turn around there is another cousin."

"I thought that was what this was about. Helping our own."

Donal felt guilty. His anger had made him speak out of line. "Sorry. You're right."

"Terri says this race will put your farm on the map."

"If we win, right?"

"You'll win."

"How can you be so confident?"

"You have more to lose, and more to gain riding on this race."

"Liam, I want to purchase one of your hounds for Martin."

"You're changing the subject."

Donal nodded.

"No problem, at all. Now or later, lad?"

"I think his next birthday. He is going to become an official Apprentice at that time. I was thinking perhaps later one for Carl too."

Donal wondered if he had imagined it, or had Liam's face closed at the mention of Carl's name. The older man's eyes gave nothing away.

"You'll have to talk to Mánus about Carl."

If Carl wasn't an O'Brien or Scanlon, who was he? Carl's strange green-brown eyes made Donal want to know who his father was.

Someday, Donal thought, *Mánus will have to share that information with me.*

☙

By race day, Donal was sure he had made the biggest mistake of his life. Grey Ghost was fast, had the endurance to see the race to the finish. The question is whether he would catch and pass Dawn Lightning.

The call for riders to mount came over the loudspeaker.

"Good luck, Donal. See you in the winner's circle," Mánus said.

His partner was wearing a lightweight blue suit, darker shirt with a blue silk tie and matching tinted glasses. Mary Catherine was wearing a cream-colored dress and large showy hat with a big blue bow. Mary Rose, their oldest daughter, and Sally Brown wore hats too. Even his sons were dressed in suits.

They all looked like they belonged to the local racing society.

Cathal stepped forward, "Good luck, sir."

Donal smiled down at Cathal.

"Just remember everything I have been telling you," Terri yelled.

Liam had on a blazer and slacks. He would walk them out to the starting gate. When he reached for the bridle, Grey Ghost snorted and tossed his head, and moved forward before Donal could rein him in. Both father and son jumped back.

"Ghost, stand, Liam is a friend," Donal said in Irish. He nodded at Liam. His friend moved forward and clicked the lead onto the bridle.

As they neared the starting gate Donal tried to calm Ghost. This would be the hardest part of the race. Ghost hated the starting gate. At the gate he balked, backed up and refused to move forward. No matter what Donal tried, he refused to enter the gate.

Sammy Day, Dawn Lightning's jockey, laughed. "Having a little trouble? Maybe he knows he is too big to fit into the gate."

"Don't let it upset you. A lot of horses don't like the starting gate," Liam said.

Donal leaned forward, closed his eyes and ran his hand along the sleek gray neck to soothe Ghost. "Easy boy," he said in Irish. "This is almost over. Let Liam take you into the gate."

Once inside, Liam climbed out of the way. And then it was upon them: the bell sounded, the gates flew open, and Grey Ghost jumped forward and reared up, his front hoofs raking the sky. Donal fought to bring him under control. He managed to turn him in a tight circle. They were facing back toward the starting gate.

Donal swung Ghost around and dug in his heels, leaned forward and told the stallion to catch Dawn Lightning. The gray stallion shot forward, gaining ground. Dawn Lightning maintained a lead of a dozen lengths. Gradually the gap between them shortened. Time was their enemy. They would run out of track soon.

Donal counted the marker posts as they flew by.

Grey Ghost ran with ease. Bred for endurance, not for speed, Donal was sure he would catch Dawn Lightning.

As they came around the first turn they still trailed Dawn Lightening by three lengths. Sammy Day, whipped his horse, he wanted more speed. As Donal maneuvered his stallion over to pass on the outside, Sammy switched the whip to the outside to try to scare Ghost.

Move over, we're coming through.

Grey Ghost settled in a head behind the smaller horse. Donal leaned as far forward in the saddle as possible, he doubted that Ghost heard him over the sound of thundering hoofs and the din created by the screaming crowd. He tried anyway, yelling encouragement to his horse. Beneath him the powerful strides lengthened.

They were neck and neck as they thundered down the home stretch and past the finish line, Donal sat up to slow Ghost down. Dawn Lightning no longer ran along side of them.

Donal glanced back over his shoulder. Two lengths back, Sammy Day whipped his mount to no avail, the race was over. The crowd roared. Among the cheers there were boos as well. He turned and headed back to the winner's circle. The track management waited for the winner. Only after he weighed in and they completed a drug test would the results become official.

CHAPTER FORTY

"Hello."

Donal glanced up from feeding Grey Ghost. He was surprised to find Barbara Sedgwich standing in the open door.

"Your partner told me where to find you."

Ghost eyed her from his stall.

Donal didn't know what to say to Barbara. They hadn't talked since the night they had parted outside O'Flaherty's. He fed Ghost another carrot.

"This is quite a trailer," she said, looking around.

"Yes, quite a change from the truck we brought him over to the track in. It's a gift from my two partners. It can hold four horses and has a sleeping deck over the cab."

"You're on your way now."

Unsure how to proceed, he said, "Yes, we are." Did he want to make up with Barbara? "I saw you in a private box with your mother. I didn't know you were interested in horse racing?"

"I'm not. Terrence Strickland invited my mother and me to share his box. I'm here with him tonight.

He needs to settle his bets. I can't stay long. I just want-ed to warn you to stay away from them."

"Away from them?"

Ghost snorted and tossed his head. Donal made sure he had both leads on the halter.

"Strickland and the others at the country club, es-pecially Terrence. He thinks you cheated on this race. He'll be out to get even."

"He'll get over it."

"Take this seriously. You've made some powerful enemies today."

Donal fed Ghost another carrot.

"Listen," he turned back to her, "I've been think-ing, Barbara..."

He was alone. Perhaps this was for the best he told himself.

Liam relieved him so he could join the party. Donal closed the trailer door and walked across the parking lot, slipped his keycard into the slot, and entered the hotel.

The party was in the Trinity ballroom.

Terrance Strickland held court by the bar with the group from the country club. In the far corner Terri Leahy held court with a group of men. Donal only rec-ognized the man he had talked to two weeks ago in the stable.

Mánus walked over to him, he held up a bottle of twelve-year-old Jameson.

"What is that for?" Donal asked.

"I was thinking that we could have a private party up in our suite or back in the trailer."

Before Donal could respond, Strickland held up a hand to try to silence the crowd. He yelled that he had an important announcement to make. He waited for the room to quiet down.

"That one is no better than he should be," Mánus said.

Strickland turned to Clancy and asked him something. Clancy looked in Donal's direction, pantomimed what was needed. Donal nodded. Clancy reached under the bar, pulled out a microphone and handed it to Strickland.

There was an irritating buzz over the intercom system, before Strickland said, "I want to thank our hosts," he looked over to where Donal and Mánus stood. Everyone in the room applauded and held up their glasses. When the crowd quieted down again, he said, "We were going to wait, but we, Barbara and I decided that this is a good time to announce our engagement."

Around Terrence, his friends offered congratulations and applauded. The people around Donal remained silent.

Strickland smiled down at Barbara, not a warm loving smile, but the smile of a man looking over his newest possession.

Donal didn't know too much about Terrence Strickland. Of course, it was Barbara's choice to make. He had to be the gracious host, even if it went against his personal feelings. He made his way through the crowd to the bar.

"I'd like to be the first to congratulate you," Donal said. "And offer a toast to your happiness."

Callie Weston, the young woman Mánus had arranged for him to bring to the party, joined him. Strickland gave them a smile that didn't touch his eyes. It reminded Donal of Barbara's warning.

"Clancy, champagne for everyone."

When everyone had champagne, Donal said, "To your future. May you have years of happiness."

Mánus was right about Callie looking good on his arm. She was tall with a stunning figure and long blonde hair that fell almost to her waist. The look on the faces of the men from the country club reminded Donal of children looking at candy. After another toast and some small talk, they moved back to where Mánus waited with the O'Briens.

"You didn't get any Krug, Mánus?"

"I was never one for that French stuff. Irish whiskey is good enough for me."

Mánus looked upset.

"Callie, would you see if the children are okay." Without a word Callie moved off.

"What's up?"

Mánus sipped his glass of Jameson. "No good will come of this, lad."

"You know something?"

"Your man there hates you. This is his way of getting even. Best to watch your back."

Before Donal could respond to his partner's comment. The man he had talked to two weeks ago in the stable came over.

"Hope I'm not intruding on anything?"

"Not at all," Mánus said.

"I wondered, you both had such serious looks on your faces. Let me introduce myself. I'm William Saunders."

Mánus held out his hand, "Pleased to meet you, Mr. Saunders. Have you met my partner?"

"Unofficially. Mr. Tolan, it is a pleasure to meet you again. I'll get right to business if you don't mind, then we can get on with the party."

For Donal the party was over.

Mánus never got right down to business. Like Liam, he liked to relax and talk, then over desert get down to business.

"Let's have a seat over in the corner," Donal suggested.

They sat down at a round table. Mánus placed his bottle of Jameson at the center. Donal signaled for a waitress.

"I never drink during negotiations."

"Bring us glasses," Donal told the waitress. "We'll save the drinks for later."

Mánus kept quiet while William Saunders outlined exactly what he wanted.

"You've seen Grey Ghost run once and you want to breed him with one of your mares?" Donal asked.

"I'm looking for fresh bloodlines," Saunders said. "Let's face it, you won by luck as much as by speed. Your horse is big and fast, I don't think he could keep up a long racing career. Therefore, we breed him into racing bloodlines. I was wondering if there are any other offspring from the match between Donegal Lass and your original stud."

"Warlord sired several promising foals," Donal said.

"Have I heard of any of them?" Saunders looked from Donal to Mánus.

"You should have, Spring Morning." Mánus said.

"Yes. She has potential. That proves that my idea is sound. I'm willing to pay seventy-five thousand, but a colt or filly must come out of the union."

Donal glanced at Mánus. His partner gave him a slight nod of his head.

"Before we shake, I'd better tell you I'm working hard to get your trainer to join my farm."

"Ms. Leahy isn't under contract with Forest Lake."

"Good," Saunders said, leaned forward and held out his hand, "Well, gentlemen?"

Donal took the hand offered, "You have a deal."

"Done," Mánus said, as he shook hands with Saunders.

᠀

Osgar's growl pulled Donal out of an euphoric dream. His arms were wrapped around Callie. Carefully, he disentangled himself and moved away trying not to wake her.

He slipped on his jeans.

On bare feet he padded to the door. "Guard, Osgar," he whispered to the hound.

The door handle rattled slightly.

Then there was silence, followed by a slight scratching sound, almost indiscernible in the early hours of the morning. Donal figured it would take them only seconds to pick the lock.

The door opened slowly.

Donal took a firm grip on Osgar's collar.

Osgar growled menacingly at two men framed in the doorway. The flashlight beam went from the Donal to the hound.

"Don't make me turn this dog on you."

The first young man dropped his flashlight, bumped into his partner as he turned, knocking him down. The other man scrambled to his feet and ran after him.

Seconds later an engine roared to life, tires squealed as a vehicle pulled out of the parking lot unto the street.

Behind him, Donal heard a slight noise. He turned, surprised, should he smile or raise his hands. Callie stood feet apart with a gun held two-handed in front of her. She reminded him of a Celtic warrior ready to do battle. No. Not a warrior, a Celtic Goddess.

All Callie had on was a green O'Flaherty's T-shirt; it came to mid-thigh, exposing her beautiful long legs. Donal wanted her more than he wanted anyone in his whole life. He forced himself to get control of his emotions. At the end of this weekend, they would go their separate ways.

"You can relax."

"Sorry," Callie said as she lowered the gun. "I saw what was going down, thought you could use some backup."

Going down? Backup? She sounded like a cop.

"Who are you?"

"A cousin."

"You don't look like an O'Brien or Scanlon."

"I'm a second cousin from Georgia," Callie said, flashing him her dazzling smile.

Her eyes gave her away. She didn't look him in the eye, looked to the left a little. She was lying to him, making up a story as she went.

"Really." He noticed she didn't name herself either an O'Brien or Scanlon.

Donal walked over to the door, picked up the flashlight and checked the lock. The lock looked undamaged, he pushed the door closed and locked it again, then tested it.

"Guard, Osgar."

Osgar moved over to the door and lay down facing it.

"That means you must be Tuathall and Anne's daughter. They live near Brunswick."

"Yes," Callie said, then looked puzzled. "What?"

"Let's try this one more time. There are no Scanlons or O'Briens of our clan in Georgia. I've met them all, including all the Ryans."

"Mánus said you wouldn't believe me if I said I was a cousin. You're too sharp for a ploy like that. I was hired by Mánus and Liam as part of security."

"I see."

"He also said you wouldn't like having a bodyguard."

"As usual he was right. Do you sleep with all your clients?"

"It just sort of happened. You're an extraordinary man, Donal Cullan Tolan."

He glanced at his watch. "It's late. I don't think those kids will be back."

"Are you sure they were kids?"

"I'd say they were punks who have burgled other property in the area. We have been having a rash of breaking and entering of late. Osgar will warn us if they come back."

"I could dress and keep watch."

Donal didn't want to think of Callie out in the parking lot keeping watch from a car or van. Perhaps he just didn't want to spend the night alone, not after his victory.

"It's late, let's go to bed."

She ran her fingers over the scar on his right side. "How did you get this scar?"

"A fight in my youth."

Donal followed Callie back to the ladder. He let her climb first, before joining her on the sleeping deck.

༄

"You should have told me about Callie, Mánus."

"You would have said no. This way I had you covered."

"I guess I had too much to drink at the party, I got a little carried away."

"Not you."

Mánus never brought up Donal's bout with drinking after Cynthia died.

"You needed company. Where is our lovely Ms. Weston?"

"After we drove back to Forest Lake, and settled our champion in his box stall, I drove her to the airport in Middleton. She made a connection in Chicago."

"Too bad you didn't keep her around a little longer."

"Nothing would come of our weekend together," Donal said. "Next time let me know what is going on, and while we are on the subject. Liam and you can stop trying to be matchmakers. I don't plan on marrying again."

"I'll pass the message on to Mary Catherine and Peggy Joyce. I don't think it will do any good. They feel that someone of your position should be married."

"See what you can do."

"I can only try, Donal."

CHAPTER FORTY-ONE

Donal sat at his usual place at the bar in O'Flaherty's reading the cyber news on his laptop. It was late afternoon, the quiet time between lunch and dinner.

"Did you read the sports section?" Tabitha Lynch asked.

"Not today, anything of interest?"

"Tom Spence, the sports writer, interviewed Terrence Strickland. They talked about the race last month."

"Is he still angry about the race?"

"Strickland says that the race was fixed."

"Really."

"He didn't come out and say it, but he alluded to the fact that he thinks Grey Ghost is a genetically enhanced horse."

"An Altie horse, interesting. Not true. I don't think he can prove it one way or the other."

Donal didn't like where this was leading. Strickland was a heartbeat away from saying that Donal was an Altie.

"What else?"

"Strickland said the racing commission should check into you and your horses."

"People will believe what they want to. Sometimes even when there is proof to the contrary."

What would he do if Strickland came right out and said he was an Altie? He would cross that bridge when he came to it. Worrying before you came to a problem was counterproductive to living.

Fred Scalla, a reporter from the Prescott Herald called a week later. Fred wanted to interview him for the weekend edition. Donal agreed. Publicity for the pub was good for business.

They set a time for the next afternoon.

After asking a few questions about O'Flaherty's, Fred Scalla asked if Donal had a comment about what Mr. Strickland had been saying.

"I'm not part of the country club scene. Even if I were, I wouldn't take anything Terrence Strickland had to say too serious."

"Well, you should be interested in this. He is saying that your horse is genetically enhanced and that he thinks you are too. He's telling anyone who will listen to his theory on how you won the race against an experienced horse and jockey."

Donal kept his face unreadable. "That's a new one on me."

"Then you are saying it isn't true."

"Of course it isn't true. I'm no different than Strickland or you."

"Can I quote you?"

"Of course."

❦

Tabitha Lynch put down the telephone. It was another cancellation. She told the caller that they would forfeit their deposit.

"This isn't good, Donal. This is the fourth cancellation for next weekend. We're going to have a lot of extra food. Should I call and change the food orders?"

"I hate to do that. It puts our suppliers in a tight place. Do you have any idea what is going on?"

Tabitha Lynch was a cousin of Liam O'Brien's late wife Deirdre Ryan. It was her idea to bring over several people from Ireland to staff the pub; it gave the place an authentic feel. She updated the menu and added a few Irish meals, and had married the barman, Thomas Lynch.

"Strickland is going around saying you're an Altie. Most people laugh at him. But if you say something long enough people begin to wonder if it could be true."

"People are afraid I'm an Altie?"

Tabitha nodded.

"Will this affect our business, our staff?"

"It sure looks like it will. Most of your employees are loyal to you. Anyone who leaves wasn't worth keeping in the first place."

Donal picked up his laptop.

"I'll be upstairs in the small snug. When Martin comes in after school, both of you come up."

Upstairs Donal closed the door for privacy, sat down and placed his laptop on the table. Placing his thumb on the track-pad, he keyed in Mánus's code and waited. He should have talked to his partner sooner.

Mánus appeared on the screen. "What can I help you with?"

Donal explained to him what was going on.

"It wasn't so long ago that people were afraid the Alties would take over the world," Mánus said.

"This could ruin the pub. First the private parties cancel; next our lunch and dinner crowd will drop off."

"Certainly it will be bad for business. However, in the long run I think not. I'll notify Dominic, see what his thoughts are on what to do. Strickland can't be serious, this is something that is too easy to check."

"What?"

"There are tests. At least that is what I've heard."

Donal didn't doubt for a second that his partner knew what he was talking about.

"So how do I get checked?"

"You don't, Donal."

"But..."

"Stay calm. The people who are interested in Alties will get in touch with you."

"Government men?"

"Yes. I'm afraid you are about to find out how good your identification really is."

"I'll have to cut back on the food orders until things settled down." Donal thanked Mánus and signed off.

Tabitha and Martin came in.

Donal filled Martin in on what was going on.

"What do we do in the meantime?" Martin asked.

"We stay calm and try to figure out what to do."

"Perhaps Jeff Lewis can help," Tabitha suggested.

"Good idea."

From a pocket in his computer case Donal took out a flash drive. He pulled off the protective sheath and slipped it into the USB slot. Then keyed a work form and wrote up an advertisement with coupons. The first coupon would be good for lunch or dinner, buy one get one free, equal or lesser value. The second coupon offered 25 percent off special dinners.

Donal went over all the extra food they would have on Friday and listed the dinners available. The second coupon was only good for next weekend.

He didn't bother to do a spell check; his system was set up to do it automatically. He hit eject, slipped the drive out, and put the sheath back on.

"Martin, take this down to the printer on Sycamore. I want five hundred fliers made up."

"Yes, sir. What if he can't print them today?"

"Bring it back and we will buy a printer and paper and do it ourselves."

Martin hurried out.

"Tabitha, the coupons are only a stopgap for our problem. Notifiy are suppliers that we have to cut back on the orders, in two weeks. We will have to wait and see if things get better or worse. Call Jeff, set up an appointment with him, see if we can see him this week. We need to go over with him all the options that might help us get though this."

❦

Tabitha worked every other weekend. Even though it was her weekend to work, Donal told her to take it off. He would work her shift.

She came in anyway.

"With Thomas working I might as well come in. My neighbor can watch TJ."

Donal was satisfied that the coupon helped, but they still had plenty of food left over on Sunday night. Donal had food packages made up for each employee to take home.

Through autumn business continued to drop off. To increase party bookings for the holidays they offered a discount of 25 percent with a nonrefundable deposit required. Donal wondered how long he would be able to keep the whole staff working.

He decided to wait until after the New Year before he made any drastic decisions.

CHAPTER
FORTY-TWO

On January tenth two men entered O'Flaherty's. Thomas Lynch said, "I've might be wrong, but it looks like the gardai."

Tabitha sat them in the side room. She came back immediately to talk to Donal.

"They're asking for you. I told them I would see if you were in."

"I'm sure they know I'm here. Tell them I'll be right over. See if they want anything to eat or drink. Then get Jamie and his brother down here."

"Cool as a cucumber. Doesn't anything upset you?" Tabitha asked, flashing him a smile.

"I've faced worse." He didn't feel that confident.

Donal watched Tabitha go around the bar to the side room. He wrote down a telephone number on a napkin.

"Please call this number, Thomas. Tell Dominic his special order is in."

In the side room, Donal glanced at the identification card that Special Agent Owen Smith held out to him. "This is my partner, Special Agent Eugene Camp," Smith said. Eugene held up his identification. "You have to realize, Mr. Tolan, that the FBI takes things like this very serious."

Sitting across from the two agents, Donal said, "Am I under arrest?"

"Come with us to our Springfield office," Camp said. "And we can get this over with."

"You'll have to wait until my lawyer gets here. You're dead wrong on this one. I was born in Ireland, not in some laboratory somewhere in the States."

"We checked your records and what you say is true. We still have to check out all complaints. Make this easy on yourself; come with us now. This way no one will know there was any question about you."

"I think it is too late for that."

Dominic had already warned him not to go with them, to wait for him to arrive.

"Who filed a complaint?" The agents wouldn't tell him, still Donal asked.

"That's restricted information, Mr. Tolan."

Donal sighed, exasperated, they were getting nowhere. "Fair enough, but I'm not going anywhere until my lawyer gets here."

"I don't understand the problem here. If you're not an Altie, then let's go get it over with."

"You have my records, I have nothing to hide. I just want to wait for my lawyer."

Jamie Ryan and his brother occupied a table across from the booth where Donal sat with the two agents. They made no pretense at being customers. Agent Smith's partner glanced in their direction from time to time. Both agents were aware they were there to protect Donal.

"We will be back, Mr. Tolan."

I'm sure you will be.

When Donal stood to go back to work, he was surprised to find Martin and Thomas sitting in the next booth.

Thomas Lynch picked up his shillelagh. "We just wanted to make sure they didn't try anything."

"Everyone can go back to work now."

"We'll see you home tonight, Mr. Tolan," Jamie Ryan said.

ᕲᕔ

Dominic arrived in time to have dinner with Donal.

"This has to be public, we don't want them spiriting you off to Springfield. We want your name cleared out in the open. I'll alert the video-stations and the local newspapers."

"You're going to force their hand."

"Oh yes. There is a precedent already. They'll be back and we'll be ready for them." Dominic paused, "There is nothing to worry about."

Did Dominic mean his identification?

Donal often wondered about Dominic, what was his story. Someday he would try to draw the lawyer out, and find out what was in his past.

༄

The light in the communication room changed as each new photo came on the screen. Strom J. Elliston studied each photo. Earlier he had glanced at the file Special Agent Smith had sent along with the photos. The face displayed seemed familiar. After working in law enforcement all his adult life he wasn't surprised, after a while you begin to think you had met everyone.

Elliston buzzed the control room to stop the program. He had seen enough. When he reached his office, he told an agent directly under him to contact Smith; he wanted to talk to him ASAP.

Smith had let things get out of hand. It was time to stop fooling around and bring in the alleged Altie. When his telephone rang half an hour later, he reached for it, intending to read the riot act to his senior agent. As he yanked the receiver off the cradle, the telephone slipped sideways into a pile of folders, sending them against the silver frame at the corner of his desk.

The frame wobbled and fell over.

Years ago, in an angry fit, he had knocked the frame off his desk breaking the foot that held it up. It had been a stupid thing to do. Beth, his late wife, had given him the frame their last Christmas together. He had fixed the frame with tape and put it back on his desk. Now the frame held a photo from last Easter of his daughter, son-in-law, and two grandchildren.

Elliston checked the tape on the back of the frame, and returned it to its place of honor.

As he picked up the receiver the memory of the fight with his daughter came back to him. Another memory followed it, unbidden. An encounter on a lonely road near Prescott, it was late, somewhere around midnight. The memory had faded to a point it seemed more dream than reality.

Now he remembered where he had seen the young man in the photos he had reviewed earlier. It was the man from the dream. He was older now; it had to be the same person.

He remembered then that Smith was waiting for him to answer. "Elliston here."

"Is there a problem, sir?"

"You've let this case get out of hand. I think it's time I came out to see that it gets resolved."

Special Agent Smith protested Elliston getting involved. Elliston wouldn't budge his position; after all, he was the boss. He needed to meet this man, make sure that it wasn't anything more than just a coincidence.

CHAPTER
FORTY-THREE

"I don't like this, Donal," Dominic said. "The director of the FBI doesn't get involved in cut-and-dried cases like this."

"Do you think they found something?"

"Perhaps, let's see what he wants. Let me do the talking."

Donal didn't like this new complication anymore than Dominic did.

"This must be him now."

The man that entered the room was in his late fifties, heavy-set, square-jawed, with hard eyes that stared out through aviator-style glasses.

Special Agent Smith made the introductions.

"Gentlemen, this has gone on far too long. At our regional office we can get this over once and for all," Elliston said in a no-nonsense voice.

"All we want is to have this taken care of locally and have a doctor of our choice do a second set of tests," Dominic fired back.

"Before I would consider something like that I need to talk to Mr. Tolan."

"No problem."

"Good. If you will wait outside with my agents."

"Wait a second." Dominic looked shaken. "I can't let you do that."

"Then I am prepared to take you both into custody."

"On what charges?"

"I'll throw every one of the hundred plus Patriot Acts at you. You'll find yourself and your client tied up in court for a long time."

Donal put his hand on Dominic's arm; the lawyer turned to him and shook his head.

"I don't like this at all."

"I'll be all right," Donal tried to reassure him.

When they were alone, Donal walked over to the windows. Below on Main Street nothing seemed different. The afternoon traffic moved along unaware of what was going on in the Prescott Hotel.

"Please, take a seat."

Donal turned to find Elliston watching him.

"Please?" Elliston asked again.

"Your name and the glasses threw me off for a second," Donal said. "Did you call your daughter?"

Strom Elliston went pale. He sank down on the couch. "So it really happened. After awhile I began to think I only dreamed that night."

"Why?"

"I don't usually pick up hitchhikers, but something about that night. The fight with my daughter and there you were."

"You told me your name was Jackson."

"It is, Strom Jackson Elliston. I..." Elliston stood and walked over to the bar and poured an inch of golden liquid into a glass and added ice.

He turned to Donal. "Can I fix something for you?"

Donal shook his head.

"I never told anyone about you."

"I was going home; the farm I inherited isn't far from where you dropped me off."

"I know. This morning I had City Hall send me all the information they had on the land along that stretch of the county road."

Elliston took a sip of his drink. "It was the way you were dressed in those old-fashioned boots and pants. Under your parka you were wearing a strange tunic and I could just see a leather lace, you had something hanging around your neck. The only modern thing, besides the parka, was your watch. It was as if you had stepped out of time."

Only someone who paid attention to details or someone in law enforcement would have noticed.

"You know I'm not an Altie."

"True, so why not just get this over with."

"You never answered me. "Did you call your daughter?"

"Yes. We patched everything up. The fight seems so juvenile now, but at the time I thought she would never speak to me again."

Donal sat down across from Elliston. "There is someone in town who wants to ruin my reputation. If the tests are done out of town he has won. I need to have them done here, very public, and with a local doctor, and yours too if you agree."

"If I say no I'm screwed, if I say yes I'm screwed."

"I don't follow your line of thinking."

"If you're not an Altie," Elliston said, "Then who are you?"

"Just a man like you, like agent Smith, my lawyer."

Elliston studied Donal over the rim of his glass. His eyes said he didn't believe Donal for a minute. He put down his drink. "Perhaps a man who likes to dress up in strange clothes and go hitchhiking around in the middle of the night, in the dead of winter. How could you have known that I should call my daughter?"

"I put myself in your daughter's place."

"I wish that is all there is to it. I read in the report about your wife. I'm sorry about your loss."

Donal nodded.

"I'm not asking for a favor."

"Good, because the director of the FBI isn't in the business of granting favors."

❧

Every newspaper and video-station in the Midwest sent reporters to cover the story. Security guards stood at the entrance to O'Flaherty's to keep the video-crews out. The once-sleepy farming town became a three-ring circus. News satellite vans clogged Main Street, taking up most of the parking places. Pat Junior, the mayor, met with the City Council, though there wasn't much they could do.

Wandering video-crews interviewed customers coming out of the restaurants and stores.

Business picked up at O'Flaherty's and all around town. Most of the Main Street merchants didn't complain too loud; they were seeing a boom in business. At O'Flaherty's people wanted to get a look at the man accused of being an Altie. Donal's notoriety would only last as long as he was the hot story. Eventually something more important would break and he would become yesterday's news.

He decided it was best if he stayed away from the pub and let Tabitha and Thomas run things.

Three days after the meeting with Strom Elliston, Dominic called Donal to let him know it was all set up.

"They agreed to what we want?" Donal asked.

"Yes, don't ask me why, but they did. Agent Smith wasn't happy. We set a date for February twelfth."

CHAPTER
FORTY-FOUR

Donal parked his Jeep behind Stan's Roadhouse and entered by the side door. Clancy was working behind the bar. Only a few customers sat on the far side of the room. It was quiet now; on Friday and Saturday nights the place would be crowded, the noise level so high you had to shout to be heard.

Clancy smiled at him and nodded toward the back rooms.

Donal walked around to the right side of the bar; in the back a chain blocked access to the private booths, set up when Stan's was a hangout for gangs during the bootlegging days. On the wall a sign read: Employees Only.

He unclipped the chain, stepped through, re-placed it, and walked down to the private booths. He stopped at the entrance to the left-side booth so he could watch Callie Weston. She had a compact out and was checking her makeup. As usual she looked gorgeous, her long golden hair perfect, makeup flawless, and stunning blue eyes.

Why had she gone into the security field? With her good looks and figure she could have become a model or video-star.

Callie sensed his presence, looked up and smiled.

"Callie," he said as he leaned over, he intended to kiss her on the cheek. He changed his mind and kissed her on the lips. They tasted like ripe strawberries. He slipped into the booth across from her. "Thanks for coming."

"Is this about your current problem?"

"No. I hope to have that resolved soon. This is about something else."

Callie had a slight accent that surfaced at odd times. Probably when she didn't think about what she was saying. He wondered if she grew up in the south somewhere.

"I have a position for you to consider. How long will you be working in Chicago?"

"About six months, perhaps a little less. What do you have in mind, Donal?"

"When your current contract is up, consider working for my company. We are thinking of branching out into the private security field. We could use your expertise."

"You could have called me on the phone. So what do you really want?"

Donal placed a manila envelope on the table between them. "I've been getting some nasty letters."

Callie pulled the envelope closer. Before opening it, she pulled out a pair of thin plastic gloves folded neatly in her purse. Donal noticed that she had a gun tucked into a side pocket.

She pulled the gloves on her long thin hands, before pulling the top envelope out of its plastic cover and read it out aloud, "Go back to where you came from or I'll tell. Interesting, do you think they are referring to the accusation of you being an Altie?"

"Yes. I think it is Terrence Strickland's idea of a sick joke."

She read another one. "Wow, vicious. Are they all about the same?"

"They are getting worse."

"If it wasn't for the content," she said, "this could be a joke of sorts. People just don't do this kind of thing anymore, they don't paste words together."

"Really."

"If it is Strickland, he has watched too many old cop videos. When did you start getting them?" Callie asked, all business now.

"After I formed TOSE, Tolan, O'Brien and Scanlon Enterprise."

"Could it be an inside job?"

"No," Donal answered a little too fast. The person, was referring to where he really came from. The implications were scary. To know where he came from you had to be one of the clan members that made up TOSE. He didn't want to believe that someone on the inside didn't like him.

"I wish it were as simple as a sick joke. I have a friend who is a profiler, helps out the Chicago Police Department. Let's have him take a look at them, see what he comes up with. I take it your partner couldn't find out anything."

"There are a dozen or more fingerprints on the letters, mostly postal workers, and mine. There is nothing to tell us who is sending them. The paper you could pick up at any office supply store, nothing on the newsprint either."

"They know what they are doing. Let's see what my friend says. Then go from there."

Callie slipped the letters into their plastic sleeves and placed them back in the envelope.

Donal was about to make the biggest mistake in his life. Worry about that tomorrow, he told himself.

"Have you eaten?"

"No."

"Good," he said and pushed the button on the wall.

After lunch, Donal walked Callie to her car. He kissed her again before she drove off. He went back inside and found Clancy waiting for him at one of the four-tops in front of the bar.

"I was hoping you would come back inside."

"Is there something I can help you with, Clancy?"

"Jason Strickland is back in town."

"I've never met him. He left town about the time I came back here to live."

"He was in here last night. I'd like to say he is a brick short of a full load. I think it is a little more serious than that. I think he is an arrogant, vindictive little bastard."

"That nice?"

"He thinks that you cheated his father and hopes that you get run out of town over being an Altie."

"I'll try to stay clear of him. My twins are several grades ahead of Barbara's oldest boy, and her daughter is four or five years younger than Rónán. I'll remind the boys to stay clear of all the Stricklands."

Chapter
Forty-Five

On February twelfth, Donal entered Prescott General Hospital through the delivery entrance to avoid the crowd that had gathered outside. Dominic, Mánus, and Cathal accompanied him; Jamie Ryan stayed with the car.

After the tests Donal planned to give a statement to the press and video-crews. He wasn't worried about the retina scan or the DNA profile. He wasn't an Altie. He had submitted to an extensive DNA profile when they formed TOSE. The results showed he was related to both the O'Briens and Scanlons.

At eleven-thirty the government doctor, John Lacy, performed the first set of tests, then Stan Updyke, the senior geneticist at Prescott General, preformed the second set.

Donal and his friends waited in an office for the test results to come back. Jamie brought in lunch, and later dinner. It was after nine when the test results came back. All four tests were negative.

"Mr. Tolan, no hard feelings," Special Agent Smith said. "We have to check into each complaint. There are some very sophisticated identification forgers these days."

"I'm just glad it is over."

From the safety of the hospital Donal stood with his friends; they watched the two doctors talk to the press.

When the doctors were finished, Donal pulled out his estate-linc and pressed the phone button, "Jamie, bring the car around."

As soon as Donal and his entourage stepped outside, the reporters surrounded them and thrust microphones in his face. Flashes went off like lightning on a stormy day.

Reporters yelled their questions at him.

"Are you going to sue?"

Dominic X. Monaghan, tried to quiet the crowd, had to raise his voice to be heard over the din. "Ladies and gentlemen, we have a statement to make."

"Mr. Tolan, are you innocent?"

"I came forward to clear my name," Donal said into the microphones. "This malicious attack on myself and my family is unfounded. I am not an Altie as you have already heard from the doctors."

"Are you going to sue?" a reporter shouted again.

"If I find out who started this rumor," Donal looked into the cameras, "I will consider a civil suit against them."

"Thank you, ladies, gentlemen," Dominic said. He slipped a card to Dan Kirk, the reporter from Channel 4.

Cathal and Mánus forced an opening in the crowd. As soon as they approached the car Jamie Ryan jumped out, opened the passenger door, and helped Cathal keep the reporters back.

"What did you pass to Dan Kirk, Dominic?" Donal asked as the car pulled away from the curb.

"He'll meet us tomorrow for an exclusive interview."

"It is time we looked into Strickland," Mánus said.

Donal wanted the feud to end here. It was too late to stop it.

"Check into his two friends, Charles Blesstin and John Tillman, while you are at it."

"Done."

Chapter
Forty-Six

The octagon-shaped building had four rollup garage doors on the west side, they were up today to let in the afternoon sun to warm and brighten the room. Jax DeVos gave the carousel one last inspection. Rob and Don Tolan were at the front of the group of more than a dozen boys and girls. Rónán waited with Martin along the railing. Not one of the children cared that it was an antique PTC Carousel. All they wanted to do was ride it.

From the Wurlizer Band Organ came the old-fashioned strains of music from a bygone era. The scrolls for the organ were imported from Germany. Donal had taken one look at the old gentleman who made them and ordered extra rolls.

Mánus watched the children for a minute, before he turned back to Donal. "You spoil them outrageously."

"They need extra love, they're orphans."

"They have you."

Donal turned to watch Sally Brown and Mrs. Murphy setting the tables for the birthday party. The twins were thirteen today, teenagers.

Perhaps he did spoil them too much.

Mánus broke into his thoughts. "It isn't every day that someone buys a carousel for his boys."

"It isn't really theirs. I set up a trust to see to the running and maintenance. They can come here and ride anytime they want to. Even bring their class for a field trip. Rob suggested that we have their party here. It's a great place for children to come for their birthday parties."

"Well, I'm glad to hear this carousel isn't a gift for them. I was worried that when they turned eighteen you would buy them a sports team."

"I plan to wait until they're twenty-one," Donal said, without missing a beat. "Haven't decided on the Cubs or White Sox yet. Or do you think I should go for the Bears?"

Mánus' mouth dropped open, he closed it and smiled. "You're having me on."

"Of course I am."

The Ryan clan entered by the back door. The two oldest Ryan girls wore skirts far too short for an afternoon children's party.

Donal frowned at his partner.

"I'll speak to Mr. Ryan."

"Have Dom speak to him, make it unofficial. If it happens again, we can decide if you or I will speak to him. Though thinking about it, I think you should talk to him, if it comes to that."

"You know what they say, Donal. You can pick your friends, but not your relatives."

Jax DeVos opened the gate. As one the children surged forward, a herd of pushing, screaming teens and tweens.

They scattered in different directions once inside the gate. The youngest Ryan children hurried to catch up. Rob headed for the lead horse. Don took the next horse in line. Martin lifted Rónán over the railing. He headed for a chariot with a pair of white horses with blue accents on the bridle. They would get one ride before the party started, then after the cake and ice cream it would run the rest of the afternoon.

"Seriously, Donal. I worry that Rob always gets his way. Everything just falls into his lap. One day something will go wrong and he won't be able to handle it."

Donal hoped that his friend was wrong.

They watched the carousel turn, lights and mirrored sounding boards giving it a festive look. Martin stood with the older boys, who were admiring the Ryan girls.

Sally signaled DeVos.

"Time for lunch." Donal stood, froze. Taydan stood on the far side of the carousel, just inside the building. Cold sweat broke out on Donal's brow. He blinked. In an instant Taydan was gone.

"Are you okay?"

"I'm fine."

"You should get serious about your friend in Chicago."

"I'm not going to marry again." Donal almost added, he didn't want to jinx another person he loved. Nor did he want to talk about it, even with his partner. How to get out of this without seeming rude?

Sally Brown saved him by announcing that the food was ready.

⌒

Mánus knocked on the door to Donal's apartment no the third floor. Inside Donal called for him to enter.

"Would you like some company?"

Donal closed his laptop. "Your company is always welcome. Can I get you something to drink?"

"Yes. Midleton straight up."

Donal stood and walked over to the bar. Into two old-fashioned-style glasses he pour several inches of golden liquid from a tall bottle.

They moved into the living room and sat down on matching wing-backed chairs.

"That was wonderful of you to save that old PTC carousel from being broken up and ending up in a private collection."

"We talked about this earlier," Donal said. "So what is on your mind?"

In answer Mánus reached inside his coat; from the pocket he pulled an envelope inside a plastic sleeve. He handed it to Donal.

Donal slipped the envelope out of the sleeve and read the message out loud: "Your partner isn't listening... he must go or you will both suffer the consequences."

"When did you get this?"

"Three days ago. It looks like the ones you received. I had MSS check it. They didn't find anything to help on it."

"It has to be someone on the inside, someone in our clan."

"It would explain why we haven't caught him or her."

"You aren't surprised?" Donal said.

"No. I've been thinking along those lines for a while. We'll start with the Ryans and go from there."

"Do you really think it could be one of the Ryans?"

"Shirttail relatives, everyone of them."

"Check them out. But I think it is someone closer."

"We'll check into it. Then, as Liam likes to say, we will know what is what."

CHAPTER
FORTY-SEVEN

Rónán hurried along Fourth Street. His brothers would be looking for him. At almost twelve it wasn't often he was allowed to go to the library on his own.

At Elm he ran around the corner, dodged around a man only to collide with a young girl knocking her off her feet. As he helped her up he realized it was Jennifer Strickland.

"Sorry," he said, waiting for the tirade that would follow.

"My fault. I should have seen you coming," Jennifer said. "I guess I was daydreaming."

Rónán smiled at her.

This was the first time he had met Jennifer. They didn't have any classes together. She was several years younger than he was. She had her mother's good looks and none of her father's surliness.

"Listen," he said. "Let me make this up to you. How about tomorrow? We could meet under the First Street Bridge."

"Sure, tomorrow, after school."

Rónán nodded agreement and hurried off to meet his brothers.

৵

Martin paced at the corner of Second and Main Street. Where was Rónán? Martin walked to the corner, was relieved to see his young charge hurrying down Main Street toward him.

Rónán waited at the light on Second; when the light turned green he joined his foster brother.

"What took you so long?"

"Sorry, I stopped off at Polreath's. They have the cutest black and white bunny."

"Have you asked Donal if you can get a bunny?"

"It's not for me. Carl has been talking about how one of the boys in the foster home where he lived had a bunny. It would make a great present for him. He graduates in June."

Martin was amazed. Carl hardly said two words to anyone, including Donal. Rónán seemed to have a way with people; everyone liked him, trusted him. He had more friends then the two twins combined.

Rónán glanced around. "Where are the twins?"

"Rob was hungry so they went on to the pub."

They crossed Main Street and continued walking along Second. At River Street they turned left. River Street, originally a towpath along the Prescott River, ran one way behind the businesses that lined the south side of Main. At O'Flaherty's they cut through the parking lot and entered by the kitchen.

Don Carlos, the new chef, smiled at them.

"Dia dhuit," Rónán said.

Don Carlos gave the appropriate reply in Irish, and said in English, "Can I make you something?"

"Sure," Martin answered. He was growing fast and needed all the protein he could get. "One of those super steak sandwiches with sweet potato fries would be great."

"And you little one?"

"An order of fries and a Harp, please."

"Sure, coming right up." Don Carlos winked at Martin.

Martin and Rónán moved into O'Flaherty's.

Donal was at his usual place at the end of the bar.

"How was school today?"

"Fine," Rónán said, looking around for his brothers.

"They're upstairs. As soon as you eat, Jamie can drive you home."

❧

Rónán turned left at Spruce, then onto River Street. He never thought of it as a street, more of an alley, or rather a boreen. When he was almost across from the parking lot behind O'Flaherty's he scrambled over the steel guardrail and hurried along the path that ran along the river.

He headed for the First Street Bridge.

Ever since the day he ran into Jenny Strickland, they met once or twice a week under the bridge. She was far different than her older brother Joseph, who enjoyed being the center of attention in school. Jenny liked to keep to herself. Rónán had never met the oldest brother Jason.

In the future, he would have to be careful. He was supposed to be at the library. Not exactly a lie, he never said he went, nor said he didn't. He hoped Jenny would be waiting for him.

Jenny sat tucked up under the bridge reading a book.

She glanced up, as if it was an accidental meeting and smiled.

"I won't be around for a few days. My dad and I are going to check out Andover. He wants me to take some summer classes there."

"Perhaps we should stop meeting," she answered. "If your father finds out you even spoke to me...I shudder to think of what would happen."

Jenny was in one of her dark moods.

"Listen, Jenny, my father is more understanding than most people think."

"Really. Then tell him about us."

His father would understand, he told himself. Then why didn't he tell him?

"I can't stay long. After I get back from Massachusetts. Perhaps we can meet over by the lake?"

"I don't know, Rón. I don't want to get into trouble, or cause you any. My father speaks about your father as if he were the devil incarnate."

"He isn't." Rónán bit his lip. This wasn't going as he had hoped it would.

"That race years ago gave my father one more thing to yell about. He never lets mother forget she used to be friends with him."

"I think they were more than friends. Anyway, that was when I was much younger."

Jenny smiled at his comment.

"I've got to go." Rónán was almost to a place where he could get back up to the street when she called to him.

"Rón, I hope you like Andover. I'm going to take a few classes there next summer too."

He turned, smiled, and waved. He hadn't been sure about going until now.

CHAPTER
FORTY-EIGHT

Robert sat down on the bench and began his afternoon ritual of tying his running shoes.

"I'll be right back," Martin said. "As soon as Rónán is done with his class we'll join you."

"Don't be late, you'll miss my run."

"You and Donald warm up. I'll be back in time."

Martin looked around. It was strange; the usually busy three-school campus was deserted. He shrugged off the feeling of unease and headed across the street to the middle school.

Inside, Theodore Roosevelt Middle School he found the halls a little busier. Jay Tealy was waiting for his younger brother.

Martin nodded at Jay.

"I see you got the warning too."

The bell rang, doors opened with loud bangs as groups of children came out yelling, pushing each other, gesturing with their hands. Rónán came out a few minutes later, surrounded by his friends.

Puzzled, Martin asked, "What warning?"

"That something was going down at the track this afternoon. Everyone was told to stay away."

"The track?"

Martin turned and ran to the door. Behind him Rónán called to him to wait. Martin crossed the street at a dead run without bothering to check traffic. He slowed at the gates to the athletic field.

It was empty.

Where were Robert and Donald?

He ran along the bleachers looking for Robert or Donald. Near the end he heard angry shouts from back near the fence. The shouts turned to screams of pain.

In a second Martin took in the scene.

Robert lay on the ground curled up on his side clutching his right knee. Donald was being manhandled, two young men held him by the arms, while the leader, bat in had, swung in an arch, as if taking a practice swing. He laughed when Donald flinched in fear as the bat was laid alongside his head.

"Not a word to anyone about this," said the youth with the bat. "It was an accident, he slipped on the track. Remember, or I'll come back and get you too."

Martin didn't wait for an explanation. He charged into the fray.

Someone shouted, "Shit, it's Martin!"

The two young men holding Donald ran, leaving their leader to face him. Now Martin recognized the face: it was Jason Strickland.

Jason pushed Donald, "Get away, skank."

Donald stumbled back, regained his balance and hurried to help his twin. Jason moved to meet Martin head on.

Unarmed, his father, had taken down armed men. Martin had to stay calm, outsmart this amadan. Jason held the bat over his shoulder as if he were waiting for a pitch. But to Martin's surprise, Jason flung the bat aiming for his head.

Martin sidestepped the missile.

From his jacket pocket Jason pulled a long knife with a spring-activated blade. His opponent meant business. This was more than just a casual mugging. Martin feigned to the left hoping to draw Jason that way. When Jason shifted his position, Martin switched to the right and came up under his defenses.

They fell backwards in a tangle of arms and legs. Martin grabbed at the hand holding the knife to keep Jason from using it. Jason managed to slip out of his grip and roll away.

Martin struggled to his feet.

With the knife poised for action Jason came at Martin again. This time Martin caught Jason's arm, pulled the knife out of his fingers. As he pushed Jason back he heard a cracking sound. It reminded him of the sound dry wood made as it snapped in two.

"You bastard, Jason screamed. "I'll see you in jail for this." Tears streamed down Jason's face. He made it as far as the end of the bleachers before he collapsed on the ground, pulled out his cell phone and started to punch keys.

Martin pulled out his estate-linc, switched it to phone, and waited for the call to go through. He looked around, surprised to see KC Little sitting under the bleachers smoking, watching the fight as if it were a video-show.

Down toward the gate there were shouts. Rónán was running along the back of the bleachers toward him with an older man that must be one of his teachers.

In the distance sirens wailed.

❧

At O'Flaherty's, Donal received a series of calls, each one worse than the one before. He called Dominic first, then a local attorney. With Jamie a step behind him he went out the back entrance to his car.

His first stop was the hospital. There he found Donald and Rónán sitting in the emergency waiting room with Fred Weiss, one of his youngest son's teachers. Both boys had been crying. When they saw Donal they ran to him. Donal knelt and held his sons close. They needed reassurance that everything would be all right. He gave them the comfort they needed. When the tears subsided, he stood.

Jamie handed them tissues from a box on a nearby table.

Donald told his version first, before Rónán told what he had witnessed.

"Jamie, take the boys down to the cafeteria. I'll join you as soon as I talk to the doctor and see Rob."

"It's down the hall and to the left," the teacher said. When they were alone they moved over to a deserted area of the waiting room.

"What happened?"

"Robert said that Jason hit him across the knee with a baseball bat, hit him several times. And as Donald told you, he threatened him. Scared him pretty bad."

"What did you see?"

"I came later. Jason must have called Terrence; he arrived first. The police came later. The way he tells it, Martin and the twins jumped him and his friends. That Robert got hurt while they were trying to protect themselves."

Donal studied Fred Weiss. "I understand one's reluctance to take on Strickland. Hopefully, later on, you will remember what you saw."

Fred Weiss's face turned red.

Donal stood. "Thank you for waiting with my boys."

"No problem. Your sons will be suspended over this."

"I'm expecting the worst; that they will be expelled from school."

Donal had to wait a few minutes before the doctor had time to talk to him. The news wasn't good.

After that he went in to see Rob. As he walked along the small makeshift rooms with curtains for walls, he realized he hated coming here. Cynthia had died here. Be fair, he told himself, they had helped Rónán years ago.

Rob looked so small and young lying in the hospital bed. His eyes were closed. Donal leaned over and placed his hand on his son's forehead. They must have given Donald some thing to ease the pain, his eyes looked glassy

"Take it easy, son."

"They arrested Martin. This is all Jason's fault."

"Easy. I know."

"Am I going to be all right?"

"I'll get the best surgeon in the country. But there is only so much they can do. Some things have to be borne."

"But you can fix it, right? Mom said you could fix anything."

"I'll do everything I can."

Donal's next stop was the jail. He hoped that Dominic would get here before Martin was arraigned.

He had to make a lot of noise before they would let him in to talk to his foster son.

They were allowed to talk in an interrogation room. Someone was watching from behind the glass panels so Donal spoke to Martin in Middle Irish.

"Dominic is on the way. I also have a local attorney ready to be with you if he doesn't get here in time."

"I'm sorry to bring this trouble down on you."

"You didn't start it. Maybe next time Jason will think twice before fooling around with us."

"Will I be expelled?"

"Probably. Don't worry about it."

"I don't want to have to go to school out of this area."

"I don't think you will have to. I've given it some thought on the way over here. If we are forced into home schooling, so be it."

Martin nodded.

"I don't understand why Jason wasn't brought here after they fixed up his arm."

"I don't know where he went. After the ambulance arrived, I lost track of him."

Donal had a bad feeling about this. Jason could be on a plane headed to Canada, or more likely France. He didn't tell Martin that.

"Jason's two friends are backing his story. Was anyone else present that you remember?" Donal asked.

"KC was there."

"KC?"

"Keith Charles Little was sitting under the bleachers. He witnessed it all." Martin paused. "He had a cell phone with him. He might have recorded the fight. There is also Rónán and his teacher. They were close enough to see that Jason pulled a knife on me."

"I figured he might have seen something. Now all I have to do is get him to tell what he saw. What do you know about KC?"

"I would say a pretty standup guy."

"Good. Things aren't looking as bleak as they did before. Don't worry, no matter how high they set the bail, I'll cover it."

Donal told Jamie to take Donald and Rónán home and to explain things to Mrs. Murphy and Sally Brown, then meet him at the courthouse.

After the arraignment, Martin was allowed to return with Donal to Forest Lake. As Jamie drove them home, Donal's thoughts were about Rob. His oldest son prided himself on his running. He hoped to make the Olympics next year. Not likely now; he would be lucky to walk without a limp. Of course they would try everything, including stem-cell replacement.

◦◦◦

Keith Charles Little came forward the next day. With the graphic evidence recorded on his cell phone, charges against Martin were dropped. Donal expected to hear any day when Jason's trial would begin.

Donal was surprised when Dominic called to tell him that Jason's lawyer had advised him to throw himself on the mercy of the court. He was sentenced to two years in a readjustment center; his two accomplices were given a year each.

In a way, Donal was glad that there wouldn't be a trial. He didn't want the twins and Rónán to have to appear in court and relive what had happened that horrible day.

It wasn't going to help Rob, he was having trouble dealing with his injury.

CHAPTER FORTY-NINE

From the second floor the sound of something crashing against a wall or floor reverberated through the silent house.

Donal hurried up the stairs with Sally Brown close behind him. On the second floor he turned left to the direction the sound came from. He found Donald standing outside his twin's room.

"What happened?"

Before his son could answer him, the door flew open and Dr. Peliteir hurried out. Abusive words were aimed at his back. He shut the door with a bang that made it vibrate in its frame.

"This is it!" Peliteir said as he hurried in the direction of his room. "I won't take this kind of abuse."

"Sally, go down and let Martin know the good doctor will need a lift to the airport."

Donal opened the door to Rob's room. His son's leg brace lay on the floor near the door. Without making a comment he closed the door and picked up the brace, placed it on the chair by the dresser.

Rob sat up in bed, ready to throw his alarm clock. When he saw it was his father he placed the clock back on the nightstand and leaned back against the headboard.

Donal waited for his son to tell him what had happened. What had triggered his latest bout of anger aimed at his doctor.

Rob crossed his arms over his chest.

When Rob didn't say anything, he asked, "What happened?"

"I can't stand that brace."

"The brace will help you walk."

"I want to walk like everyone else. I want to be normal again."

Donal sat down on his son's bed. "You are normal, son."

"I want to run again, to do all the things I did before Jason Strickland ruined my life." Before Donal could respond, he said, "I want to try stem-cell surgery."

"The best doctor is in Boston. You can recuperate with your grandfather after the operation."

"Is it expensive?"

"That is beside the point. If it helps, that is all that matters. Rob, you have to understand that it doesn't work for everyone."

"I have to try it"

"I'll call the doctor today."

CHAPTER FIFTY

Donal called Mánus, asked him to keep an eye on Jason and let him know when he was released.

Before signing off Donal asked him a question that had been nagging him since the fight.

"Do you think this will put an end to the letters?"

"At least until he is released. If they start up after that, I will have someone follow him, try to catch him in the act."

The subject of Jason Strickland came up again when he was released early for good behavior.

"It looks like Strickland gave Jason a one-way ticket to California to live with a cousin," Mánus said. "That's where he was sent last time he had to leave town."

"So I don't have to worry about another confrontation between Jason and my sons."

"I don't think he will ever return to Prescott."

After Donal told Rob that Jason was not returning to Prescott, he wondered if he had done the right thing. As Rob matured, his anger at having to wear a brace grew. For a long time his anger was centered on Jason Strickland.

Now his anger seemed to turn toward Donal.

Everything came to a head on the Sunday Martin was to drive Robert and Donald to the airport in Middleton, from there they would fly to Chicago and then to Boston. They were going to stay with Robert Long over the summer.

Rob's cruel words found their mark, ending with; "I am never coming back!"

Donal doubted that he would ever forget the words his son shouted at him. All he wanted to do is erase to-day's heartbreak from his mind.

He never would.

He hurried to the stables.

Inside the stable, he flung his sports coat over the half-door to Ghost's box stall before he swung the door open. He whistled a few notes. Ghost moved out of the stall and waited for Donal to put on the bridle and saddle. Instead, Donal led the tall stallion outside to the stable yard.

"Sorry, old friend, no carrots. Perhaps later."

Donal grabbed a handful of mane, jumped onto the broad back. With a gentle squeeze of his right knee the stallion turned along the practice field and corrals. At the end they turned north. When they passed the last fence, Donal gave Ghost his head.

To the sound of Ghost's thundering hoofs came the words Donal wanted to forget.

Never. Never. Never.

I am never coming back!

At the lake they turned northeast and rode around to the back. When they reached the dock, Donal slowed Ghost to a walk. He sat on the dock, letting Ghost drink at the edge of the lake. After a rest, they were racing across the estate again. With the silky gray mane whipping him in the face, and the wind stinging his eyes. They didn't stop until they reached the northwest corner and the back gate.

At the back gate they rested again. Streaks of gold and blue in the western sky told Donal that it would be dark soon.

At a slower pace they returned to the stable.

It was dark and well past the dinner hour. He hoped Carl had gone to his room. Donal was tired, more from the words his oldest son had shouted at him earlier in the day than his long ride. He walked Ghost down to his stall. Before putting him to bed for the night, he untangled the long silky mane and tail, brushed down his coat and checked each hoof. He closed the bottom door.

From the small refrigerator in the back he took out carrots to feed to Ghost. When the carrots were gone, he filled the manger.

At the stairs he debated going into the house though the kitchen. Sally Brown would wait up for him. He entered through the solarium, locking the door behind him.

On the solarium table he found a tray with several covered dishes and a pot of tea and a mug. Carl most have heard him in the stable and let Sally know he was back. He picked up the tray.

He decided to go into the library. They would never look for him there.

The large library in the west wing, with its tall windows and floor-to-ceiling bookcases, in the center stood the Four Horsemen in bronze. They rode upon a seven-foot solid oak table. The statues were over five feet in height and took up most of the table. Placed around the table were two couches and several armchairs. Donal set the tray on an end table and walked over to the statue.

On the open second floor gallery of the Celtic Studies Building in Chicago hung lithographs of his late wife's Four Horsemen; the original paintings were on loan to the Museum of American Artists in New York.

Donal sat in one of the armchairs. Here in this house, where the twins had grown up, it was hard to forget what had happened earlier. Surely Rob would rethink his words. He reminded himself that Rob wanted to be called Robert now.

Tomorrow Donal would talk to their grandfather.

After Donal finished his meal he moved over to the leather couch, leaned back, and let his eyes close. In a minute he told himself he would go up to bed.

Donal woke, surprised to find he was lying on the couch in the library, sunlight streamed through the windows. Someone had placed a comforter over him. On the table sat a fresh pot of tea and several slices of wheaten and brown bread with a monkey dish of Sally's homemade blueberry jam.

He poured tea and helped himself to a slice of bread. It was still warm. He applied a generous layer of jam before taking a bite.

Mánus's words came to Donal, "Your son is spoiled. He gets his way all the time. One day, mark my words, he will have to face something you can't fix and he won't be able to handle it."

Did he spoil Rob?

Perhaps.

Donal finished his breakfast, dismissed thoughts of his son and Mánus. He hadn't changed for his ride yesterday. Time to go up to his room and shower. He left the food tray on the table in the main hall.

After his shower, he would go below to the stable and see what he could help Carl with. Willy John, Carl's helper, had two weeks off.

Donal planned to fill in for him.

CHAPTER
FIFTY-ONE

Carl closed the back door, crossed the mudroom and stepped into the kitchen. Sally Brown stood at the stove preparing lunch. Mrs. Murphy was setting the table. Both ladies turned to him as he entered.

"You're early," Sally Brown said.

"I need to talk to Rónán."

"He's in the solarium with Martin. Go on through."

Carl hesitated, he never felt comfortable in the main house.

Sally Brown turned from her cooking. "Go on. You're not going to see the King of Ireland."

No, just the crown prince.

Carl moved into the house, past the main stairs and into the living room. He crossed the long room with its fireplace and antique furniture. On the baby grand piano stood the latest photo of Donal and Grey Ghost.

At the French doors Carl paused, before he knocked on the wooden frame.

Both Rónán and Martin looked up.

"Did you want me?" Martin asked.

"No. I need to talk to Rónán."

Martin stood. "I'll go up and change before lunch. How are thing going below?"

Carl looked away, how could he answer the question? And still be both civil and honest.

"That bad," Martin said, he exchanged a look with Rónán. Then, to Carl's surprise, Martin closed the French doors and motioned for Carl to take a seat.

Carl sat; a request from Martin was almost the same as one from Donal.

Martin moved to the sideboard, poured tea into a cup, and set it in front of Carl. Rónán closed his laptop and set it aside. Martin refilled their cups and sat down again.

"So what can we help you with?" Rónán asked.

Carl didn't know where to start; after a minute he blurted out, "It's your father."

Martin exchanged another look with Rónán and sat back, an unreadable look on his face. No one said anything. Carl was worried. Had he made a mistake?

"I'm sorry, I...shouldn't..."

"Don't feel bad, Carl. There is nothing to apologize for. We know what you are going through. Martin and I were discussing it earlier. In a few days your helper will be back and things should settle down again."

"I don't think I can last another few days. Your father is working me to death, I can't keep up with him."

"I'll talk to my father. Where is he now?" Rónán asked.

"He took a few horses out to the north pasture to graze."

"You go ahead and have your lunch. I'll wait for my father to return and talk to him."

Carl gulped down his tea and stood. "Thanks."

∽

Rónán heard his father calling for Carl before he heard the sound of his boots on the flagstones outside the stable office. He wished he had taken Martin up on his offer to stick around.

Donal entered the office. He looked surprised when he found Rónán sitting at the desk.

"Where's Carl?"

"He went up to the house for lunch."

Donal didn't glance at his wristwatch, instead he turned and glanced down the hall to the open stable door. His father often told time by the sun.

He turned back to Rónán. "It's a little early for lunch."

"I told him he could go up early."

Donal started to say something, then closed his mouth, and moved over to the desk. He grabbed the folding chair leaning against the wall. Opened it and sat down.

"Did that hurt?" Rónán asked.

"What?"

"Did it hurt when you were cut by the whip?"

"You've heard the story before, son."

"I like hearing it."

"You're the only one..."

"Da, I am sorry."

"Don't be, son. It wasn't any of your doing." he paused. "I guess I brought it on myself. Did Carl ask you to speak to me?"

Rónán nodded. "Da, you have to slow down, you'll kill yourself. And us too," Rónán said and smiled at his father.

"It helps to forget what Rob said to me. If I keep busy I don't think about it."

"Really?"

"Well, not as much." Donal sat back, resting his head against the wall and closed his eyes for a minute. He opened them again, "It helps me to sleep too. And not see things..."

"Are you still seeing Taydan?"

"My partner wants to get into my head and you want to shrink it."

"Sorry! It is just that I worry about you. How does he do it, or you for that matter."

"Do what?"

"How do you keep Mánus out of your head. Or vice versa."

"Someday I'll try to explain it to you."

But not today, too bad, his father needed something to take his mind off of Rob.

"I guess Martin could pick up the slack until Willy gets back."

Rónán watched his father. His thin face looked haggard, with dark circles under his eyes. He asked Martin why he hadn't stepped in that day. Simple, he said, "You never get between a father and son."

What a time for me to be in town, he had missed the whole thing. Later Martin had given him the terrible details.

"Did I spoil him too much?" Donal asked more to himself then his son.

How to answer the question? "Not any more than Donald or me."

"Well, what is done can't be undone."

"Perhaps, Da. Time will tell." He loved his father more than he could ever tell him. Why didn't Donal see this day coming? "Let's go up and eat in the kitchen like old times."

There was indecision in his father's eyes.

Things would never be the same again.

Never.

Not when it came to the Rob.

CHAPTER FIFTY-TWO

Rónán walked straight to the back of O'Flaherty's to pick up his father.

Donal looked up and smiled. "You want to drive?"

"Sure, Da."

As they drove home in silence, Rónán thought about Jenny. Would Donal understand about her? At some point he would have to tell his father.

Jenny had been his friend ever since the day they met under the Main Street Bridge. Later they met in the park on the other side of Elm Street.

"I've been thinking of going to a local college."

Donal turned from watching the passing shops on Main Street. "Why?"

"I don't want to commute back and forth to Chicago."

"What brought this on? You don't have to make a decision right away, you have time to think about which college to attend. I thought you might want to go to a college out east. You could stay with the twins or your grandfather."

"I would prefer to go to some place nearby. I received a letter from grandfather, he said the twins started college early."

"Yes he told me. It's your choice of course. It would be nice to have you home on the weekends. Are you still thinking of going into the medical field?"

"Psychology."

"That sounds heavy. Plenty of time to think about your future."

"You've been alone for a long time. You should think about getting married again."

"Are you afraid I'll be lonely when you go to college? Is that why you are thinking of going to a local school? Martin will be here."

"You're still young, you should take Liam up on one of his fix-ups."

"I'm too old and too set in my ways. Besides, I'll never find another lady like your mother...she..."

Rónán waited to see if his father would finish, when he didn't he said, "Martin says his aunt, Moya, cares for you."

"Moya is a young girl. One day she'll grow out of her crush on me and fall in love with someone closer to her own age."

"She must have grown up by now, you've been saying she is nothing but a girl for a long time."

"Son, I don't plan on getting married again."

Rónán glanced over at his father. They were at the road that would take them to Forest Lake. He turned the car right.

You're afraid to marry. *Every woman you have ever loved has died.*

"You look tired. When you're not working around the farm, you are at O'Flaherty's. You have competent help. Take a vacation. Spend some time in Chicago, or go home for a visit."

"I know...but..."

"You're always relaxed when you come back from home.

CHAPTER
FIFTY-THREE

Donal took Rónán's advice and went to his other home in Cwillan.

He sat halfway down the incline among small bushes. From here he had an unobstructed view of the young boys below swimming in the Glas River. Their work done for the day, they played at the edge of the river jumping from the rocks into the green water.

He turned at the sound of footsteps on the path above. Fionnbar came into view. Donal waved at the boy so that he would see him. Fionnbar the youngest of Lord Niall's sons was thin for his age and looked much younger than his true age.

Donal welcomed his company.

When the boy began to cough, Donal reached over, "Are you okay?" he asked in Middle Irish. Fionnbar gave him a weak smile.

Donal handed him his water bag.

Fionnbar unstopped the bag and took a sip. He handed the bag back to Donal. "Have you decided yet?"

"Not yet."

Lord Niall felt it was time for Donal to foster one of his sons. He wanted Donal to make the decision. It had been easier with Martin. He stood out among his brothers, showed good leadership skills even at a young age.

With Niall's boys it was different. Kenn the oldest and Fionnbar the youngest had the Power in varying degrees, neither were strong like their father. Only Fionnbar seemed interested in joining him.

"Did you need something?" Donal asked.

"Moya sent me to tell you your meal is ready."

Donal stood and stretched.

Fionnbar watched the boys below. Their happy cries echoed up to them on the late afternoon breeze. There was longing on Fionnbar's young face. Donal wished as he had on many an occasions that he had the Power to heal.

"Come. If we are late Moya will be angry with us."

What Fionnbar lacked in good health he made up for in a gentle spirit and intelligence. At the top they turned south along the path that paralleled the river. Then up hill on an old dry streambed for a league; at the top was a small glade.

The cottage Donal used when he visited Cwillan stood at the far side almost hidden among the trees. He whistled to let Moya know he was back.

Before they entered the cottage Fionnbar stopped him. "If you spoke with Moya, she could teach me what I would have to know to care for you."

Surprised and puzzled, Donal asked him, "Is Moya going somewhere?"

"She was betrothed last winter. When she marries, she will leave Faolán."

"I will speak to Moya about it."

Donal had to stoop to enter the low doorway.

"Good, you are back," Moya handed Fionnbar a bowl. "On the hill behind us you will find early berries, pick as many as you find for later."

Fionnbar hurried out, always happy to help.

Moya busied herself with the evening meal. She was kin to Lord Rónán. Martin called her his aunt, but they were actually second or third cousins.

After her father's death, her mother had taken Moya and her younger sister to live with her clan. At the age of eight summers her mother had died. Mór brought both girls back to Faolán and raised them with her own children.

Moya had gladly taken on the care of Donal whenever he returned to Cwillan.

Watching her work around the cottage gave Donal a peaceful feeling. He remembered her as a thin, quiet child. Always helping Mór with the many children at the seat of Guardians. She used to sit upon his knee, until she grew too tall.

When she married everything would change between them.

"I understand that congratulations are in order," Donal said.

Moya glanced up at him, before she shrugged her thin shoulders before returning to her work. She wore her long auburn hair pulled back into a long braid.

Donal was treading on dangerous ground. They had spoken about this matter before. Up until now Moya had refused every suitor, held out for the man she loved. The man she loved was too old for her and he had told her so.

Still she waited.

He was glad she would marry soon, sad too. They had become good friends.

"Is it a good match?"

"As good as can be expected at my age. He is an ambitious man, hopes to move up. I fear he uses my foster father's clan as a way to gain prominence, and perhaps also land."

"Is it official?"

Moya nodded.

To break a betrothal, the husband to be or head of the clan of the bride would have to go before a brehon with a valid reason why they wanted the arrangement set aside. There would be a heavy debt of compensation paid to the wronged party. It would be a great hardship on any clan.

Before he could respond to her answer, Fionnbar hurried in, put the half-filled bowl down on the table with a thud, and ran to the niche by the hearth where Donal kept his sword.

"Someone is riding up the path. I saw him from the hill," Fionnbar said, struggling with the heavy sword.

Donal met him halfway to relieve him of his burden.

Moya already had the escape door in the back corner open; she called to Fionnbar to join her. Donal hurried to the front window to peer through a small hole in the wooden shutter.

Across the glade, someone had stopped in the gloom at the edge of the trees.

In the stillness of the late afternoon came the cry of a curlew. Donal waited. Then came the up-scale and down trill that was the second signal. One taught to him by Fred Tolan years ago.

"Friend," Donal said and smiled at his companions.

Donal stepped outside and gave the answering call. At a walk Kenn, Niall's oldest son led his horse across the glade.

"Welcome, son of m'anam chara."

Kenn sketched a bow. "Lord, my father sends his greetings. He would have me remind you of the wedding in three evenings."

"I will be honored to attend. Will you break bread with us?"

"I am to return tonight, with my younger brother." Kenn looked back toward the trail on the far side of the glade.

"Is there something wrong?"

"Coming up from the river path I had the feeling that someone had followed me. He smiled down at

Fionnbar, reached over and tousled his hair "I am sure it was only my imagination."

"I am to be trained to help Cullan Donal." Fionnbar stood to his full height. "Later when I grow up I will be his Guardian."

Donal watched Kenn over his brother's head, fixed the young man with a questioning look. Kenn turned from Donal to busy himself with his horse.

Moya broke the silence. "Do not dishonor your lord," she said from the doorway. "It is late and a long way to your father's holding. Stay with us the night."

"It will be my pleasure."

"And you," she said to Fionnbar. "We still need those berries."

When they were alone Donal questioned Kenn. "Why was Fionnbar never told?"

"This is something you will have to take up with my father."

"I will bring Fionnbar with me to the wedding," Donal said. "At that time I will speak with Niall."

"Mar is mian leat."

After the evening meal, Kenn and Donal sat on wooden benches before the hearth. Kenn filled him in on what had been happening in Cwillan since his last visit. He never mentioned Feargus, but stuck to affairs of the different clans in the immediate area.

Moya brought them ale.

It was a pleasant night, but soon Kenn excused himself to go to his bed. The young man would sleep with his horse in the small shelter behind the cottage. At first light he would return to his father's holding.

Fionnbar shared the bed-box in the small side room with Moya.

Donal, deep in thought sat by the fire. Years ago he had slept before a hearth in the small cabin owned by Fred Tolan. So much had changed since those days. The years had piled one on the other; they were full years, lonely years at times.

If only he were ten years younger, he sighed. Even ten years younger he would still be too old for Moya. In his heart, he loved her; in his mind, he was too old for her. She deserved better, a young man who would give her children.

Donal's thoughts turned to why Niall had not told his youngest son that he had the Power. He found no answer to why. It had been a long day. Soon his eyes began to close on their own. He pushed back the benches and made his bed on the warm stones in front of the hearth.

Fionnbar hurried through his morning duties and was off to catch fish for their evening meal. When he hadn't returned by the time the sun was high in the sky. Donal went to look for him. He found the boy lying on a large flat boulder that hung out over the Glas River.

From his inside pocket Donal slipped out a tiny photo disk and recorded several frames of Fionnbar. The boy sensed his presence and looked up. Donal took one more photo before he returned the disk to his pocket.

"What was that that you had in your hand, Cullan Donal?"

Donal slipped a flat stone out of his pocket. It was the same silver-blue color as the photo disk. "Just a strange blue stone I found up in the hills."

Fionnbar took the stone from him to examine it. After making sure it was only a stone, he returned it to Donal.

"What do you see in the water?"

"Fish, they hide in the shadow made by the boulder. I was hoping to catch one more." He hurried across the boulder, jumped to the grass. At the edge he leaned over and pulled out a string of fish. He held them up for inspection, pride on his young face.

"You did good. I will make you Master Fish Catcher."

Fionnbar beamed up at him, pleased that Donal thought he had done well.

"Do you know how to clean them?"

"No. Will not Moya clean them?" Fionnbar asked without guile.

"Yes she would, but she works very hard, so I will show you how to clean them when we get back to the cottage."

Donal took the string of fish from him and they started up the path, Fionnbar in the lead.

"I was hoping I could meet your brothers before I have to make the decision."

"Neither of my brothers wants to go with you."

This morning Donal had decided on a plan for his friend's youngest son. "And you, do you feel the same?"

Fionnbar stopped on the narrow path, which forced Donal to stop as well. Did Fionnbar also fear going with him. Niall's youngest son turned slowly, a strange look on his young face.

"My father said that I would also be considered for the honor. Until now I never really believed him."

"Why would you not believe your father?"

"Rea, my older sister, laughed at me when I told her I was going to be the one you picked. She said you would never consider someone as sick as I am."

Donal knelt down to face Fionnbar. "You've been sick?" Fionnbar nodded. "You are well now. Of course I would consider you."

"My father has been worried, but It is not important now."

There was something Fionnbar did not want to tell him. He could see it in his eyes. Now he was sure he had to speak to Niall.

Donal stood. "We better hurry now, Moya will wonder what has happened to us."

CHAPTER
FIFTY-FOUR

At Forest Lake, Martin took his Wolfhound, Scolán, down to the stables. Then they crossed over to the garage. From there they walked up the drive to the second gate, then along the wall to the first gate. Both gates were locked.

Satisfied that everything was as it should be, he walked around to the kitchen entrance and went up to his room on the second floor.

Scolán took his place by the short hall that led to Martin's walk-in closet and beyond that his office. He never had trouble sleeping; he drifted off in minutes.

When the familiar tune on his estate-linc began to play, Scolán jumped to his feet and barked. Martin was awake in seconds; only a few people had his personal number.

"Is Donal back?" Mánus asked before Martin could say anything.

"I expect him any day now," he said, noting the strange quality to Mánus's voice. "Has something happened?"

Scolán paced the room, at the window he barked, giving Martin an eerie feeling.

"Is that your hound?"

Martin told Scolán to lie down. Instead the tall hound paced to the door, then back to the window, put his huge front paws on the sill, and barked again.

"Quiet, you'll wake the whole house."

Scolán returned to his place and lay down.

"Sorry. Did you say there was a problem?"

"I've had this strange feeling all day. Tonight I had a dream about Donal. When I woke up I couldn't remember the details, only the unease. Now your hound senses something is wrong."

"Nothing strange there, he saw a rabbit this afternoon on the front lawn, he wants to go catch it."

"I suppose I'm making too much of this. Sorry to call so late."

"No problem. I'll have Donal call you as soon as he gets back."

Martin turned off the light and lay back in bed. He stared at the ceiling unable to get back to sleep. The security light from the front of the house made strange patterns on the Belgium Swirl ceiling. He was too deep in thought to see them. Mánus wasn't flighty. So what was really behind his call?

Strickland came to mind whenever there was trouble. Thoughts of the last time he had seen him filled his mind. He was standing with Donal on the street in front of O'Flaherty's. Terrence's limo pulled up, he jumped out before his chauffeur had a chance to open the door for him.

"Are you satisfied?" he shouted, his face purple with rage. Martin remembered wondering at the time if he would have a stroke.

"Your son started this. In the future stay away from me and my family."

"I'll get you for this," Terrence said, getting in Donal's face. Martin moved to get between them. To his surprise Donal signaled for him to back off. He turned away from Strickland, dismissing him, as if he were of no importance.

"Let's go."

Martin didn't know how long he stared up the ceiling, thinking about Terrence Strickland. When Scolán stood, his collar tags jingling, he padded to the hall door and scratched at it.

"Easy, boy."

Martin slipped out of bed and moved silently to the door and opened it with a jerk. Farther down the hall someone was standing near the stairs.

"Rón, is that you?"

"Sorry, I didn't mean to wake you. I came down to see if you were still up."

Martin flicked on the bedroom light. "I wasn't asleep. Go down to my office. I'll slip into something and meet you there."

When Martin opened the connecting door to his office, he found Rónán studying the sketches on his office wall.

"They're lithographs of four of the sketches that became the 'Four Horsemen'. Do you want something to drink?"

"No, not really," Rónán said, as he examined the sketches. "I wish I had a chance to get to know my mother."

Martin didn't know what to say to his friend. He moved over to the couch and sat down. "So what has you up so late?"

Rónán sat down across from him. "I had this strange dream. I can't remember just what it was about, but it left me with the feeling that my father might be in trouble."

"You too?"

"What?"

"Not me. Mánus." Without explaining, Martin pulled out his estate-linc, keyed it for an outside call, and dialed Mánus. He made a connection almost immediately.

"Sorry to disturb you, sir. I think you need to talk to Rón."

Martin handed Rónán the phone, stood and walked over to the liquor cabinet. He took out two glasses, poured an inch of golden liquid into each.

Rónán wasn't on the phone long. Martin handed him a drink. "So what did Mánus think?"

"He says he will be here as soon as he picks someone up."

Martin stepped over to his desk, opened his laptop, and placed his thumb on the track-pad. When it came on he typed a note for Mrs. Murphy, alerting her that Mánus and Cathal would be visiting and probably with at least one guest.

~

Mánus arrived late the next afternoon. Cathal drove, they had Brid and Tomás and their daughter, with them.

"This looks serious, if he brought Brid with him," Rónán said to Martin.

Brid introduced Rhyianna, their daughter.

"Shall we go back to Donal's office," Mánus suggested.

Brid stopped inside the office door. "His presence is strong in this room."

"Please, sit down." Mánus motioned toward the couches at the other end of the room."

Instead Brid wandered around the room touching this and that. After going from one end of the room to the other, she sat down behind Donal's desk.

"What has happened?" Mánus asked.

Brid didn't answer right away. She placed her hands palm down on the polished desktop.

"One world is out of balance. It has been for some time." Three coins rested in an ashtray on the right hand side, old Irish punt coins. Brid picked them up. "Our worlds are like these coins. She set each one up and spun it. The three coins spun around and around.

The coin on the right wobbled and ran into its neighbor, sending it into the third coin. All three coins fell over. "One world out of balance affects all worlds."

She set two coins spinning.

"Something that should not have happened, happened, creating an imbalance. Each year the spin becomes more erratic. Now, without correction, not only that world but ours is in danger."

"Is my father okay?" Rónán asked.

Brid spread her hands out on the desk again. Rónán began to worry when she didn't speak.

"His future has always been uncertain," she paused, then said, "Only your father can right his world, for this affects him the most."

"I don't understand."

"If your father returns, both worlds will be in balance again. If not, something terrible will happen there! And here!"

CHAPTER FIFTY-FIVE

The wedding of the brother of Lord Niall's wife, Siobhán, to a clan from the south followed the old traditions. After a service in the chapel at Boweayn, they sat down to a sumptuous banquet. At that time the marriage contract would be read.

The bride wore a long linen shift with an overdress of pale silk, in her braided hair she wore a wreath of early summer flowers. The groom wore a tunic and leggings of linen, his hair and beard were trimmed and combed. The bridal party sat at a long table at the front of the hall, with the guest's tables arranged so they faced the couple.

Donal was seated at the first table closest to the bride and groom. He stood and gave a toast right after his host. He stayed through several rounds of toasts to the newly wedded couple. Later, after the guests had drunk too much, the toasts would become lustful and very descriptive.

As soon as he felt he could leave without appearing rude, he slipped through the side door and out into the night.

Overhead in the vaulted sky millions of stars twinkled. He climbed the steps and walked along the top of the curtain wall. At the eastern side he stopped to look out over the valley of Boweayn.

He remembered the fateful day he had fought Artúr in this valley. It had been close, the battle could have gone either way, yet they had won. Artúr had panicked when he thought himself caught in his own trap.

"Evening, lord."

Donal turned from his musing.

Had he met this man before? He had not been introduced to all the wedding guests. It would seem rude on his part to ask his name. He wished they were still in the hall where he could get a better look at him. Donal became uneasy when the man spoke not a word, just stared at him.

Laughing voices below broke the spell.

"Forgive me for disturbing you." The man turned and walked along the curtain wall, disappearing into the night.

"So this is where you are hiding."

Donal turned at his friend's voice.

"I was hoping we could talk, Niall."

"Kenn mentioned as much. Whom were you speaking with?"

"He did not say."

"One of the wedding guests, I am sure. Is this about Moya?"

Donal sighed. "This is not about Moya, though I do worry about her as well."

"If you married her, you would not have to worry."

"We have been over that before. I need to speak to you about Fionnbar."

His friend turned to look out over the valley. "There is not much to tell. It was a hard winter, he took to his bed with a bad cough." Niall turned and leaned back against the wall. "We feared he would never get up again. His illness left him pale and very thin. He kept to the room he shares with his older brother. Nothing brought him joy."

"What does your healer say?"

"Another bad winter and he will not live to see the summer."

The news saddened Donal. "Fionnbar seems better now."

"I told him that you were in need of a foster son to accompany you to your land. It was like a miracle; he rose from his bed, put on his clothes. Each morning, he forced himself to walk a little farther to build up his strength. He even talked Moya into letting him help her."

"You were not pleased, Niall?"

"When you leave, I fear the worst."

"Would you allow him to come with me? My healer might be able to help him."

The silence between them stretched on, finally Niall spoke, there was hope in his voice. "Are you sure?"

"Yes. The other boys do not wish the honor. I am sure that Fionnbar will say yes. If by chance he says no, I will speak with his brothers."

"Let us hope he will say yes."

In the morning Donal would speak to Fionnbar.

If he agreed to come with him, he would come back for him at Samhain.

Rónán joined them.

"What news of Ciarán?" Donal asked.

"Feargus keeps him busy. He will try to be here before you leave. How is my son?"

"Your son is a credit to the clan of Guardians."

CHAPTER FIFTY-SIX

Carried on the wind, the curlew call pulled Donal out of his thoughts of Moya. He turned back to see what the problem might be. Kenn pantomimed to him that someone was riding along the trail they had just come down. They dismounted and led their horses off the trail, trying to move silently through the brush. They left their horses in a copse of trees. Behind bushes they waited to see who was following them.

Fionnbar rode by at a canter, clinging to the horse's mane, barely able to keep his seat on the large horse.

Kenn stepped out into the path and called to his younger brother.

Fionnbar reined in his mount, fought the horse to turn it, and rode back.

Donal helped him dismount.

"You must come back. Moya has been called to Cwillan, the brehon wish to speak to her. Please, Cullan Donal, you must save her."

"What are you going on about, little brother?" Kenn asked, as he came up with the horses.

"Moya needs Cullan Donal's help."

Donal gathered the reins of his horse and sprung onto the animal's broad back. He tugged on the reins to turn back the way they had come.

"Cullan Donal, wait," Kenn yelled and grabbed at the headstall to stop him.

"I can make faster time alone."

"You will need another mount. There is a farm at the western crossroads. Give Old Sheeny my name, he will give you a fresh mount. May the Father and Son go with you."

Donal urged the horse into a canter, then into a gallop. If he rode all night he could be in Cwillan by first light.

The day turned hot even in the shade of the tall trees. Donal rode all day, only pausing to rest and water his horse. It was dark by the time he came to the crossroads. He waited, impatient, while Old Sheeny's son saddled a horse for him.

As the sun came over the mountains, Donal rode his mount up to the gates of Cwillan. He called to the guards to open the gates. After much grumbling the small window in the gate opened.

"Who wishes entry here?" said a sleepy voice.

"Lord Cullan Donal, kin to Feargus."

"Forgive me, lord."

Without closing the window the huge gates began to open. As soon as there was enough room to pass through, Donal entered and rode up to the summit.

He left his mount at the stables and hurried across to the main entrance. The guards lounged on either side of the door. When they saw Donal they came to attention, crossing their long spears, barring his way.

"Do you know Ciarán?" Donal asked.

The youngest of the guards said he knew Ciarán.

Donal fumbled under his brat, found what he wanted. He held up two gold coins for the guards to see.

"Wake Ciarán, tell him the man he wishes to foster his son with would speak with him. I will be in the stable." He handed the guard one coin. "The other when you bring Ciarán to me."

⟲

Arms crossed, Donal leaned against the rough stone wall. Ciarán paced back and forth, telling what he had heard about the summons.

"Rónán says he is an ambitious man, perhaps he has found a better match. If so, he will use Moya's care of you to break the betrothal. He will say that she is no longer a virgin."

It was a lie; Donal had never even given Moya a brotherly kiss.

"If the brehon rule in his favor, it will be a great burden to her family," Donal said. "Does Mangan know who I am?"

"I think not, and neither Rónán nor Moya will drag you into the matter."

"And if I come forward?"

"Perhaps Mangan has paid off the brehon."

Politics were the same everywhere. No one was beyond taking a bribe.

"I could appeal to Feargus?"

"You would take your chances with the Ard Ri?"

Ciarán knew how things stood between Feargus and Donal. Would his son help him?

Donal didn't hesitate. "To save Moya, yes. This is not fair to her or her clan."

☙

From the shadows of the gallery above the High King's hall, Donal watched the proceedings. Mangan pleaded his case for breaking his betrothal before the brehon. He wanted compensation; his honor and reputation had been wronged. The young man stated the facts: Moya was staying with a man in the hills.

When he became suspicious of her absence at her foster father's holding. He had a servant follow the son of a friend to a cottage in the woods.

"I was told that he was an old man, yet when I met him at the wedding feast, I found that it was a lie."

So it was you that night.

Moya sat at the front of the hall, head held high, as befitted a daughter of the clan of Guardians. When

Tole asked her if she had anything to say, she told him her father would speak for her.

Rónán stood to give their side of the story. "The daughter of my heart cares for an old friend of our clan. There is nothing between them."

Mangan jumped to his feet. "Then bring him forward. Let us meet this *old* friend, so we all might judge the truth to the matter."

"It is not fair to drag my friend into this," Rónán said.

The hall fell into silence as Tole, the head brehon at Cwillan, conferred with the brehon who had accompanied Mangan to Cwillan.

Donal had promised to wait until called before the brehon. He could wait no longer; he hurried down the stairs only to find a guard at the back door. He explained the situation to the man.

The guard would not budge.

"I was not told that one of the witnesses would be entering by this door."

"Speak with Ciarán, he will vouch for me."

"Stay here.

Donal hoped to slip inside as soon as the guard was away from his post. However, when the guard stepped into hall, another came out to take his place.

Donal paced back and forth.

When the door opened and Ciarán came out, he looked none too happy. Before Donal could speak, he saw the problem. Pilib, Feargus' reachtaire, followed him.

"Rónán wishes not to involve you, lord," Ciarán said.

"Then I will come forward on my own."

Pilib turned to the guard. "Escort Lord Cullan Donal to the main entrance, where he can give his name and he can tell us what brings him here."

Donal followed the guard down the passageway. As he entered the Hall, Pilib bent to speak with Feargus.

"I understand we have someone who would like to speak," Feargus said in a deep voice so that all assembled could hear. "Come forward and state your name."

Donal moved to the front of the hall, bowed to the Ard Ri and to the brehon, then to Rónán and Moya.

"So you have come forward at last," Mangan said.

Tole stood. "Careful, this is no common man that has come forth this day."

Mangan studied Donal for a moment, before he turned to lodge a protest with Feargus.

Feargus held his hand up to silence him.

Was Mangan blind that he did not see the likeness between the High King and Donal? It was the hair that threw everyone off. Feargus' dark hair, like his mothers was very different then Donals. Feargus had Donal's eyes, the same set of his mouth when he was displeased with something.

"State your name for the court and tell us what brings you here," Feargus said. He was pleased with the idea of hearing what Donal had to say.

"Ard Ri," Donal said, bowed again and turned to the Tole. "My name is Cullan Donal. It is true; Moya brought food to my cottage and saw to my needs. Sometimes she would stay the night."

Mangan jumped up. "See, it is true!"

Feargus gestured for him to take his seat. "Go on," Feargus said, enjoying seeing his father's discomfort.

"On the nights that she stayed at the cottage, the son of a close friend stayed with us. Moya and the boy shared the small bed-box in the side room. I slept in front of the hearth."

Feargus leaned forward. "Moya is this the truth?"

Moya nodded, then turned and looked at Donal. For the first time he saw in her eyes what he had been trying to deny to himself for years. He saw her love for him.

Tole stood. "Will you swear before the Father and Son that this is the truth?"

"Yes," Moya said, in a strong voice.

Tole hesitated, before he said, "Do you also swear that this is the truth, lord?"

"Yes, by all I hold holy, this is the truth." Donal glanced over at Mangan; the young man scowled back at him.

The brehon did not take long to come to their decision.

"Your betrothal will be set aside, Mangan," Tole said. "But only because there is no trust between the two of you. If there is some compensation owed, it certainly is not to you. You may go."

Before Donal could speak with Moya, Ciarán came forward.

"Feargus wishes to speak to you."

"Do you know what he wants?"

"All he said was that it is important."

∽

Up in the Ladies Bower, Donal sat in the shade of the grapevines that grew along a framework set against the inner wall. Clusters of grapes hung above his head, in time they would ripen and made into wine. Bees buzzed among the vines, the only sound in the lazy afternoon.

From the river below a dragonfly appeared, flitted around, then turned and landed on the wooden table. Its iridescent wings and blue body with large green eyes looked more like a fantastic jewel fit for a ladies' shift than an insect. Seconds later, it was off again, on the hunt.

As the sun moved toward the horizon a servant brought out ale. Donal wanted to refuse the ale, wanted water, but pure water for drinking was not always available.

As the afternoon turned toward twilight Feargus and his Queen, Niamh, came out of the inner rooms accompanied by Ciarán and two personal guards and several of the queen's ladies.

Donal stood and bowed to the High King and his Queen. She held out her hand to him. He took it and kissed it.

"It is always good to see you," Niamh said, a slight asperity to her voice.

She would be happier if Donal went away and never returned. How his son felt he was never sure.

Niamh clapped her hands. From her apartment an older woman hurried, carrying a small child with dark brown hair, dressed in linen with a thin golden circlet around his head.

"Our son, Fintan."

Donal's first instinct was to reach for his grandson. He held back though, waited for Niamh to make the offer. When she didn't, he said, "A fine name, for a fine son. May the Father and Son protect him always."

"I need to speak to Cullan Donal," Feargus said, dismissing everyone.

Only Ciarán remained.

They moved over to the benches below the grape arbor.

"If you had married the girl, we would not have the problem we had this morning," Feargus chided him as he removed the gold circlet from his brow. He rubbed his damp forehead, reached up and found a place among the grapevines to hang the circlet.

Long ago, Donal remembered doing the same thing.

Before he had a chance to respond, his son turned and signaled Ciarán, who disappeared inside for a moment.

Servants brought bowls of warm water for them to wash their hands. Before placing a bowl of washed grapes from Solaria and ale on the table. Donal was surprised that his son had taken to his suggestion that hands needed washing before eating. Feargus helped himself to the grapes.

"This problem should have been resolved long ago." He fixed his eye on Donal. "No comment?"

Donal was about to tell him it was none of his business, thought about it, and changed his mind. Perhaps his son was trying to close the gap that always seemed to be between them.

"Moya deserves better than me, someone young who can give her children."

"Better than you? I have heard it said that there is no better man in all Cwillan than Prince Cullan, the hero of Boweayn. Though many do not know you by that name." Feargus chuckled, "You could have stood Mangan on his head." He reached for another handful of grapes. He took his time, eating one grape at a time. "There is the matter of compensation owed to Moya and her clan. By saving her you have condemned her to a lonely life."

Donal expected the worst as he waited for Feargus' judgment.

"Tole and I discussed it. Two horses of the very best quality would be about right, do you not think?"

Donal let out his breath with a sigh of relief, he was afraid that Feargus would command him to marry Moya. "I will see that it is arranged."

"Take the horses yourself. It is your problem, you must deal with it."

"I will take care of the matter before I return to my own land." To change the subject Donal said, "You have been up to Carracán. Do you plan to restore it?"

"My grandmother died there, along with innocents. I keep it as a place to go when I have things to think out. If the slaughter there had never happened, everything would be different."

Donal waited.

"Your life was shaped by the horror of that day and your exile in Wyneth. If it had not happened you would be Ard Ri here and I..."

"Would be my tanist."

"No, father. I might not even be. For Briana and your daughter would not have died. If you had no male heir, your daughter would be your heir."

Donal was surprised at how deep his son had thought this out.

"If things were different I might not have even met Briana and might have married your mother anyway. The past is to learn from, not to worry over. You can not rewrite history."

"Yes, you are right. Come, Ciarán, join us."

CHAPTER
FIFTY-SEVEN

Rónán studied Moya. "Child of my heart, do not take news of the horses seriously. I am sure they are for compensation, nothing more."

Moya shook her head. "He will come for me. Matched horses, a bride's gift, I am sure. Foster father, we must be ready for Cullan Donal when he comes."

Rónán sighed. Why was life so difficult?

ᕲ

Normally, Donal would be happy to have Ciarán's company. Today, he represented the High King, his duty to see that Donal kept his word and delivered the horses to Faolán.

East of Cwillan, near the Gap of Laoghaire, Donal and Ciarán rode south. The fortress of Faolán, the seat of the clan of Guardians, was a four-morning ride.

The village just outside the fortress was busy as they rode through.

They could not help but notice the garlands of flowers hung over doorways. Men and women, in their best clothes, bid them a good day as they rode by.

"It must be market day, or perhaps a local feast day."

"On the way back," Donal said, as they rode out of the village and on toward the fortress, "perhaps we can stop for an ale."

"I am surprised that you have any coin left to think about ale, with the price of these two beauties," Ciarán said.

Donal glanced back at the two matching chestnuts. He did not comment; for some unfathomable reason he would be in need of strong drink soon. He dismounted before they reached Faolán; he wanted to walk the rest of the way or perhaps delay what was to come.

Ciarán dismounted also. "I will stay back." He held out his hand for the reins of Donal's horse.

Donal sighed and nodded. The sooner this was over, the sooner he would return home.

Why was home always were he wasn't?

With a pull on the leads, he led the chestnuts across the drawbridge. He glanced up at the portcullis; above in the winch room men watched all who passed beneath them. The guards came to attention as he passed into the courtyard.

Just inside the gate a fat matron moved forward, bowed, and offered him a cup of ale.

"To wash the dust of the road from your throat, lord."

The ale was cold and nicely spiced; a young girl stepped forward to take his empty cup, a second maid held a bowl with water to wash his hands.

"My compliments to the Ale Master."

"Welcome to Faolán," the maid holding the bowl said, sketching a bow.

Dubhloach, Rónán's second son, and his reachtaire hurried across the courtyard to meet him. "Lord, you should have sent word that you would be joining us so soon."

"How did you know that I was coming?"

"News travels fast here. My younger brother heard from a farmer to the north of the beautiful matched chestnuts you bought at the Clairdh horse fair."

This was not good. Did they think that the horses were more than compensation? Was it possible they thought the horses a bride's gift?

The head groom, came forward to take the horses.

Dubhloach escorted Donal up to his father's solar.

One look at Rónán's face told Donal that something was wrong. He sat down on a bench with his back to the windows. He listened to what the head of the clan of Guardians had to say. Then he tried to explain his side of the story.

As his partner liked to say, he made a dog's dinner of the whole thing, a total mess.

"I was afraid that this would be the outcome. Is it Moya's age?

"How old is she?" Donal asked, remembering her as a child.

"Twenty and six this summer."

She was far too young, Donal thought.

"I see by the look on your face that she is too old. She would still make a good wife."

"This is all Feargus's fault."

"Do not be so hard on your son, perhaps he only wishes to save your life."

"Save my life?" What did his friend mean? Save my life, indeed! Complicate it was closer to the truth.

Rónán looked at Donal as if he were one of his many children. "Your youngest will be grown soon. Think about it, Cullan Donal. When he marries, what will you do? You have devoted your life to caring for him and his older brothers. A man needs more than his horses. And a cold bed becomes colder as we grow older."

Rónán stood. "If you do not wish Moya for your bride, it is best that you tell her yourself. Perhaps then she will understand, and the matter will be settled once and for all."

࿔

Donal followed the path from the fortress to the meadow half a league to the south. After four days on horseback, he welcomed the chance to stretch his legs.

The late summer meadow bright with afternoon sunlight was empty. He followed the tracks left in the tall grass to a stand of Rowan trees. Through the dense growth of trees, patches of blue were all that showed of Loch Faolán and Half Moon Bay below.

The sound of old and young voices drifted up to him on the breeze. They were happy voices. Now and then, several voices joined in song as the women worked, getting ready for the feast day on the morrow. Younger voices added harmony to a song about life.

Donal thought it best to wait until they came up to return to the fortress. He walked along the headland. Here the trees grew lower down on the ridge and he could see out to the blue sparkling waters. Halfway down the loch a dark object detached itself from the rocky shore, a colorful blue sail lifted into the air, billowing out as it caught the afternoon breeze. The flatboat moved down the length of the narrow lake toward the fortress.

At one time flatboats were common on the lakes and rivers of Cwillan. The use of the cumbersome raft-type boats had given way to modern boats that were faster and easier to handle.

As he returned to the path in his mind he tried to arrange the words to tell Moya.

Harsh words pulled him out of his thoughts.

"What would you know about love with the dullard you have chosen?"

Donal smiled at Moya's voice.

"Old is old, and he is old. Perhaps it is you who are mistaken."

"Don't bother with the óinseach," yelled a voice similar to Moya's.

Minutes later, a dark-haired woman emerged from the path. Startled at seeing Donal, she dropped her basket. She hurried to pick it up. Turning quickly so he would not see she had blushed crimson as she fumbled the clothes back into it.

"Forgive me, my lord," she mumbled.

Confused, he watched her hurry back toward the fortress.

Next a group of women came up the path. The youngest were girls in their early summers, they giggled as they passed, giving him shy glances when they thought he was not looking. The older women nodded at him, following the girls. The oldest, a grandmother, stopped to talk to him.

"Is there something I can help you with, lord?"

"I seek Moya, mother."

"Moya and her younger sister stopped to watch a boat on the lake."

"I saw it from the headland."

"They won't be long, the boat will put in at the bight closer to Faolán."

He watched the women and girls. Soon they were lost to sight. Time passed and still Moya and her sister did not appear. Worry nagged at him. What if there had been an accident? He started down the path of split logs, pegged into place to form steps.

"Fóir orainn!"

Startled by the cry for help, Donal quickened his pace, he was right; there had been an accident. The sight that greeted him when he cleared the trees stopped him in his tracks.

At the water's edge the flatboat rested, sail down, oars on the deck. The steersman on the right side waited, the steering board pulled out of the water as far as possible, so the boat could get in close to shore. At the bow stood a robed and hooded man, he jumped to the sand.

Donal recovered in a heartbeat, pulled out his dagger and ran toward the men dragging Moya and Siúi, her sister, toward the boat.

When the hooded man saw him he shouted to his men, turned said something to the steersman and jumped aboard again, with an oar he pushed the boat out into deeper water. They stopped the boat a dozen paces off shore.

"Hurry!" yelled the hooded man.

The men pulled their captives into the water.

Siúi managed to pull away from her captor, who held a knife at her side. She struggled through the water to throw herself at the man that held her sister. Outweighing her by many pounds the big man handled her with ease. He fisted his hand, she flew backwards from the blow, disappearing beneath the water.

Slowed by the water, Donal hoped to help Siúi before she drowned. "Release Moya," Donal yelled, as he pulled Siúi up.

Through his mane of long, tangled black hair and full scraggly beard the big man scowled at Donal. He dismissed him and turned dragging Moya closer to the flatboat.

"Kill him," shouted the hooded man.

The voice sounded familiar, but Donal didn't have time to think about it. The big man turned back to study him; a smile split his hairy face revealing broken yellow teeth. He turned to his companion. "Take this one. If the young one gives you trouble, kill her."

Siúi, still coughing up water, tried to pull away from Donal and resume the fight. "Let me go, they will have Moya on the boat soon."

"Stay here." At the men he yelled, "Stop, before it is too late!"

"I think it is too late already," the big man said. "We would have returned the women when their clan paid the ransom."

Ransom?

Did he really believe that?

There would be no return; no witnesses left to go before the brehon. Donal splashed through the water, closing the gap between them.

With a bellow of rage the big man charged. He wrapped his arms around Donal in a bear hug, before he had a chance to use his dagger. Donal was lifted off his feet for a minute before he was dragged toward the beach. They fell on the wet sand at the water's edge. The air was knocked from Donal's lungs as his assailant came down on him. His dagger flew from his hand. He barely had time to pull his legs up tight before the next onslaught.

With all his strength he kicked; the big man reeled backwards, caught his balance, and rushed forward again. His large hands bit into Donal's neck. In the heat of the moment, Donal was unable to concentrate enough to put an end to the fight.

He was struck hard across the face. His vision darkened, sparks of light flashed before his eyes. When he came to his senses, the big man was holding a rock to bash him with. He struggled, rolled away, and regained his feet. Missing his target, the big man turned and headed for the boat.

Donal ran after him, catching his arm before he reached deep water; he yanked him around to face him, fisted his hand and hit the man hard. The shock from the blow sent pain shooting up his arm, yet it seemed not to bother the big man.

"So you have not had enough," the big man said as he tried to catch Donal in another bear hug. Donal ducked driving his fist into the man's stomach. The big man caught him, they rolled over; dark water closed over Donal's head.

How long could he hold his breath?

Not long enough!

He clawed at the man holding him down. With his lungs aching, he thrashed out with his arms.

His fingers closed on something hard. He struck at the man, fear or an adrenalin rush gave him a new strength, he struck over and over, hoping to hit him on the head. The full weight of the man came down on him again, then seemed to rise, and lift a little.

Donal struggled, choking and gasping for breath. As he rose from the water he blinked, pushed the hair from his face and scrubbed water from his eyes. As he threw the rock away, he glanced at the dead man floating face down in the water, a red stain mingling with the water.

Moya fought like a tigress, but in the end was no match for the men as they pulled her aboard the raft. Donal reached the boat just as the sail was raised. He pulled himself aboard, found his balance and grabbed an oar. He stood facing the three men, ready for battle.

The men stared at him. The hooded man picked Moya up, threw her into the water, turned, and yelled to the steersmen to drop the steering board and move out into the lake.

Moya disappeared beneath the dark water.

Donal dropped the oar and dove in after her. He swam to the area where he thought she had gone down. He dove down, searching for Moya, found no sign of her. He came up gasping for air. He dove down again. Panic set in when he didn't find her. He broke the surface for air, and went down again.

His hands closed on something soft, lost his grip and had to search again. When his fingers found her again, he gripped tighter and pulled her to the surface.

She coughed up water, and resumed the fight, only to relax when she recognized Donal. He let her catch her breath, before he had her move behind him. With her arms around his neck he swam toward shore. When they were in shallow water again, he helped her stand.

As the flatboat slipped out into the lake, the hooded man let his hood slip back.

"Mangan!" Donal shouted.

"This is not over!"

"You are damned right!"

Siúi waited at the water's edge for them. Donal put his arms around Moya and her sister. Moya hugged him; her body shook as she cried against his chest. He kissed the top of her head.

"It is over, grá."

One minute Siúi was standing with them, the next she slipped down to the sand, clutching her side.

"Siúi? What is it?" Moya cried.

Donal turned her over, noted the seepage of blood through the tear in her shift and apron. He picked her up and carried her higher on the beach, laying her on dry sand. All the color had drained from her face.

"Do you feel well enough to run to the fortress for help?"

Moya did not hesitate; she kilted up her skirts, turned, and hurried toward the stairs.

Donal placed his hand on Siúi's forehead. Her skin was cold to the touch and getting colder by the second.

"Siúi! Hear me, open your eyes!"

The warm afternoon sun, the deserted beach faded away; he stood on a windswept road that snaked through a wilderness that seemed to go on forever. He hurried to catch up with Siúi. No matter how hard he tried to catch her, she always remained a pace or two a head of him.

"Siúi!"

She kept on walking. Perhaps she had not heard him.

"Siúi, wait," he yelled at her back.

Siúi paused and turned. Her face white, her coppery hair plastered against her head, eyes dull, lifeless.

"Siúi it is not your time. Come." He darted forward and caught her arm. Donal blinked, suddenly warm by degrees, then cold again. They were back on the beach.

Siúi moaned, her eyes fluttered open, "Moya! What of my sister?" she gasped.

"Moya is fine." Donal put his finger to her lips. "Do not speak. Save your strength, rest now. Moya has gone for help."

He checked the wound. She had lost a lot of blood. He pulled off his tunic, ripped a length of cloth from the edge, and fashioned a pressure bandage to slow the bleeding. He covered her with what was left of his tunic.

Please Father, let help get here in time!

CHAPTER
FIFTY-EIGHT

Donal let the horse come to a stop at the far end of the courtyard. He slipped off and held up his hands to help Moya dismount. A groom hurried forward to take the horse.

He sighed; tomorrow he would be stiff and feel every one of his years. Moya's movements were slow. She had not spoken to him since she brought help. Was she tired, or had she guessed at the truth about why he had come to meet her at the lake?

Siúi was placed on a narrow makeshift bed. Men and women from the fortress followed Mór and her children inside.

Rónán called for riders to go out to the headland where the boat had come from. He sent riders to each village and holding along Loch Faolán, and to Cwillan to let Feargus know what had happened. Word would spread; Mangan would find himself a hunted man.

Donal doubted that he would be caught. They would abandon the boat and make good their escape.

"Thank you for saving my sister, lord." Moya turned to go inside.

"Moya, mo ghrá."

In the light from the torches her eyes were bright with unshed tears.

"I will bother you no longer," she whispered.

"Forgive me for being a fool. It never occurred to me why I came back so often. I should have recognized love when I felt it." He caught her hand before she had a chance to leave him, pulled her toward him.

Moya refused to look up at him.

"I will not take no for an answer."

As he put his arms around her, she began to shake. He held her against his chest, trying to hold at bay the shock of what had happened earlier, what was happening now. He would never know how long they stood holding on to each as if their life depended on it.

Nearby a gasp, pulled him back to the present. He glanced around. Mór stood next to Ciarán, staring at them.

"Mór will take you up to your room." Donal smiled down at Moya, and kissed her.

"Lord, I..."

"Go with Mór. I will speak with Rónán tonight."

Mór stepped forward, put her arm around Moya, and led her toward the fortress. At the door Mór turned and looked back at Donal, before she helped Moya inside.

Ciarán remained watching him.

"What upset Mór?"

Ciarán hesitated, before he said, "I saw it too, you and Moya just now... It was as if the years had fallen away and you held Briana in your arms again."

"She is very much like Briana, different too."

"Come, Cullan Donal, let us join the men. They will want to hear firsthand what happened."

Ciarán pulled the heavy oak door open.

Donal was about to step inside; he needed something hot to warm him. Behind him a sound not part of the silence of the courtyard made him let go of the door and turn. In the shadows stood a woman, a shawl over her head.

"The circle is complete."

Donal stepped closer to the woman. "Do I know you, mother?"

"Peace be with you. May the Father and Son watch over you."

"You said something about a circle?"

"The circle is complete."

"I thought you were right behind me."

Donal turned when he heard Ciarán's voice. "I stopped to speak with this woman."

"What woman?"

Donal looked around the empty courtyard.

"Come, the men are waiting to toast you."

"I did nothing more than any man would have done under the circumstances."

"You have forgotten, this is the anniversary of the day you rode into Cwillan in triumph."

"All that seems so long ago." Donal paused at the door, looked back one last time. The woman was gone, if she had been there at all.

Glossary of Names

Aoife   -   Donal's second wife

Ciarán   -   Donal's former Guardian

Cynthia Ann Long   -   Robert Long's daughter

Dominic X. Monaghan   -   Lawyer

Donal Tolan   -   assumed the name and surname of Fred Tolan

Liam O'Brien   -   dog breeder

Lord Niall   -   friend, one of the Four Horsemen

Mánus Scanlon	-	friend and partner of Liam
Robert Long	-	financial advisor
Taydan	-	old enemy
William Dylan Long	-	Robert Long's son

GLOSSERY OF WORDS

Ab	-	Abbot
Amadan	-	male Fool
anam chara	-	m'anamchara -my anam chara - my soul mate, but not in the sense of the love of your life, more of a religious term -mentor
Bean Sí	-	Ban shee
bia	-	food
eon corr	-	odd man out
ficheall	-	Used here as chess, a board game
fómhar	-	Autumn

Glas River	-	Green River
Grá	-	Love
Leann	-	Ale, Beer
Mar is mian leat	-	As you wish
Mna	-	Women, as in women's room
Og	-	Young person, Youth, Cullan Og (Young Cullan)
óinseach	-	female fool
seanchaí	-	Story teller
Taoiseach	-	Chief

Many Thanks

To Ken Gangwer, without his help this book would
never have been possible.
Many thanks to my editor, Heather Murray.
And for Fred P. Wessells, you are missed.

To my father, who gave me the chance and the
opportunity to write this book.

To the real Donal Tolan and Mánus Scanlon, May the
Father and Son keep you always. May you never lose
your Celtic Soul

Cover Photograph By

Celtic Cat Photos

www.etsy.com/shop/Celticcatphotos